Dear Steve

Beyond the Wall:
The Journey Home

Thank you for walking with us today.

Thank you!

Anin

Beyond the Wall

The Journey Home

—A Novel—

Alivia C. Tagliaferri

Foreword by Jerry Beightol,
Vietnam veteran and retired licensed clinical social worker.

Featuring the poem 'Home' from the collection
UPROOTED: Searching for Serenity by
Michelle McCloskey-Alicea.

IRONCUTTER MEDIA LLC

Manufactured in the United States of America

Cover by George Foster, Foster Cover Designs
Interior Design by Barbara Shaw
Author's photograph by Paul Kline, Paul Kline Photography

Published by:
Ironcutter Media
4600 Benedict Drive, Suite 203
Sterling, Virginia 20164

ISBN 0-9788417-2-7
978-0-9788417-2-0

This book in second edition is
again dedicated to the loving memory of my father,
Anthony M. Tagliaferri, for continuing to teach me death is not final.

Acknowledgements

FIRST AND FOREMOST, I would like to thank Dennis M. Butts for sharing with me stories of his experience in Vietnam and subsequent battles with PTSD. I was honored he entrusted me with the keys to his past. Dennis, my sincerest hope is for you to know one day of true happiness.

My humble thanks to the USO-Metro for opening the door into your world and to the staff at Walter Reed Medical Center for providing warrior care to the thousands of wounded who have entered your doors over the years—there is nothing more beautiful than healing another human being.

I am blessed with the love and support of good family and good friends. To each of you, I share my immeasurable love, gratitude and respect.

To my mentors, thank you for teaching your invaluable lessons. The student was ready.

To Jerry Beightol, my heart is happy to call you friend, thank you for penning such a beautiful foreword.

And with deep gratitude to the men and women in uniform who serve our country, you were and continue to be the inspiration and reason I wrote this book. Thank you and welcome home.

Foreword

I AM THRILLED to say a few things about the book *Beyond the Wall: The Journey Home*. This novel is an amazing journey of what it is like returning home from war, describing the loss of innocence and the quest to find one's self again while confronting bitter truth and biting pain upon the return home. As a Vietnam veteran, retired therapist and social worker, I found myself gripped by the in-depth knowledge this book covers in terms of the psyche of someone who has been riddled with post traumatic stress disorder. I was almost shocked that such a young author with no military background or experience could pen such an insightful approach to both an old and new problem about men and women coming home from war.

Beyond the Wall: The Journey Home is a must read for anyone who deals with veterans who have been in war. As a therapist who has dealt with and treated those dealing with post traumatic stress disorder, I believe this book powerfully wields a new pathway for teaching about combat trauma. The novel not only describes the incredible journey of recovering from the wounds of war both physically and mentally, it cleverly takes one through the pathway of warrior-ship.

It is important to note that there is an almost esurient appetite for knowledge and information about what really occurs in war and the changes that take place in a person. This book not only captures these aspects with a fresh perspective and astuteness about the lasting symptoms of war, it illustrates the importance of mentoring programs and the healing force that it evokes. Mentoring was pathetically missing from the Vietnam era, yet, it is a force not only for those being mentored as well as by those doing the mentoring.

I am not afraid to admit that when I came home from Vietnam my life was a mess. I was glad to be home, but my mind kept wandering back to friends left in the jungle I knew were still witness to destruction and devastation that is beyond description. After my service in-country, I was assigned to the XVIIIth Airborne Corps at Fort Bragg in North Carolina to work with a small detachment for troop movement deployment and was quickly immersed with the details of sending the 3rd Brigade of the 82nd Airborne to Vietnam to assist in the Tet Offensive of 1968. Many of the men in this unit had already been to Vietnam and some were still recovering from wounds seen and unseen from previous tours.

When I was honorably discharged from the Army, I had no job and no place to go except back to live with my parents in a small town in central Pennsylvania, but sadly, it was a horrible experience, and one that left me feeling I was being scorned for my service to my country. I was angry and upset that no jobs were available and the only one ever offered was planting trees. To unearth my old feelings that some people were spitting on the sacrifices of our generation along with other indignities is best left to the past. With no job, an alcohol problem and a desire to go back to school, I learned that Salem College in West Virginia might allow me entrance for the fall of 1969. I acted fast and furiously and was granted admission starting late August.

The chance of finding out about Salem was truly a critical juncture for me. If I were not to have pursued that window of opportunity I think I would have become a lost soul. I was drinking heavily at the time and my head was full of anger, discontent and grief as names of friends kept coming up as KIA in 'Nam. Salem was not well known, although it was a golden opportunity for many reasons. The professors were genuine and highly respectful of my military experiences and were a great challenge for me academically. The student body primarily matriculated from the east coast and many had older brothers in the service and several had experienced the loss of a sibling due to the war.

I completed my degree in Psychology and Business Administration by 1972 and was hired to work at the Department of Veterans Affairs Medical

Center in Clarksburg, WV as a Psychology Technician and it was here that I really began to learn about my generation of warriors. The man who hired me, Dr. Robert Bell, was extremely interested in this new group of men coming home from war. He said he felt almost ashamed of the labels being cavalierly tossed around about the Vietnam veterans. He felt there was something interesting happening in this group of warriors and could not quite put his finger on it. He was incensed that just dismissing this group as a loser generation or as the drug users was not quite accurate.

Dr. Bell insisted on researching this phenomenon and found many highly interesting documents about men coming home from war after WWI, WWII and Korea as well the Civil War. He did have an uphill battle to convince his other colleagues because many of the veterans admitted to the hospital at that time were there as a result of taking or using drugs (mostly pot). Underneath that layer of drug usage was deeply rooted anxieties about the war. As it turns out, the West Virginia veterans suffered the highest percentage of casualties based on populations of 100,000 or more. Dr. Bell felt there were a cluster of symptoms that demarked this group and was reluctant to diagnose schizophrenia as a major malady.

During my time with him, he always felt that the symptoms he saw were naturally occurring as a result of stress and trauma from the war. He was highly gifted in the use of projective techniques which a clinician often used to aid in the diagnosis of psychosis and schizophrenia.

The diagnosis of PTSD was not yet in the literature and he had the use of the Diagnostic and Statistical Manual II that had not been updated since World War II. He emphatically maintained his view about stress and trauma and often spoke at numerous community functions discussing his work with this new warrior group of Vietnam veterans. I personally saw how many communities were willing to dismiss the Vietnam veteran as someone causing the rise of prolific use of drugs and other ill-fitting claims to the cause of the downward trend in the country. Heaping the woes of the country onto the warrior's back was cause for alarm. By the mid- to late-1970's there were literally hundreds of other professionals in the field dedicated to finding better ways to treat the veteran, especially Vietnam veterans, and not place blame on them. It has often been said that nary one of the warriors made the decision to go to war or designed a frame work to regulate the policies. Perhaps it is, then, wise to not heap blame onto their psyches.

The early seeds planted in my mind grew and a great passion to find out not only what went on with me, but to share new knowledge with my veteran brothers. It was as important to hear their stories of the war and their journey coming home. Great tragedies were told, many sleepless nights were shared, and hundreds of tears shed as we learned how to speak about the unspeakable. And over the course of my career at the Department of VA and later as a consultant for Re-Entry Associates, Inc., a program designed exclusively to treat veterans suffering from war traumas, I have been blessed to share many amazing and humbling experiences with my veteran brethren.

While it is true that PTSD has its unique and qualifying nosology, each warrior group has a distinct set of cultures that is enormously important to each of them. That does not mean that they should be treated separately or quantifying them as greater than the other. It is as important today to listen to what this warrior has to say as it was to listen to warriors from the ancient past. That is why I feel this novel is so important to therapists, veterans and their friends and families alike. Alivia Tagliaferri has demonstrated the incredible capacity to listen while also possessing the unique ability to tell a great story of unusual depth and understanding. *Beyond the Wall: The Journey Home* is reminiscent of a Vietnam veteran's combat experience but embodies all the nuances of this recent war that is expressly and possessively of this generation.

This novel captures the passion and idealism of this new warrior group, as well as discussing fear and perseverance in the face of enemy fire. It is a story well told, as it is able to exact the feelings ignited about the loss of friends, the anger that swells and the sadness that lingers, and the homecoming that is so difficult to articulate. What makes *Beyond the Wall: The Journey Home* stand out is the author's cognizance that a warrior's experience in battle has been a high point in his or her life, and despite the horror, terror, and weariness; the grime, and the hatred, participation with others in the chance of battle has an unforgettable side. While understanding that those who have not experienced war or combat for themselves have a difficult time comprehending it – of which, as noted, the feelings are hard to comprehend for the participant, let alone trying to explain it to anyone else – the novel's combination of earnestness and lightheartedness so often noted of those who have borne the battle is articulated with profound dignity and grace.

A few years ago I had the privilege and honor of meeting Alivia, whom I now cherish as friend. She has a passion and energy that is simply amazing. Not only is she a gifted writer, but a musician as well, and I will never forget listening to her play a piano ballad she composed for a capacity filled room of warriors and therapists after a discussion session – it was a great welcome home for all.

To the many men and women who have survived the carnage of battle and who happen to be ambivalent about reading anything about war, I would put this on the number one list to read. This book is one that makes you look at life a little differently. It is cathartic and poetic all at once.

Jerry Beightol,
Vietnam veteran and
retired licensed clinical social worker (LCSW).

Home

By Michelle McCloskey–Alicea

Home is the place where one's heart resides—
A secure dwelling with a framework of pride.
Physically made of bricks and stones,
Emotionally cemented by the bonds of the home.
With rose-tinted windows that allow sunlight,
And doors that barricade the dangers of night.
Decorated and embellished over the years
With love and compassion; laughter and tears.
It envelops the heart, the spirit, the mind
With an identity that's truly one of a kind.
But the house modernizes and changes with time
As life experiences shape its design.

The place where most of life lessons are learned,
It's the home to which one longs to return.
Especially when life gets heavy and weighted—
The home is the remedy so dearly awaited.
For it's the place that restores and revives
The inner spirit trying to survive.
For the home is not just a structural space,
It's family, support, and a welcome embrace.

A temporary structure with a permanent hold
Of one's mind, one's heart, one's spirit, one's soul.

Home is a featured poem in the collection titled UPROOTED: Searching for Serenity by Michelle McCloskey-Alicea, published by Ironcutter Media (November 2009). www.uprootedpoetry.com

Prologue: The Dream

DENNIS MICHAELS INSPECTS HIMSELF in the mirror. His Marine uniform is neatly starched and pressed, his face clean-shaven, his hair close-cropped. A flash from the scarlet and gold Marine emblem pinned on his shoulder reflects brightly in the mirror. The eagle perched atop the anchored globe blazes under the banner of two words: Semper Fidelis. *Always Faithful.*

Dennis' eyes harden like steel as his gaze burns into the emblem. The reflection begins to grow stronger, like a flame; quickly becoming so magnified it seemingly penetrates the glass forcing Dennis to shield his eyes with his hands. It feels as though the rays of the sun itself are beating mercilessly upon him.

It *is* the sun, perched high in the sky on a warm summer afternoon. Dennis stands under it solemnly; his mood in stark contrast to the landscape of rolling green hills, minted valleys and sky the perfect shade of blue. *This place looks familiar.* It reminds him of one of his childhood homes in New Jersey. *Was it number six, or seven?* He can't remember; he lost count long ago. A large maple tree stands stoically in the foreground, offering its shade. He notices it for the first time. *How did I not see it?* It is just like the one Harry used to describe.

Harry.

Immediately, Dennis' focus becomes involuntarily narrowed as a tunnel-like sensation of pressure wraps itself around his eyes much like blinders worn by a horse, an apocalyptic horse. And suddenly, a deafening noise drowns out all other sound. It is unlike anything he has ever heard before and he imagines it to be the roar of a run-away train barreling down the tracks, conducted by a phantom who waves his ghastly arms in delight as a diabolical musical score is unleashed inside Dennis' head, growing louder and louder until it transforms sensory perception from the surreal to the corporeal.

Dennis looks down at his feet. He is startled to find a gray tombstone before him. Inscribed in the granite are the words:

HARRY E. WILLIAMS
BORN MARCH 20, 1947
DIED APRIL 5, 1967

Dennis falters backward. *Harry's grave.* He can't breathe. Rigid, a futile gulp of air gets caught in the lump forming in his constricted throat and he feels something dangling around his neck, something that feels eerily like a noose. He grabs for it, wishing it to be just his imagination but to his horror, he makes contact. Rough bristles of braided rope feel course in his grasp. Seizing the braids, he rips it furiously away from his body, but something is attached. A camera. *Harry's camera.*

Dennis stands above his best friend's grave clutching that friend's sole possession, and he can't shake the feeling something else is horribly, dreadfully wrong. Beads of sweat streak down his face. Finally, a realization dawns —he is missing something. *What?*

Searching his uniform, he thrusts his left arm deep into his pocket and fumbles around as if looking for a lost set of keys. Curiously, his right arm doesn't budge. Something is very wrong. He wants to shake himself, cross his arms over his shoulders, and tell himself, "Get a grip!" But he can't. A sickening feeling sweeps over his body. *Oh my god.*

"No . . . !" Dennis shouts at the top of his lungs.

His right arm is gone. Amputated. His uniform hangs limply from the severed stump of his shoulder. His stomach turns as if a thousand-pound weight has just been dropped from the sky, hitting him squarely in the gut. Bulls-eye. He groans loudly, expelling every ounce of air from his lungs.

His body jerks upright.

Dripping with sweat, heart pounding, Dennis looks over at the clock. It is 4:10 am.

"Good friggin' morning." Dennis bids himself a sarcastic greeting as he shakes his head in disgust. *The same dream. Always the same damned dream.*

The Moving Wall

IN THE PRE-DAWN DARKNESS, inside a white pitched tent, Dennis Michaels, age 46, is slumped in a folding chair with his arms crossed. His head hangs heavily as he fights the urge to sleep; it is a losing battle. He bobs down, nearly smacking his forehead on the table but quickly snaps back to attention before making contact. *Gotta stay up.*

He wishes he had slept more the night before, but the dream woke him up. Twice, actually. Once at two o'clock, and again at four. Nothing new, it's been the same nightmarish routine since he was nineteen. Since 'Nam. He shakes off the urge to sleep, knowing he needs to stay awake; rather, it is his *duty* to stay awake. Tonight it too important. It is the first night the Moving Wall—the half-size replica of the Vietnam Memorial—is hosted by Martinsburg, West Virginia and he is keeping the first night's vigil.

Inspired by an Army veteran named John Devitt, the Moving Wall was created twelve years prior for the purpose of bringing the powerful experience of "The Wall" to those who could not make the pilgrimage to Washington, D.C. Two replicas were built and have toured the country ever since, one of which is here now for a week long stay. Once the flag is raised over the Moving Wall, the veterans have already decided, it will never be left unattended.

Less than five miles away, traveling south along Interstate 81, a lone motorcyclist speeds toward the exit for the mall. The rider, a grisly looking middle-aged man clad in black juts his bearded jaw rebelliously into the wind.

His eyes are set into a hard, fierce stare. Yet, something is out of place, uncharacteristic. In his fist, balled up and held beneath the handlebar, a paper bag swings back and forth. Angled just right, it flashes a bright yellow cartoon smiley-face. *Oh Happy Day.*

Inside the tent, Dennis nudges Tom Patterson, a friend and fellow veteran who also volunteered for the first night's graveyard shift. Sergeant Tom, as he is better known, was an Air Force Rescue pilot in '67 and '68, around the same time Dennis was a Marine with Delta Battery 2/12 who often operated as an FO with 1/9. However coincidental, they didn't know each other until many years later, not until a mutual friend introduced them at a VA event.

Sergeant Tom rubs his eyes and makes a face. He doesn't have to say it, Dennis knows. The silent question being, "Man, how the hell did we do this before?" Dennis just shakes his head and laughs. *No clue.*

"So, what are you going to talk about tomorrow? For your speech?" Sergeant Tom asks, referring to the opening ceremony.

"Not sure yet. I didn't prepare anything if that's what you're asking. I was just going to talk."

"Oh? Well, maybe you should write something down. Notes or something."

"Nah, I'm just going to wing it," Dennis replies. He's not nervous about speaking in public nor is he nervous to speak about Vietnam. He's been doing that for the past two years. But it's never easy and often painful. Akin to prematurely ripping a bandage from a wound, his memories feel raw when exposed.

But beneath the surface, a voice inside his head is asking questions, fishing for answers. The voice is no stranger. *Who the hell am I to be up there talking? What the hell did I do that was so special?*

Noting with irony the only "Doubting Thomas" in the room is not the one sitting next to him, but the one sitting in his own head, he already knows the answer: *Not a single thing.* The only difference between him and many other veterans is that he has come to terms with his demons. All of them, that is, except for Harry.

The faint rumbling sound of a motor pervades the quiet night and interrupts Dennis' thoughts. The sound quickly gets louder; it is fast approaching. "Is that thunder?" Sergeant Tom wonders.

The biker, exiting off the highway, is now just outside the tent. Turning off the Harley's engine, he catches a brief glance of the shadowy outline of a long wall. His grip tightens around the smiley-faced paper bag and it crinkles loudly. Dennis and Sergeant Tom have heard the motor turn off, and know by the proximity of sound outside they are expecting company. Anticipating the impending arrival, they sit upright with ears perked and curiosity piqued.

The biker enters the tent. Both men reflexively sit up even straighter. Dennis quickly sums up the situation: middle aged man, black jeans, black shirt, faded black leather jacket with a Grim Reaper emblem on the top rocker and a patch with the 1% sign. He is a Pagan, a member of the notoriously violent motorcycle gang and nemesis of the Hell's Angels. Dennis thinks he looks more like a Viking than a Pagan, with his yellow beard, scraggly graying hair pulled back in a ponytail and gut sticking out unashamedly over his jeans. Dennis notices the paper bag. *What the hell is in there?*

No one speaks and no one moves. The awkward silence spans several seconds until finally the Pagan steps forward. He stops just short of the table and throws down the smiley-faced, grease-stained paper bag. The contents fall out. Breakfast sandwiches and hash browns.

"Here's your friggin' breakfast," he snarls.

Dennis doesn't take his eyes off the Pagan. Sergeant Tom, on the other hand, quickly grabs a hash brown and takes a bite. "Thanks."

The Pagan's attention is no longer on them, but instead focused on the replica within plain view. The first rays of sunrise have popped up over the hills, and are now gleaming off the black Plexiglas wall giving it an incandescent golden glow. Sucking in a deep breath, he slowly walks toward the replica.

His steps seem methodical, not wholly his own, as if drawn by a force more powerful than he. Ten yards away from the wall he abruptly stops. As if suddenly paralyzed, he stands frozen with fear, not able to take another step.

Dennis doesn't know who this man is, this Pagan, but he knows one thing for certain. *He is one of us.* He begins to walk over unsure of what to say or how to help but trusts he'll figure it out by the time he gets there. The Pagan hears Dennis' footsteps behind him and turns his face away. Dennis can see the man's body is shaking.

"I . . . I can't," the Pagan stammers, his voice hoarse. He shakes his head and clears his throat. "I'm sorry. But I just can't," he says again as he turns his body away from the replica.

Dennis catches a glimpse of the man's face one last time and sees the tears brimming. The Pagan quickly swipes them away and walks brusquely back to his bike. He revs the engine loudly, and peels out, jutting his jaw into the wind and setting his eyes back into a cold, hard stare. The thousand-yard stare, as called by those who were there, returns.

Dennis stands quietly with his head bowed down in silence, and listens to the sound of the engine until he can hear it no longer. Sergeant Tom is speechless.

"That's what I'm going to talk about, Tom. That's what I'm going to talk about." Dennis himself looks over at the wall and feels its magnetic pull. Transfixed, he walks over to it, instinctively walking directly to Panel 17E. Row 109. Harry E. Williams.

Dennis instantly envisions Harry, twenty years old, standing in the pouring rain. Monsoon season. Thua Thien Province. Alongside Harry is Sergeant Malloy, the most senior Forward Observer and center-post for the group of FO's in 2/12. The two are anxiously awaiting orders to begin the operation on the Street Without Joy. Preparing to move into position, Dennis passes by the two figures standing in the rain. He is startled to see Harry. *He's not supposed to be here. What the hell is he doing?* Their eyes lock. Harry calls out to him, but the words are inaudible. Dennis shakes his head. Harry yells out louder. "Hey Denny, make sure they send my body home!"

What?

"Dennis."

Dennis doesn't respond.

"Dennis?"

Still no response. "Dennis, are you alright?" It is Sergeant Tom's voice.

Dennis is still staring at Harry's name on Panel 17E.

"Yeah," Dennis calls back, "I'm fine."

Coming to terms with Vietnam wasn't something that happened by Dennis' own volition. Rather it happened by physical intervention—a tear in his arterial wall, like an internal pressure cooker that was on the brink of explosion. "Do you want to live?" the cardiologist had asked. At the time

Dennis was surprised by his response, an affirmative. "Then change," the doctor then ordered.

On a deeper level Dennis wondered if the tear in his heart was in fact a reflection of his mental state at that time. For years he had bottled up his emotions, his anger, his guilt, feeling as if he could burst at the seams at any second. It wasn't until that night when he laid awake in a sterile hospital room attached to tubes and staring out the window that he let go of his anger. Especially the resentment he felt toward his mother, who, to her dying day was blind to the changes that had taken place in her own son. She of all people did not understand who he really was. *Could she really not grasp that I changed? That I wasn't the same person as before the war? Or did she just not want to see—preferring to turn a blind eye?* He never knew.

It was during that time that he met and became friends with Jerry Brentham, a veteran himself who headed a group at the nearby Veterans Affairs Medical Center studying Post-Traumatic Stress Disorder. Previously, PTSD had been simply called "shell shock" and left at that. Jerry's team found that post-traumatic stress had much farther-ranging consequences than previously imagined. Upon meeting Dennis and evaluating his symptoms, Jerry classified him as a "100% fully functioning disabled veteran. Mentally disabled but able to function normally day to day." He would later urge Dennis to join the speaking tours organized by the VA and share his experiences. That suggestion became the catalyst for Dennis to reach out to other veterans and is the reason he is here tonight in Martinsburg with The Moving Wall.

Daylight comes, and the morning brings more veterans and tourists. The organizers and volunteers help the score of people find names along the wall. They talk with the families, share stories, and offer handshakes. Conversations with fellow Marines are usually punctuated by one word, *Ooh-rah*, emphasis placed on the first syllable.

But one girl, no older than fifteen, stands out in the crowd. She is pacing up and down the panels of names holding a white piece of paper in her hand. Dennis watches as she looks up into the faces of each passerby and asks. "Did you know my uncle?" She hands them the piece of paper with the outline of a pencil-etched name. Sadly, the response has been the same. "No, sorry."

Dennis watches her for several minutes before he is able to break free from conversation and address the young girl directly. With her head bowed in dejection, she does not at first notice the man towering above her small frame. Wisps of dark brown hair cover her eyes. Slowly, she looks up. Dennis is startled. The shape of her face, her eyes. *My god, she looks just like Lilly,* the little Vietnamese girl he had befriended long ago. Actually, all kids remind him of Lilly. He thinks it has to do with their innocence. *Lilly was innocent.*

"Miss, can I help you?" Dennis asks politely. The young girl's eyes widen with excitement at the prospect maybe this man knows her uncle. She hands him the paper. "Did you know my uncle? Jack Livingston? He died in 1969." Dennis, too, shakes his head no. "I'm sorry, I didn't know him."

Her dejection is palpable. "That's what everyone says. I just wish I could talk to someone who knew him. My father said he was brave."

Dennis looks her in the eye and speaks without hesitation. "Yes, he was brave. Very brave,"

"But how do you know?"

"I just know." It is sincere.

A faint smile crosses her face as she brushes back her hair and looks into the black reflection of the wall once more. She sighs and her shoulders relax; she seems to be at peace now. They walk together for a few steps, then, as their paths diverge, she turns to him and smiles. "Thank you."

He returns the smile. He feels good; the fleeting brush with innocence has made him whole again, if only for a moment. Turning back around to face The Moving Wall his heart nearly jumps out of his skin. He can hardly believe the coincidence of where he is now standing. Panel 21. *Dave Keating.*

Instantly, Dennis remembers the full weight of Dave's head cradled in his arms, and how he placed his hands over Dave's mutilated abdomen in a futile attempt to stop the blood from gushing. "You're gonna make it, Keating." Dennis had told him with all the conviction he could muster. But it was a bold-faced lie and Dennis knew it. "Just hang in there."

The sun sets.

The next round of veterans report for their graveyard shift vigil. Sergeant Tom bids Dennis farewell. "Ooh-rah."

But Dennis is not ready to leave yet. He wants to say good night to the guys—the ones whose names are etched on the wall—before he leaves. Standing alone in front of the replica locating Harry's name once again, he leans forward and whispers, "See ya, buddy. I'll be back again in the morning."

Dennis hears Harry's voice—the same voice that called out to him in the pouring rain nearly thirty years ago. "Make sure they send my body home, Dennis!" Harry is teasing him. No, not teasing, taunting him. *Why is he doing this? Doesn't he know he's going to die?*

Enraged, Dennis shakes his fist into the air. "God damn it, Harry! Stop messing around!"

Dennis startles himself. Facing the black wall, yelling at Harry's ghost, Dennis is overwhelmed by the feeling he is standing before the commune of souls whose names are etched into that wall, judging him, wondering the same thing he has all these years. *Why did you make it, and not us?* Emotions swirl, and his head feels light as he hears his own voice shout out. "It wasn't my fault, you stupid jerk... It wasn't my fault!"

Instantaneously, a wave of relief rushes over his body. Like baptismal waters washing over a baby's head, cleansing him, purifying him, the words still echo in the air. *Let go. Let him go back to the place from where he came.* And for the first time in twenty-five years, Dennis understands—truly understands.

It wasn't his fault. It never was.

The dream of standing over Harry's grave returns never again.

Part One

Deckhouse Five
November 2, 2004

The essence of warriorship, or the essence of human bravery, is refusing to give up on anyone or anything.

—Chogyam Trungpa, *Shambhala,*
The Sacred Path of the Warrior

All Soul's Day

THE MID-MORNING TRAFFIC on Georgia Avenue is congested with voters driving back to work from the election polls. A black SUV pulls up to the security gate at Walter Reed Army Medical Center. Right now, the main hospital and campus is the premiere stateside care facility for trauma casualties flown in from Iraq and Afghanistan. Located in the far northeastern corner of the District on a 113-acre parcel of land, the hospital and its auxiliary facilities are currently running at maximum capacity. Security is tight.

Dennis Michaels rolls down his window. A security officer checks his driver's license and verifies that he is on today's list of registered guests. "Pull over to the side, sir, while we inspect your vehicle." A security detail walks around the SUV to inspect the back seat and trunk area, and confirms the license plate number with the documents provided. "He's good."

The security officer gives him a guest badge. "Here you go, sir. The Mologne House is behind the main hospital. Just follow the semi-circle around to Visitor Parking."

Dennis nods and follows the directions. He finds a space in the crowded garage and walks toward the main hospital passing the marble water fountain. He pauses briefly in front of the main entrance of the historic landmark and reads the inscription adorning the building: *We Provide Warrior Care.* It is very fitting. The main hospital, a ten-story red brick building housing nearly three hundred beds and fourteen operating rooms, has cared for the country's wounded since the World War I, including a number of presidents

But the sudden sight of men in wheelchairs on the patio mars Dennis' appreciation. Some are missing arms. Some are missing legs. Some are missing both. Actually, it's the sight of teenagers in wheelchairs, with boyish faces that is the most jarring. *Did we look that young?* Dennis wonders, shaking his head. It's hard to see these young faces and bodies disfigured. The paradox of the current conflict is there are far fewer combatants killed in action than Korea or Vietnam, but more survivors of polytraumatic casualties—amputations, head injuries, and burns. In each successive war, there have been fewer KIA's than the previous one because of improvements in technology. Today, the military is able to quickly transport casualties to Germany and on to Walter Reed and Bethesda Naval hospitals for critical care, where surgeons and state-of-the-art equipment are ready to operate within hours of the conflict. So the likelihood of bleeding out on the battlefield is much less today than it was forty years ago. Their lives have been saved, but the lifeless look in the eyes of these veterans on the porch says it all.

Dennis averts his gaze and continues walking around the back of the hospital toward the Mologne House, a convalescence facility that houses rehabilitation patients. Don Leary, founder and president of the "Make a Difference" organization, is standing in front of the manicured lawn waiting to greet him.

"Dennis, thank you for coming." The two men shake hands warmly.

"I'm glad you could make it. Follow me." Don leads him inside the Victorian-style mansion. "I told Andy all about you"

"Oh? What did you tell him?

"Just that you were a Marine in Vietnam with three purple hearts and a story to tell."

Dennis cringes. "I hope you didn't make me out to be some kind of darn hero, Don. I didn't do anything that anybody else didn't do over there. That's not what this is about."

"No, no, don't worry," Don assures him. "I told him you were a mentor with our program."

Dennis isn't exactly sure what a mentor really is, much less how good of one he is going to be, but he likes Don, likes his passion. Although Don himself never fought in a war, he created 'Make a Difference,' with the mission of improving the quality of life for disabled veterans. So far, the group has provided financial assistance to help offset the costs of special equipment and living expenses for over a dozen veterans. And recently, Don began recruiting older veterans to help those coming home from the current conflict readjust to civilian life. After meeting at a business function, Don asked Dennis to join the mentor team; after all, he seemed the perfect candidate.

"The goal," Don had first explained in corporate terms, "is to help these guys achieve their post-recovery goals and keep them looking positively at the future."

"Look, Don, I admire what you're doing, but what do these veteran mentors really *do*?" Dennis questioned.

"They talk, they listen. . . . They do anything they think will help the guys. Don't let them get in a funk, get them living again, let them know they're appreciated and can still contribute."

It sounded good at the time, but now seeing Don, Dennis has reservations. "Wait here," Don points to the couch in the reception room, "I'll go tell Andy you're here."

Dennis sits down and studies his surroundings. The decor is welcoming. He picks up a bulletin letter listing the activities going on at the campus today, including a list of different religious services. He skims it briefly. The fact is, he's not a man to be found in a church on most Sundays; but whenever asked his response is, "there are no atheists on the battlefield."

A Catholic mass is scheduled for today at ten o'clock. It has an asterisk next to it: *All Souls Day. He remembers back to a conversation he had nearly forty years ago while in the hospital at Camp Pendleton recovering from an automobile accident. He was sharing a room with a Marine named Rocco, who was a devout Catholic. Rocco had been in-country and Dennis respected his tenure, often passing the time picking his brain about Vietnam. One day in early November, Rocco told him about All Souls Day, or Day of the Dead, which dated back to the 7th century. Rocco explained it was centered on the belief that souls of the dead are not perfectly cleansed and are barred from entering heaven until they have been purged from sin.

"So where do they go?" Dennis remembers asking him.

"Purgatory," Rocco said gravely.

"What's that?"

Rocco's voice fell to a hushed tone as if sharing a conspiracy and explained. "Purgatory, " he whispered, "is a place between heaven and hell, good and bad, a place where sins can be purged and passage granted."

Rocco then told him All Souls Day was created so that the living could pray for the dead. "Pretty much everyone goes to Purgatory, because everyone has sinned. So it helps if people here on earth pray for those who've died— you know, help them atone for their sins and move on to heaven." At the time, it reminded Dennis of something he had read in the *Odyssey*, how the souls of Agamemnon and the dead warriors of the Trojan War were cast away to the underworld Hades, which could only be accessed by crossing the River Styx. Then Rocco said something that Dennis would never forget. "War is the hell, Dennis. When you're out there in the jungle, guys will talk about home like it is heaven, like they can't wait to go home. But home is the purgatory. The only heaven you'll ever know is when you die."

Now, sitting in the waiting room at the Mologne House, it dawns on Dennis what Rocco was talking about all those years ago. Maybe purgatory is a very real place found here on earth, a personal daily confinement some veterans live in every single day of their waking lives.

Don returns and motions for Dennis to follow him down the hallway. They stop in front of a room. Don knocks lightly on the door and opens it.

"Andy, Dennis is here to see you."

No response.

Don looks at Dennis apprehensively. "Well, I'll leave you two alone," he motions to Dennis to have a seat and shuts the door behind him.

Dennis pulls up a chair next to the bed and sits down. Up close, he can easily see the outline of Andy's shortened body. The blanket lies perfectly flat against the bed below his torso. His face is turned away. "Hey there, is it Andy . . . or do you prefer Andrew?"

Again, no response.

"Well, I don't know what they told you about me. And I don't know what you're feeling right now. So I thought we'd start off by just talking. How old are you, Andy?"

Silence.

Dennis already knows Andy is twenty-two. He memorized the biography Don sent. Born: 1982, San Diego, California. Grew up in Ohio. Joined the Marines in 2001. Deployed to Iraq. Second tour. Injured outside Fallujah. Sunni Triangle. Improvised Explosive Device. Both legs amputated. Here at Walter Reed since April.

What Dennis doesn't know is that Andy was in surgery just hours ago while doctors drained an ugly puss-filled cyst that was oozing out of the sutures on his right stump. Shrapnel is still working its way out of Andy's vexed skin and will further delay the fitting for his prosthesis, as his stumps cannot yet be molded to fit socket castings until the inflammation subsides—yet another setback in the name of progress. Tired and disgusted, with his mood clouded in foulness, Andy views Dennis' visit with contempt. *This guy still has his own legs, what the hell does he know?*

Sensing Andy's skepticism, Dennis desperately wants to break the silence but doesn't know what to say or where to begin. Looking at the stump of Andy's body, he wonders if and how he can possibly help this young man. *This is all so very wrong.* He starts to feel pity, but immediately fights the temptation. *No, don't pity him. That won't do him a darn bit of good.* Dennis takes a deep breath and refocuses, forcing himself to look at Andy in a different light. *He's one of us . . . Semper Fi.*

"Look, son. War is war. It doesn't matter where it's fought, or even when. I don't know exactly what you went through, but I know it was something real bad." Dennis looks down at the floor. *Just keep talking. Maybe he'll come around.* "I also know how it feels to come home when you're not ready. The day I left Vietnam? Well, I look at that day as the day that I was born. Because the person I am sitting here today didn't exist before then. Some people may think that sounds strange. But truth of the matter is I was conceived in war. You were too."

Andy's body stiffens.

Dennis sits back in his chair as if his mind is reaching out to grasp a key that opens a long-forgotten door.

"1967." Dennis starts pensively. "I was nineteen years old," his voice grows bolder. "And I was in Vietnam for nine months—the same amount of time it takes a woman to give birth to a child. And that's exactly what it felt like. The only difference was, inside the war's womb, I was consciously aware of the changes taking place in me the entire time." Dennis pauses. "And when I came out, I wasn't born with my innocence. I was born without it."

Andy's body rustles under the covers. He turns his face away from the window and stares up at the ceiling straight ahead. He is listening.

"I can still pinpoint the days when I felt something inside of me change. Those days when I saw too much . . . did too much . . . lost too much. For me, those days happened over the course of five operations that changed my entire life. Starting with Deckhouse Five."

But just as Andy is checking in, Dennis is checking out, and his mind returns to a different place and time.

Dead Man's Breakfast

December 31st, 1966

IN THE STORMY SOUTH CHINA SEA, off the coast of the Philippines, a helicopter hovers loudly over the deck of LSD Thomasson en route to Vietnam. A middle-aged man jumps gingerly out of the chopper. High winds swirl around the officers waiting to greet him. Slinging a backpack over his shoulder, he shakes hands with the officers as they yell into the deafening winds, each pretending to hear the other. The man reaches for his note pad and jots something down.

Below deck, a long line of fresh-faced Marines snakes outside the mess hall that barely accommodates the thirteen hundred men on board. Private First Class Dennis Michaels stands in line next to his friends from Delta Battery—Harry Williams, Pete Cavanaugh, and Chet Lambert.

"How much longer? Pete sighs impatiently. A blueblood with a sharp wit and quick temper, he slumps against the wall holding his growling stomach. It's anybody's guess.

Dennis gently elbows Harry and winks. Harry is the quiet one of the bunch, shy and soft-spoken. But Dennis, a mischievous nineteen-year-old, is up to something. He yawns loudly, dramatically almost, and stretches his arms out. Bending at the waist, he pulls out his k-bar and leans over pretending to lace up his boots. Slowly, carefully, he reaches over and cuts the laces of Pete's boot.

Oblivious to what Dennis is doing, Pete stands on his tiptoes and strains to peek around the corner.

"Jesus! What the hell are they doing up there?" He mutters under his breath.

Dennis severs Pete's left boot lace then reaches over for the right boot. Suddenly, a knife whizzes through the air. It spears the ground inches from Dennis' hand, momentarily paralyzing him.

"You sonuvabitch!" Pete towers over him, glaringly livid. Dennis rises to his feet, throws his head back and laughs. Harry covers his mouth to suppress his own laughter, but a giggle escapes. "What are you laughing about, Williams?" Pete whirls around.

"Nothing." But he can't help laughing. Pete takes himself so seriously, it comes at an expense.

Chet has been ignoring the private circus; instead, his attention has been focused on a suspicious looking man, obviously a civilian, weaseling his way into the chow line. The civilian stops just a few feet away and zeroes in on an unsuspecting Marine. Chet looks the man up and down, and whispers in a low voice. "Wonder who this guy is?" Tall and imposing, standing well over six feet; Chet is not someone to willingly cross. The civilian in question stands just inches away from the Marine's face. Clutching a pen, impervious to the personal space he is invading, the civilian squints as if in deep thought. "So, tell me, how does it feel to be doing this, to be fighting against the spread of communism?"

Chet groans loudly upon overhearing the question. The man is not just any civilian; he's a reporter.

The questioned Marine shifts his feet, clearly uncomfortable, and mumbles something inaudible.

The reporter barrels ahead. "Any idea where you boys are headed?" The Marine shakes his head no.

Chet rolls his eyes, annoyed. "I can't believe they're gonna let these jesters go in-country with us. What the hell are they thinking? They want us to fight the gooks and babysit reporters at the same friggin' time?" No one answers his rhetorical question.

The reporter, unsatisfied with his first subject, turns his attention to Dennis' group.

"Oh, boy . . . Here we go," Chet mutters under his breath.

"Mornin'. Mind if I ask you boys a few questions?" the reporter asks in the most polite and non-threatening voice he can muster.

No one speaks. The reporter quickly focuses in on Harry. He is keen on exploiting vulnerability and he senses Harry might be the weakest link. "What company are you with, son?

Harry's face flushes. He doesn't like attention. "Delta Battery 2/12," he answers softly.

"Any idea where you boys are heading?"

"Uh, no sir, I don't." Harry looks down at his feet.

The reporter frowns. "You don't talk much, do you son?" Harry doesn't know what to say. Frustrated, the reporter sighs and looks directly at Dennis, wanting someone, anyone, to give him a print-worthy quote. "Maybe *you* can answer some questions?" Dennis raises his brow, but the reporter doesn't wait for a response. "Tell me, how does it feel to be stopping the spread of communism?"

"What the hell are you talking about?" Dennis' brow quickly goes from raised to furrowed.

"Well, that's why you're here, isn't it?"

Dennis looks at him incredulously. "I'm here because they're here," he motions toward Harry and the others. "And because it's the only war we have," he says bluntly.

"Sure, sure," the reporter waves his hand in a condescending manner. "But do you have any idea—any idea whatsoever—where you boys are heading?"

Dennis' eyes narrow, and he squares his body to the reporter's, a reflex action intended to intimidate the man. "I don't know where we're going, and I don't care. All I know is we're a part of Battalion Landing Force 1-9. We go wherever they tell us to go."

Sensing Dennis' hostility, the reporter puts down his pen and coolly walks away. Chet raises an eyebrow at Dennis. "Nice."

"Yeah, well." Dennis shrugs his shoulders, as if to say, "Who cares?"

But as he starts to think about his encounter, he becomes quiet, lost in his own thoughts. "I'm in the Marines, that's all that matters to me. We're here to follow the same traditions of Belleau Woods, Iwo Jima, and Tarawa. It's the Corps that matters. Like Admiral Nimitz said, "Uncommon valor is a common virtue." *Darn, now that sounds good. Wish I'd said that to the reporter in the first place.* The fact that he didn't pisses him off even more.

Dave Keating walks around the corner from the mess hall. A farm boy from the Midwest with blond hair, blue eyes, and an affable demeanor, he is known as one of the better gun crew captains in the battery. Every one likes Dave; he's just that kind of guy.

"Hey, fellas! What's going on?" Dave asks, slapping Pete on the back.

"Aw, nothing," Pete gripes. "Just got done talking to some reporter asking a bunch of stupid questions."

"Oh, yeah? Wasn't *Stars and Stripes* was it?" Dave asks. Pete shakes his head no.

Dave chuckles, "So, you guys gonna be famous now?"

"Doubt it. He just wanted to know where we were going for the operation."

"Humph, right, like we'd really know that," Dave says sarcastically.

Dennis clears his throat and says very matter-of-factly, "I heard we're going to the Mekong Delta."

"What?" Chet asks skeptically. "Where'd you hear that?"

"One of the girls cleaning out the barracks in Okinawa showed me an article in a magazine from back home. It said we were gearing up for a massive beach landing in the Mekong Delta."

Dave stares in disbelief, "C'mon! You think people back home would know we're going before we do?"

"Think it's going to be that big?" Harry asks.

"I believe it," Chet snorts. "Look, we've only got the whole 7th fleet with us. There's what? Thirteen hundred of us and eight hundred coffins on board the Iwo Jima? You do the math." Chet pauses and spits on the ground. "Wherever we're going, it's going to be big."

Dave shakes his head, "Well, I just hope my fiancé back home doesn't read that article, that's all I've got to say. See you guys later." He pats them on the back and walks away.

Pete looks around the corner. He sees a Marine carrying a tray of breakfast. His eyes light up. "Hey look! Steak and eggs! They're feeding us steak and eggs, I thought I smelled . . . ."

"Shit," Chet deadpans, without missing a beat.

"Huh? What's wrong with you?"

"Dead man's breakfast. That's what's wrong with me. They're feeding us a friggin' dead man's breakfast." Chet shakes his head disgusted. "This is not good."

Moments later, a line cook slaps a sizzling steak and a heaping pile of eggs on their plates. But their appetite is gone.

The Briefing

THE MID-MORNING SKY is gray and dreary, and the LSD Thomasson rocks back and forth in the choppy waters as an oncoming storm approaches. All of the Marines have eaten breakfast and are now on deck. They will be briefed on their mission shortly. The waves smack against the ship, spraying a misty haze around the Marines. Standing alert in the drizzling rain, they are filled with anticipation and anxiety.

"Good morning gentlemen, I hope you enjoyed your breakfast." Flanked by intelligence officers with rolls of maps tucked under their arms, the battalion commanding officer steps forward to address the men. Idle conversation quickly tapers off to silence as he flashes them a brief smile and quickly attends to the business at hand. "This morning you will be briefed on Operation Deckhouse Five." He punctuates each syllable crisply for effect. "This operation will be historic, gentlemen. It will be the largest beach landing since Inchon. You will be the first Americans to set foot on the Mekong Delta since the end of the Indo-China conflict. General Westmoreland himself will be on hand for the landing, as will news correspondents from ABC, NBC, and CBS." He lets the last sentence hang, as if to subliminally communicate, "So be on your best behavior." He holds his hands behind his back, takes a deep breath through his nose, and peers at them until he feels sufficiently satisfied they get the drift. "Captain Tate, S-2 Intelligence Officer, will brief you on your mission."

Captain Tate clears his throat and directs the Marines' attention to a map of the III Corps area. "There are three deltas where the Mekong River comes in. We will have two simultaneous beach landings." He points to the two areas marked. "Red Beach is riverside. Bravo and Charlie Companies will land here with the grunts. White Beach is oceanside. Alpha and Delta Companies will land there. Your fire support, Delta Battery, will also operate from White Beach."

He unrolls an enlarged aerial photo. "Note the terrain. When you hit the beach, there will be approximately twenty-five yards of sand, then grass, before the tree line. Aerial recon shows the tree lines are heavily fortified, so be advised. You'll have about a hundred yards of open space between the beach and tree line. There will be no cover whatsoever."

He turns back toward the men. "Reports estimate three NVA divisions, thirty-thousand strong, operate in this area. Expect heavy resistance, automatic weapons, mortar fire, and RPG's. Once both beaches are secured, you will move inland. Your objectives are as follows. One, vertically envelop the enemy and pin him down. Two, search and destroy this NVA supply center. It is their main center in the southern III Corps area. And three, kill as many of them as you can. Gentlemen, good luck and God's speed."

Dennis and Harry stand next to each other in silence. Dennis is repeating the officers' words over and over to himself as if in a trance, committing the information to memory. "Hit the beach, tree line heavily fortified, one hundred yards open space, no cover whatsoever." Dennis walks over to the maps to study them. He closes his eyes and tries to visualize where he will take his position. Finally he turns to Harry, "You know, I think I'm more nervous about getting in those dang amtracs than anything else. You never know if they're gonna sink or float."

As is his manner, Harry just nods silently.

McNamara's Grand Plan

BACK IN WASHINGTON, Defense Secretary Robert S. McNamara isn't sure if his new defense strategy will sink or float, either. It is a plan that would choke off NVA routes through the DMZ at an estimated cost of one billion dollars. Inside the beltway, it is hotly debated, falling along quasi-political lines between McNamara and the civilian analysts who proposed the idea versus the Joint Chiefs of Staff who oppose it.

The plan, originally hatched months ago by several top scientists from MIT and Harvard is considered by some to be a technical solution to the Vietnam problem. The anti-infiltration barrier system with fortified strong points along the Demilitarized Zone's 17th Parallel became known as "Practice Nine," after the number of intellectuals who conceptualized it.

The Joint Chiefs of Staff opposed Practice Nine arguing it would take six or seven Army divisions to clear and secure the terrain, and up to two years to complete the barrier. But in October of 1966, McNamara sent a memo to President Johnson outlining the failures of their previous military strategy, "Rolling Thunder," to adequately pressure Hanoi. McNamara proposed the infiltration barrier, which he said "would run from the sea, across the neck of South Vietnam and across the trails in Laos," further detailing the "interdiction system would comprise to the east a ground barrier of fences, wire, sensors, artillery, aircraft, and mobile troops." The barrier would, McNamara concluded, "be persuasive evidence that our sole aim is to protect the South from the North." President Johnson warmed to the idea, and in the coming weeks would consider giving Practice Nine the highest national priority for expenditures and authorization.

Time would soon tell if McNamara's plan for a technological fix to the Vietnam problem would be realized in the 1967 New Year.

John Wayne

BELOW DECK THE MARINES lie awake, bracing themselves in their racks as a typhoon ravages the South China Sea. In the silent darkness, an announcement crackles over the loudspeaker.

"All Marines prepare to disembark!"

The Marines jolt out of their hammocks, quickly dress for reveille and begin anxiously preparing their rifles and ammunition. This is it; they are going in-country. Dennis cleans his weapons as he watches a young Marine next to him gingerly prepare his own rifle, superstitiously kissing the barrel for good luck. Another grunt is using plexi-tape to circle around his grenades so the pins can be pulled out safely.

Sgt. John Malloy is one of the forward observers also preparing his ammo. In his late twenties, he is considered a seasoned "old-timer" having been in-country previously, and his mere presence commands the rookies' respect. John glances over at a baby-faced Marine who is attempting to pull the pin out of a grenade with his teeth. "Hey, John Wayne...this ain't the friggin' movies. You'll bust your damned teeth doing that."

The Marine shrugs for show, but nonetheless, pulls the grenade from his mouth and looks to John for approval somewhat sheepishly. "Friggin' rookies," John groans under his breath, as he gets up, walks over, and grabs the grenade from him. "Here, watch me," he instructs, and shows the combat virgin how to safely prepare the munitions without killing anybody.

The ship rolls violently, slamming gear and ammo against the racks. The glancing thought of a potential right-in-their-laps mishap detonation makes more than a few Marines sweat nervously.

Another announcement crackles over the loudspeaker: "All Marines secure!"

The announcement is immediately followed by confusion and a chorus of obscenities.

The sergeant enters the squad bay. "Gentlemen, the typhoon has delayed our landing. We expect it to clear out by January 6th. Be prepared to go that morning."

White Beach

January 4th, 1967

"TRAC ONE! LOAD UP!" A gunnery sergeant barks out orders. The Marines load into the amtracs, amphibious tractor-driven landing boats with a hatch top and hydraulic front door. They climb down through the top hatch.

"Trac Two! Take all your stuff. Load up!"

Dennis grabs his 782 gear and climbs down the hatch. He can hear the gunny sergeant give orders to the driver. "Circle around the ship a few times so everyone launches for the beach together, otherwise, they'll pick us off one by one. You've got the grunts, a couple of FO's, and the 05s with you. The rest of the 05s will be in the amtrac right behind you."

Dennis sits in the darkness next to six other Marines and the reporter who clutches his notepad, sitting rigid and scared. The amtrac circles the boat, rocking back and forth in the choppy sea. Dennis closes his eyes and tries to visualize the beach.

The smell of diesel fuel and fear fill the air. Finally, the amtrac straightens its path. *This is it.* They are heading for the beach. *No more training, no more play time.* Dennis braces himself. In the darkness, a Marine prays softly.

Dennis finds it hard to breathe, his heart is racing and he feels light-headed. He knows this is a symptom of fear. *Control your fear,* he tells himself. He takes a deep breath. He isn't so much afraid of dying as he is of being overcome by fear, allowing it to override his senses, shut him down, prohibit him from doing what he is trained to do. In Dennis' mind, FDR had it right—the only thing to fear is fear itself; and right now, the thought that frightens him the most is letting everybody down and paying the ultimate price—costing someone his life.

The amtrac begins to slow down, and suddenly Dennis feels a wave shift under the vessel and carry it forward with the ocean's immense strength. He can visualize what is happening; they are nearing the beach and the surf is bringing in more than just the tide. Dennis' eyes are stinging from a combination of sweat and anxiety. Time is warping, and the front hydraulic door begins to open at an agonizingly slow pace. The Marines, crouched down, hearts pounding, see the sunlight stream in. *Okay, ready.* The door opens more and more, exposing first the sky, then the tree line—*Ready*—and finally the beach.

"Let's go!" The platoon leader yells out.

Marines pour out of the amtracs onto the Mekong beach—rifles ready, adrenaline flowing, eyes squinting from the sudden blast of blinding sunshine. Dennis' heart races even faster than before. His eyes dart right, then left, quickly scanning the beach. *Where are they? What do they look like?* He sprints past the dune grass toward the tree line. He makes it. Hiding behind a shady tree, he watches the others sprint across the open beach. Standing on the edge of the tree line amidst the sharp elephant grass and marshy jungle foliage, it finally sinks in. *I'm here, I'm in-country. Jesus, I can't believe how unbelievably foreign this place is.*

The other amtracs come ashore. Dennis anticipates the invisible enemy in the tree line opening fire. He clutches his M-14, feeling its weight in his hands.

Silence.

Dennis listens to reports coming over the radio. "No enemy positions on the beach."

Suddenly, his attention turns to the platoon lieutenant. He is wading in the surf, shouting obscenities, pounding on the front of an unopened amtrac. The hydraulic door is jammed, trapping the guns inside. The lieutenant hollers, "Jesus Christ! Get those friggin' guns out of there, *now!*"

Dennis hears a call coming over the company radio frequency. "What the hell is going on over there?" It is the platoon lieutenant commanding from Red Beach. "Is White Beach secured?"

"Not sure, looks like the 'trac is jammed. The guns must've shifted in the storm. They can't get 'em out."

Dennis hears the response. "*What!* Get those friggin' guns out! If we don't have fire support, we'll all be S.O.L.!"

Dennis watches the lieutenant frantically try to pry the door open. He can't believe their luck. Between the typhoon, and the previous nights' bombing, there are no NVA positions on the beach; otherwise, they'd all be dead right now.

Suddenly, Dennis hears a gun crack. *Sniper!*

He whirls around to the sound of the fire. It came from the tree line. He fires fast, pouring bullets into the position. *Fire superiority.* The sniper is silenced. Wide-eyed, Dennis scans the area, looking for motion. There is none. *Is the sniper dead? Wounded? Was that my first kill?* Dennis isn't sure. The only thing he is sure of is the rifle in his hands and the furious pounding of his heart. It is a strange feeling to wonder if you've killed a man. He expected it to be harder, more emotional, but right now he has no such feelings or emotions. He feels no remorse; the only feeling he knows for sure is survival. *Stay alive. Just stay alive.*

Finally, the guns are retrieved and quickly set into position. Harry is with one of the gun crews setting up the 05s on the beach. Dave Keating is on the beach as well, shouting out orders. "Send out the surveyor. Set up the aiming pole and establish the deflection point."

Minutes later a confirmation is shouted out, "Aiming pole set. Deflection point established."

The beach is completely secured. Fire Direction Control sets up operations on the open beach with no cover or protection. The makeshift FDC consists of several tables with maps sprawled across them and scores of radios ready to receive incoming fire missions.

Dennis joins the rest of the grunts in 1/9. It is time to go in-country and locate the NVA supply center. The platoon leader makes a sweeping motion with his hand and hollers "Move out!"

The Conception

THE MARINES HACK their way through the thick jungle brush of elephant grass and marsh. Their boots squish in the mud; leeches seep through their socks. One Marine stops to pull off a bloodsucker. Sgt. John Malloy stops behind him.

"That's not going to get 'em; he'll burrow his head in there. You gotta burn those suckers off."

The Marine grimaces.

Dennis learned from the veterans back at Camp Pendleton how treacherous the jungle can be. Booby-traps, punji sticks, land mines. The platoon labors forward. It is slow going and the sun is setting quickly. Three hundred hard-fought yards from White Beach, the platoon leader halts the men. "Set up defensive positions here. Set up the killing zones."

A sergeant motions for Dennis and the others to huddle around him as he draws out the defensive position like a quarterback drawing a play in the palm of his hand. "Okay, men. I want a M60 pig with each squad. Riflemen, set up your aiming sticks. The barrel of your gun should go this far," he spreads his arms to show the area width. He turns to a rifleman. "Thompson, make sure you set up a good killing zone." He points to the area in front of them. "Lock in your field of fire for the night. Anything you see move in your zone, kill." The rifleman nods.

"Dennis, I want you and the recon team to go out and set up two listening posts. I want one LP a hundred yards out; I want the other set up behind our lines in case they try to come around the flanks."

Dennis and Mills, another forward observer on the team, look for a suitable position to set up the LP, hunting for something that will provide good cover but still have some outward visibility. They settle on a large, uprooted tree. Crouching down next to the exposed roots, Dennis squares a grid of their location on his map. He radios back to the platoon, "Birmingham 6-4 is in position."

"You sleep first, I'll listen," Dennis whispers, as they lean against each other's backs.

Night falls. The jungle and its noises keep Dennis on edge. With every snap of a twig or animal sound Dennis clutches his gun. His grenades are ready by his side; his eyes are wide open, his ears perked like those of a bloodhound.

Mills, at first fighting off sleep, finally succumbs, and rests his head on his knees.

Suddenly, a loud crack. Another sharp crack, and another. *Crack. Crack. Crack.* It is small arms fire. *Shit!* A grenade explodes, flashing the night sky. Both men jolt upright. Dennis whispers, "They're behind us! They're probing the OP."

They sit upright, trying to make out the shadows in the night, prepared to shoot at anything that moves. They stay that way, frozen in their positions for nearly an hour, well after the danger has passed.

With their adrenaline levels almost back to normal, Mills, now fully awake, whispers, "Man, you realize we've got thirteen months of *this*?"

At that moment, sitting in a dark, foreign jungle, Dennis realizes his old life doesn't exist anymore. His new reality consists of people whose sole purpose is to kill him. And his sole purpose is to kill them. Within the depths of that reality, inside the core of his very being, a new will, a new consciousness is formed.

Dennis is conceived.

The Sandbox

ANDY IS STILL STARING UP at the ceiling, having yet to make eye contact with Dennis. He hasn't spoken, but he is taking the story in, nodding at times and balling his fist. He, too, knows what it is like to be consumed by foreignness.

Now his mind is conjuring its own reel of visions and, as though it is interconnected with his body by an invisible string, he remembers the feel of the heat and the sand, the smell of diesel fuel and human odors, and the burning, especially the burning: metal buildings, the sand burning his eyes, and the smell of his own burning flesh.

Flashing through a sequence of memories, he remembers his arrival in Kuwait; the March sandstorms that brought the Allied "shock and awe"; the Third Marine Division crossing of the monochromatic tan desert into Iraq; and the entry into Baghdad. The city looked almost peaceful as the sun reflected off the caramel and cream buildings. He was surprised to see the rich architecture in the opulent areas, the impoverishment in others, and the destruction the bombardments had produced. He remembers the trash that was strewn everywhere, especially the plastic bags that rolled through the streets like tumbleweeds. *Puppets of the desert.* He can still hear the sound of helicopters flying overhead and the Islamic prayers chanting in the background five times a day; and he remembers thinking it made the perfect recording to a strange movie sound track.

His first night in Baghdad, he awoke, surprised to find that his nose felt cold. It was only 60 degrees, a temperature that he would have normally consider mild, comfortable even, but it was such a major drop from the daytime temperature his body perceived it as near freezing. He watched the fires burn in the cityscape and he fell back asleep listening to the constant rat-a-tat-tat sound of distant machine guns. *This isn't so bad.* Andy remembers thinking.

The next day on patrol Andy discovered the body of a young boy, no more than fourteen, underneath the rubble of a toppled building. The boys' crushed body lay in a heap of stone and debris, with as little dignity as that of a dead dog. Andy thought it strange that the body would be lying out here, unattended, unclaimed. Iraqis are a very tight knit, family oriented society. They pride themselves on taking care of their own. *Was this young boy possibly a foreigner, a so-called insurgent who came to Iraq to jump in the fight?*

A bullet whizzed by, catching Andy off guard. Somebody shouted out, "Snipers!" But the firefight was over before it even started. The retinue of Marines poured fire into the building where they believed the sniper to be hiding, but only silence and dust surrendered. Andy's body felt numb, overwhelmed by the adrenaline pumping into every cell of his nervous system. "Welcome to the sandbox," the sergeant called out.

Welcome to the sandbox. It was the moment Andy knew he would never be the same person again.

Now, sitting next to Dennis, Andy shakes his head. *Yes. Every veteran has shed his old skin like a snake, conceived again in war.*

Deckhouse Five

HIT THE DECK! Hit the friggin' deck!" The platoon leader shouts. Dennis slams his body hard against the ground and covers his head with his arms, squeezing his helmet down tightly.

Loud rhythmic gunfire echoes through the ravine. The Marines are ambushed from both sides of the rocky walls. Bullets fly over their heads in every direction, ricocheting off the rocks.

Miraculously, no one is hit.

Several Viet Cong soldiers clad in black pajama uniforms are hiding along the side of the ravine. With their machine guns set to zero they expect the guns to fire waist high, but because of their position atop the ravine, the bullets are flying well over the Marines' heads. A Viet Cong officer realizes the gaffe immediately, and barks out orders in Vietnamese as a young gunner frantically tries to maneuver his gun but finds the task to be difficult for the single reason that his leg is tied to the gun.

With the Marines still pressed flat against the ravine floor, the platoon leader takes advantage of the lull and motions for his men to throw grenades at the enemy positions. Dennis throws his frag grenades like baseballs in the direction of the smoke trails.

Explosions mix with renewed cracking of machine gun fire, as more grenades are hurled over the rock walls until the machine guns fall silent. The Marines, crouched low, wait several seconds before the platoon leader motions silently for Dennis and the others to breech their positions.

Sprinting up the ravine wall, Dennis holds his breath. He's not sure what he'll find, but knows it will be one of two things. *A body or a bullet to the head.* Several others reach the same location, and with a decisive nod, they jump over the ravine wall rifles ready.

The first sight: smoking machine guns buried in foxholes. The second: at least half a dozen bodies strewn around those guns.

"We've got eight over here!" A grunt shouts out after having counted the bodies. The rest of the platoon scales the ravine. The platoon leader assesses the scene, takes out his notepad, and makes an entry.

Dennis stands over the dead body of a young Viet Cong gunner sprawled in an awkward position next to his machine gun. The body is mangled, and its face is contorted in a painful grimace—a frozen scream. Dennis has never seen death at such close range before. *Jesus, he looks young.* Dennis bends over to inspect the uniform and search for any frags or rounds. He notices the enemy's feet for the first time. *That's odd.* They are bound in rope and tied to the machine gun itself.

Sgt. John Malloy walks over. He has seen this before. "He's just a kid they probably kidnapped from a nearby village. The VC put somebody they considered expendable on the guns, hedging their bets he could knock a couple of us off before getting hit."

Dennis looks down at the boy with a degree of pity. *Poor bastard.* He notices something else that's odd—the gun itself. It doesn't resemble any of the models he saw during training. It has a different looking crank than he's ever seen.

"Chinese machine gun," John points out.

"I thought the Chinese were staying out of the war?" Dennis is perplexed.

"Guess that doesn't preclude them from supplying it, does it?" John answers sarcastically.

Dennis stands up straight, his eyes no longer blind to the ways of the world.

The second recon team returns. They have scoped out the enemy position on the other side of the ravine and are now providing the lieutenant with a status report. Pleased with the information, the lieutenant scribbles down a few notes in his journal and radios back to Delta. "No Marine casualties. 19 NVA KIA."

The Marines continue their hump in-country, hacking their way through the dense jungle brush and scaling the foot trails going up and down the hills. "Don't bunch up," is pounded into their heads every ten minutes or so, as they concentrate on their footing, possible land mines, and any encore performances from the Viet Cong. For Dennis, John, Mills, and the other forward observer teams, the going is tough with the heavy radios strapped on their backs, but it's worse for the trio of Marines who are taking turns humping the M60 pig through the jungle, all twenty-eight pounds of it.

Hours later, the lieutenant gives the order to halt. They have reached a good site for a landing zone. The platoon sets up in formation with one Marine on point and the others positioned on the flanks as they scour the landscape. It's clear. The grunts begin clearing the brush and small shrubs, while the engineers use mine detectors to reveal any hidden explosives or booby-traps.

Suddenly, a whistle rings out. The platoon freezes. Someone has found a spider hole, part of the intricate tunnel network the VC built a decade ago while fighting the French. The underground networks are again being used with great success—hospitals, supplies, and booby-traps are just some of the surprises the Marines have found below the ground. The lieutenant motions for the "tunnel rat," a small, sinewy Marine who is the smallest guy in the platoon by far. Without hesitation the Marine ties a rope around his ankle. Unsure of what he'll face in the dark tunnel, he wears the rope to provide insurance that his body can be pulled out by his comrades if worse comes to worst.

The tunnel rat slowly lowers himself down, unfazed. This is his special job, his duty, his niche. But Dennis respects him most for the single reason that he himself could never do this job. He hates enclosed spaces.

Soon, the landing zone is established, and the sound of the choppers in the distance becomes more audible until they hover over the LZ. Supplies and reinforcements for the mission are dropped off. Tomorrow they will knock out the NVA's main supply center.

The lieutenant calls the platoon to huddle around him so he can give their orders. "Men," he says, pointing to a location on his map, "This is where the NVA center is located." He marks the location with a bulls-eye on the grid. "In the morning we'll move out. Grunts from Red Beach will be set up on the other side so we can vertically envelop the enemy position." He tucks the map under his arm. "Set up defensive positions for the night. Tomorrow will be a long day."

This is Dennis' second night in-country, and although he is tired—exhausted from humping all day—his mind is churning full force on what may lay in wait for them tomorrow. He lies awake, restless most of the night, and no sooner does he close his eyes than he hears a voice shout, "Saddle up!"

A surge of adrenaline courses through his body, and that, coupled with the caffeine jolt provided by the most bitter tasting coffee he has ever brought to his lips, fuels him throughout the morning miles they log.

By mid-morning the Marines are crouched low in the tree line, like tigers ready to pounce on their prey as they look down on their target in the valley below. There is no visible movement in or around the supply center, a concrete structure believed to store the enemy's equipment, ammunition, and medicines.

The lieutenant huddles around Dennis' team and instructs, "Lay low. We're throwing in naval gunfire. Once the big guns destroy the complex, move in quickly and secure the location."

Dennis understands. "Roger." He feels a giddy nervousness churning in his stomach as he anxiously awaits the impending combat.

Minutes later, rockets fired from the destroyers out at sea whistle overhead as they streak through the sky, leaving miniature white and gray comet-like tails.

Booooooooommmmmmmmbbbbbbbbbbbbbbbb!

A deafening explosion rocks the ground beneath them. Smoke billows up in the sky like an ash-filled mushroom cloud. Dennis covers his head, awed by its sheer force. He looks down at the valley below. The supply center is completely leveled; only rubble is left. Dennis stares down at the destruction in amazement.

"Let's go!"

The Marines sprint across the open field to secure the site. The ground is torched black; there is no grass left. Charred bodies and body parts are strewn around the ground with pieces of concrete and wood. There are no survivors. Legs, torsos, and other limbs lie around haphazardly.

The putrid scent of burning flesh is overwhelming, and as Dennis bends down to pick up a mutilated body, he feels an immediate urge to vomit. He covers his mouth and nostrils as he carries the body over to the area where it will be body-bagged. He returns to the center of the devastation, and re-trieves another body. This one is more or less intact. Dennis stares into the man's lifeless eyes. He beckons his mind to go numb, and pay no further at-tention to the death mask before him as he focuses on searching the uniform for anything useful. He hears paper crinkle and assumes it is a map; but pulling it out, he finds instead a picture of a beautiful Vietnamese girl. Her face is smooth and heart-shaped, her smile coy.

Dennis closes his eyes and feels the first recognizable wave of sorrow he has ever felt in his life. *They're just like us . . . . Just a bunch of nineteen-year old guys with girlfriends waiting for them back home, too."*

Kill Ratio

DENNIS CLEARS HIS THROAT and his voice grows stronger, less distant, as his thoughts and attention return to his surroundings inside the Mologne House.

"General Westmoreland and some big-shot Hollywood actor greeted us back on White Beach. Everyone was gung-ho. Gunners celebrated by firing rounds for inspection and we were congratulated for an operation well done. He praised our kill ratio: ten to one. At the time I supposed McNamara would be happy with it too, but I couldn't stop thinking about what I had seen."

Dennis pauses and looks at Andy, then he lowers his voice and reveals something he has never shared with anyone before. "I felt like I lost a piece of myself," he whispers. "A piece I knew I'd never be able to retrieve again."

A nurse knocks on the door and excuses herself. "Andrew, time for lunch."

Andy turns to face Dennis for the very fist time. They lock eyes, and then Andy extends his arm. Dennis reaches out. He can feel the blood coursing through Andy's veins as they shake hands, squeezing tightly. Andy tries to speak, but his voice is weak. After he clears his throat, he tries again, "Come back tomorrow."

Dennis nods and rises to his feet. Just before he reaches the door he hears Andy's voice call out to him.

"Dennis?"

Dennis turns around.

"Ooh-rah."

Dennis stops in his tracks. The ballast of that one word fills him with a sense of recognition that he's rarely known. Dennis smiles. "Ooh-rah."

He thinks of Andy the entire drive home. Andy reminds him of someone. *Of Harry? Of his son? A mixture of both?* Sadly, Andy's face is like that of so many of the other veterans he has seen over the years—faces that are no longer innocent, naïve, and gung-ho but rather disenfranchised, fractured remnants of their former selves, no longer believing in the grandeur and glory of war. Andy reminds Dennis of himself. *The smoke has cleared and the mirrors have been broken, but the wounds remain.* And now he can't shake the overwhelming desire to patch Andy up, make him whole again. *But how? How can I help this kid?*

He pulls up to his empty townhouse in suburban Virginia. His ex-wife has long since gone, the kids have grown up, and the pets belong to his neighbors. He doesn't even own a fish. Dennis walks up the stairs to his unit just as a delivery man holding a floral arrangement knocks on his neighbor's door. The neighbor opens the door and gushes at the sight of the beautiful bouquet of roses. Dennis smiles. Harry used to send his girl back home flowers just like those.

Roses

DENNIS LIES ON HIS COT opposite Harry. The rain hits the dirt outside with forceful thuds as a monsoon soaks the firebase perched atop a remote hill overlooking the Co Bi Than Tan valley east of Dong Ha. Camp Czzowitz, informally named after a corporal who had been killed during their last tour, consists of eight pitched tents, twelve men to a tent, enough to house Delta Battery and the grunts. All in all, fewer than one hundred men occupy the hill. Big droplets of rain descend from holes in the shrapnel-torn canvas and smack loudly on their cots.

Drip . . . Drip . . . Drip . . .

Harry places his helmet on his stomach to catch what he can, and Dennis fumbles around for his poncho to cover the puddle of rain forming on his cot. The two exchange a quick glance and laugh at their feeble attempts.

"This rain is so friggin' miserable," Dennis chuckles.

"I was just thinking the same thing," Harry replies. Then he pauses and thinks a moment about something he had heard earlier that day. "Speaking of miserable, Chief got a letter from Gomez. I guess he's not doing so good."

"Who's not doing so good?"

"Gomez. I guess he's having a tough time being back home."

"Oh hell," Dennis says wearily. They've all heard stories about guys having a hard time readjusting to home life back in the States. "Hope he doesn't pull an Ira Hayes."

"Yeah, me neither."

Dennis still remembers the day he heard the news of the legendary Ira Hayes' death. Dennis was seven years old. It was just two months after Dennis visited the Iwo Jima Memorial and saw for the first time the larger-than-life image of Ira lifting the American flag. Ira had been made famous by raising that flag atop Mount Suribachi. But that image belied reality.

The photographer, Joe Rosenthal, who snapped the picture that inspired the statue, wasn't present for the original raising of the flag, so when a different group of six Marines, including Ira, began to hoist a second, larger flag to replace the small, tattered original, Rosenthal captured the picture.

That photograph became iconic and those in the photo became national heroes. But Ira knew the truth—and he couldn't live with that. No one knows if it was the celebrations or the word "hero" being conferred on him, if it was his help promoting war bonds or the ghosts of guys who had died on that sandy island that bothered him the most. Whatever the cause, after the Iwo Jima Memorial was commemorated, Ira disappeared from the public eye and went back to his Indian reservation, finding solace in a bottle. There, he continued to drink until he drank himself to death, and was found face down and frozen in a puddle of mud, forever immortalized in the Johnny Cash song, "*The Ballad of Ira Hayes.*"

Dennis and Harry think about this for a moment in silence. Death by the enemy is one thing, but death by your own hand is another, and unfortunately, reports have surfaced of guys back home who have taken their own lives.

Dennis changes the subject. "Hey, Harry, did you ever hear back from that girl, Joyce?"

"Yeah, she wrote me back... sent me a picture too!"

"She did?"

Harry pulls a picture out of his shirt pocket and hands it to Dennis.

Dennis whistles. "Well I'll be, Harry! She's cute as hell! So, what'd she say?"

"Just that she can't wait to finally meet me. And that she loved my letter."

"She did, huh? Damn, and to think you only signed your name at the bottom!" Dennis winks.

Harry looks sheepish.

"That's okay, Harry, pretty soon you'll learn the fine art of writing your own love letters."

"Her birthday's coming up next month. I want to send her something nice. What do you think I should send?" Harry asks excitedly, nervous at the prospect of properly courting a girl.

"Well Harry, you gotta treat her like gold, and make her feel special. Make her feel like she's the only girl in the world." Then Dennis leans over and hushes his voice so that only Harry can hear what he's saying. "Listen, don't pay any attention to these other guys. You know, the stuff they talk about doing with their girls back home. They're just talking. Half of 'em are full of crap anyway."

Harry nods. "I know Denny. So, what do you think? Should I send her flowers?"

"Oh definitely. You gotta send her roses though; all women love roses. Just mail the money and a description of what you want to my buddy in New Brunswick, and he'll call the florist for you."

"Roses . . . . Okay. I'll send him money for a dozen red roses."

"*Red?*" Dennis jumps up off his cot, alarmed. "You can't send her *red* roses! Red means you love her! No, Harry, you gotta watch sending those." Dennis pauses to think while Harry sits on the edge of his cot, frightened and excited at the same time like a kid at camp listening to a good ghost story. "White could be an option, though," Dennis says, scratching his head. That doesn't sound right to him either. "Nah, on second thought, white roses look too much like a funeral. How about pink?" It is more an exclamation than a question, a directive rather than an option.

"Pink?" Harry wonders. "Think she'll like 'em?"

"She'll love 'em, Harry. Trust me."

Harry leans back on his cot, still holding his helmet to catch the rain, but this time with a smile on his face.

Part II

Quang Tri
November 3, 2004

"The life I touch for good or ill will touch another life, and that in turn another, until who knows where the trembling stops or in what far place my touch will be felt."

—Frederick Buechner

Fallujah

DENNIS WAKES UP TO his alarm clock radio. *"The Bush campaign is emphasizing the big numbers in the president's victory, driving home the legitimacy of this reelection."*

Bush is still the president. Dennis is indifferent. For the past few months, his friends had often asked what he thought of the Kerry campaign, if he had an issue with Kerry's participation in the "Veterans against Vietnam" organization. And although Dennis' feelings used to be conflicted, he has reconciled them long ago and has since come to believe that any man who fights in a war has earned the right to say what he wants about it, come what may. But right now, he doesn't want to think about the election, or politics, or Vietnam, he just wants to go back to sleep. Just a few more minutes .... He groggily pushes the snooze button.

Ten minutes later, he hears: *"In other news, the Pentagon confirmed that a Nevadan was one of nine Marines killed. Eight other Marines also were wounded in the attack Saturday when a car bomb went off next to a truck outside Fallujah in the Anbar province of Iraq ...."*

Fallujah again. Part of the Sunni Triangle. He's been following news of the insurgency brewing since March, when the Marines replaced the 82nd Airborne and 3rd Cavalry. The Marines had first laid siege to the city in April in an operation called Operation Vigilant Resolve. They lost close to

40 men. Now, signs are pointing to another major offensive against the rebel stronghold.

Fallujah, known as the "city of mosques" for the two hundred holy structures located in and around the city, has long been considered one of the most important places to Sunni Islam. But now, because of its position on the main road west of Baghdad, and its high population of Sunni Ba'ath supporters and Saddam Hussein loyalists, Fallujah is known mostly as a breeding ground for insurgents. Coincidently, the origin of the name 'Fallujah' is derived from the word "division." And the city is certainly on par for the course to divide.

Dennis turns up his radio before walking into the bathroom to brush his teeth.

"Reuters reports that U.S. Warplanes bombed targets in Fallujah overnight, destroying an arms cache and an insurgent command post. Witnesses say seven explosions shook Fallujah. A hospital official says a woman has been seriously wounded and a teenage girl lost her right leg in the strikes."

Dennis pauses before he spits out his toothpaste. *God damn it, leave the kids out of it.* Women and children aren't supposed to be hurt by war, it's not natural. But he knows the callous reality all too well—there's never been a war where they haven't.

A Lilly in the Valley

February, 1967

THIS VILLAGE IS a prime target for the NVA to infiltrate. It is our mission to get to know the villagers," the platoon leader tells his unit. "Show them that we are their friends." He looks each Marine in the eye. "Any questions?" There are none. The attempt to befriend the villagers is part of the pacification program to make the Marines' presence known and discourage them from safe-harboring the enemy. "Good," he says. "Saddle up."

The grunts and forward observers pack their gear to go on yet another operation to patrol the villages and hillsides in the Quang Tri province. It is a routine that has characterized Dennis' daily existence for the past two months, ever since the Marines were re-deployed to the I-Corps area.

Dennis is not aware, nor is the majority of officers and grunts of the 3rd Marine Division patrolling and pacifying the villages along the Demilitarized Zone, that within the bowels of the Pentagon, a full-swing battle is being waged over the defense secretary's anti-infiltration plan. The Joint Chiefs of Staff has formally rejected the "MACV Practice Nine Requirements Plan," that Westmoreland submitted on January 26th.

The only rule for the Marines out in the jungles of Vietnam is *"Stay alive."* Operations are long, hot, and miserable. A Marine stepping on a land mine has become a daily occurrence.

Dennis slings his gear over his shoulder and adjusts the weight of the radio on his back, making sure the antenna isn't sticking up too far. He looks over toward the battery and sees Harry setting up the gun positions. The grunts have been cracking jokes that the gunners have been on vacation, and that the guns might as well be collecting rust as they've had little use for artillery on these daily patrols. Dennis looks over to Harry and nods. *See you later.* Harry averts his eyes and looks down at his gun, ignoring Dennis. *What's with him?* Dennis wonders.

The Marines walk down the hillside toward the villages of bamboo thatched huts and rice paddies. Nestled in the valley, the villages are mostly populated by women, children, and the elderly, who smile at the Marines as they tend to their rice paddies and water buffalo. The Marines try to convey friendliness, but they dart their eyes back and forth looking for any sign of NVA.

An elderly villager carefully tending to his rice paddy looks up from under his coned hat and politely acknowledges the Marines. The beautiful country and seemingly friendly villagers belie a great danger that the Marines know is always lurking.

"This place is so backward," a young grunt mutters through his teeth, pretending to smile.

"It's not backward. It's just simple," Sgt. John Malloy corrects him. "These villages have been here for thousands of years. These families have lived in the same huts for generations. It's just their way of life." The young grunt doesn't respond, but he doesn't seem convinced.

A group of children play in the field. One little girl stands out. She is no more than eight or nine years old, but she is wearing a bright red hat—a fancy hat—with a large red plume. The girl notices the Marines and immediately stops her play. She stands up, tall and proud, her hat covering half of her face. Some children, upon seeing the Marines, run and hide or at the least show expressions of confusion or wariness. Not this little girl; instead, she pushes up the brim of her red plume hat and smiles.

Dennis feels a palpable tug in his heart. This little girl is special. He reaches into his flak jacket and holds out his last candy bar. She hesitates at first, but eventually gives in to her curiosity. Dennis places the bar in the palm of her hand. She opens the wrapper and takes a bite. Tasting the sweet chocolate, her eyes light up, and she smiles with delight. Dennis turns to the others and asks, "Hey, does anybody remember how you say 'I'm an American Marine, and I am your friend?'"

It's anyone's guess. Dennis smiles down at the girl and he tries his best to phonetically sound out the phrase he learned back at Camp Pendleton.

The girl cocks her head to the side, confused. He obviously said it wrong. Dennis looks down, discouraged. Suddenly she giggles and sticks her thumb up. "Maries nabbah one! Maries nabbah one!"

They all laugh.

"What's your name?" Dennis asks. The girl shakes her head and smiles; she does not understand.

"Let's call her Lilly. Like Lilly in the Valley," Dennis suggests.

Everyone shrugs, as if to say, "Sure, why not."

Dennis kneels down and smiles, "Well, Lilly, it's nice to meet you." She beams as she watches him walk away.

The Marines continue patrolling the village, scouting the area for mines. They find none. Making their way back to the perimeter, the young grunt on point begins walking up a trail leading back to the base.

Suddenly a loud scream pierces the air. Dennis whirls around, ready to fire. It is Lilly. She is running toward them, waving her arms wildly and pointing to something. She is pointing to the trail.

"What's wrong with that kid?" The young grunt yells over, continuing to head toward the trail.

Lilly shouts out again and waves her arms even more frantically. Dennis immediately understands. "Stop! Don't move! Stay right there!" He yells to the grunt on point.

Dennis walks gingerly to the trail where Lilly is pointing. Her eyes are still frantic; she is out of breath. Stooping over, Dennis uncovers twigs and old grass and discovers a hole. It is a booby trap—three sticks, covered in buffalo dung, stick out of the hole like spears. The young grunt covers his nose.

"Jesus, that stinks! What the hell is that?"

"Punji stick." John answers him. "Bamboo sticks covered with crap and poison. If you'd a stepped in it, it would've impaled your foot, or worse, your balls. The dung would have caused an infection quicker than you could've gotten to help. You'd be dead before the day was done."

The young grunt looks horrified. "Disgusting bastards."

Dennis turns to Lilly. He bows his head to say, "Thank you." Lilly stands up straighter, and triumphantly smiles, showing off her chocolate covered teeth.

The platoon leader shouts out to the Marines. "Time to move out!"

Dennis looks back as Lilly waves goodbye.

Angels of Mercy

DENNIS CHECKS IN at the Mologne House and registers at the front desk as a visitor. "Andrew will be back shortly. He was scheduled for a last minute appointment with his team of surgeons," the desk attendant tells him.

"Oh?"

"They're checking on that shrapnel again. They hope to fit him with prosthetic limbs soon." She says optimistically; it is obvious that, having been here for so long, Andy is one of her favorites.

"I see. Will you please tell him that Dennis is here to see him when he gets back."

The attendant smiles and assures him she will.

Dennis walks across the campus to the little deli in the main hospital and orders a coffee. He is excited for Andy. He knows he's been waiting several months to be fitted with his C-legs; the new prosthetics are giving amputees everywhere a better quality of life. If anything will lift Andy's spirits it will be the freedom to walk again. Dennis has seen pictures of veterans with C-legs out running, golfing, doing normal activities; he even heard about one amputee in the Air Force, who after successful rehabilitation, returned to active duty to fly supply planes.

The prosthetic limbs of today are a far cry from the plastic or metal limbs of yesterday, which were made with limited hydraulics. Based on revolutionary technology, the lower-limb prosthetic of choice today is the Otto Bock

C-leg, or "computer leg," made of lightweight titanium and high-strength aluminum that can support up to 330 pounds. The C-legs use microprocessors with lithium-ion batteries and on-board sensors to function like a control-center, recording and matching the patient's movement fifty times per second to mimic natural gait and movement. The response from amputees has been overwhelmingly positive, and the orthopedic teams at Walter Reed, and those of the U.S. Army Amputee Patient Care Program, are quickly becoming experts in their use. *Angels of mercy*, Dennis thinks.

While he is walking back across the campus his cell phone rings. It is Don Leary from "Make a Difference." The first thing Don asks: "Hey, how'd everything go yesterday?"

"Good. I'm here again right now."

"I'm glad to hear that," Don pauses. "Listen, Dennis, something has come up that I wanted to talk to you about."

"Oh? What is it?"

"A Marine from West Virginia was shot and killed last week outside Fallujah. They're sending him home to be buried in Arlington on Saturday. He arrives in Dover tomorrow."

Dennis shakes his head. *Another one.* Don continues, "The family is flying in on Friday, and will be staying at the Fisher House. I was wondering if you would mind escorting the boy's mother to the funeral."

Dennis takes in a deep breath. This is a big responsibility. "I don't know Don, I . . . ." He stops short. *Is this something I really want to do? Something I want to see?* He's not sure if he's the right man for the job, but despite his misgivings he doesn't want to say no. *Not to something like this.*

"Will you do it?" Don asks anxiously.

Dennis pauses for several seconds before finally responding, "Yes."

"I was hoping you'd say that. I'll send you the arrangements."

Dennis hangs up and immediately second-guesses himself. He always feels somewhat numb when someone dies; it's as if the news, with all its weight, enters a hollow shell where it perpetually reverberates but never cracks the shell itself. It's a throwback to a response he learned in Vietnam he calls the "Body Bag Syndrome." *When they're gone, they're gone.*

He tries to shake it off, but an errant thought even more morbid than the first enters his mind, the one-two punch that never fails to surface. *Did that Marine know he was going to die?*

The Letter

DENNIS KICKS OFF his boots, rubs his feet, and reaches for his c-rations of pork and beans before plopping down on his cot. Harry watches him intently. Dennis seems to possess more energy than usual after a patrol.

"Harry, I wish you were out there today," Dennis tells him, describing Lilly and her role in saving them from harm. He pauses for a moment, and reflects, "She kind of reminds you of what we're fighting for in the first place."

Harry listens quietly. Instead of responding, Harry reaches into his jacket pocket and pulls out an envelope. "Here," he holds out the envelope for Dennis, "I want you to hold on to this for me."

Dennis is confused. He looks at Harry strangely but proceeds to open the envelope; it contains yet another envelope, this one with a letter inside. "Harry, what is this?"

"Just hang on to it for me."

Dennis scans over the letter, reading the first section aloud. "I want you to know I love you very much. I know you'll have a good life. I want to be buried by the tree on the hill where. . . ." He stops, and reads over the rest silently until he reaches the last few lines. "My best friend Denny will explain everything."

Dennis furrows his brow and throws the letter on the bed, annoyed. *You've got to be kidding me.* "Harry, what the hell is this?"

"Denny, I want you to send that home to my sister if anything happens to me."

"Happens to you?" Dennis practically shouts. "Harry, you're on the guns! You stay on the base all day. The chance of something happening to you is next to nil!" Dennis realizes he's shouting and lowers his voice. "Besides, your tour is almost up. You've got nothing to worry about."

Dennis grabs a stack of brochures next to his cot and hands them to Harry. "My mom sent us the Virginia Tech applications. We gotta fill these out and send them back in so we can go to school together. I thought that's what you wanted?"

Harry stands defiantly, refusing the brochures and Dennis' attempt to change the subject. "Just promise me you'll do it. Promise you'll send that letter if anything happens."

"What's wrong with you?"

"Just promise me, Dennis."

"Fine, Harry," Dennis says tersely. "If it makes you friggin' happy, I promise." He throws the brochures and application down on Harry's cot and walks out of the tent.

Under the Armor

DENNIS RETURNS to the front desk.

"Andrew still isn't back yet. They may just keep him over at the main hospital and take him directly to his physical therapy on the third floor."

"Do you have a piece of paper and a pen? I'd like to leave him a note."

The attendant pleasantly smiles and fetches him a pen and a scrap of paper. He jots down a brief note, folds the paper, and hands it back to her.

Truthfully, Dennis is somewhat relieved, as he wasn't sure what to talk about next. His mind has been flooded with questions for the past twenty four hours: *Does he even want to hear this? Is he benefiting from this, or am I just being selfish?*

Selfish isn't a term he would normally use to describe himself, but what is he really trying to do as a mentor? *Am I helping this kid, or am I just grasping at another chance to redeem all of my past wrongs?* Dennis doesn't know why he signed up to be a mentor, but now above all else, he just wants to see Andy walk out of here with his future in front of him, not behind him. So many people live their lives in the past; and he can only imagine how especially difficult it must be when your past involves an IED exploding under the belly of an inadequately armored Humvee, blowing off your legs.

The more obvious part of Dennis' question is what to talk about next. He is still unsure. After Deckhouse, his unit had gone back to Okinawa to re-supply then spent the next three months in the Quang Tri province patrolling and pacifying the villages in the I Corp tactical region. And while every day they got more and more indoctrinated into the ways of death, those first three months—the first "trimester" in-country—didn't change him significantly. That wouldn't happen until April, when they were to leave for The Street of No Joy, the operation that changed everything. But it wasn't the kills or the patrols he remembers most about Quang Tri; it was Lilly and Harry, the conversations and the guys. He didn't realize how much those conversations meant to him. Until they stopped.

Harry

HEY, SHUT UP back there!" the lieutenant scolds. The daily patrols of the hillsides and villages have become predictable for the grunts and forward observers, and the lieutenant knows that conversations can lead to carelessness, which can lead to someone getting killed. They walk in hushed silence, scouring the fern canopies for suspicious looking indents or protrusions, placing each black-booted step carefully. Caution prevails. That is, until boredom sets in again.

"Hey, pssst . . . Denny," someone whispers over to Dennis loudly. It is Vincent, a loud, obnoxious grunt from the Bronx.

Dennis is caught off-guard; his mind is preoccupied with other things, specifically the letter that Harry gave him. He touches his chest and hears the paper crinkle against the nylon. The letter's presence in his flak jacket bears an indelible weight, a burden rather, that still upsets him and he hasn't been able to stop thinking about how stubborn Harry had been.

"Hey Denny!" Vincent's whisper is louder than most people's normal speaking voice, so he's not exactly whispering at all. But then again, no one ever considered him to be the brightest guy in the platoon.

"Huh?" Dennis realizes he is talking to him.

"What'a ya gonna do when ya get back home? Ya got any plans?" Vincent asks in a thick Bronx accent.

"I'm gonna go back to school. Me and Harry are applying to colleges together."

Another grunt jumps in the conversation. "I can't see Harry as a college man. Too quiet. Looks like you're breaking him out of his shell though. He didn't say two words last tour."

The sergeant cuts them off, shushing them to be quiet again and follow the lieutenant's orders.

Vincent pays no attention. "So what a ya gonna be, an engineer or something like dat? I heard you raced cars back home. What kind a car d'ya drive?"

"A C-Factor Experimental."

Jones—or Jonesy, as he is referred to—a tall black grunt from North Carolina who is walking behind Dennis, snorts. "That ain't nothing. My hog can outrun that!"

"Hey, you girls shut the hell up back there!" The sergeant snarls, now thoroughly pissed, and he shoots back a menacing glare.

Twenty minutes later, they reach the valley without further incident, stopping only to survey the rice paddies and the villagers tending to them. Everything appears to be normal with no sign of NVA. Suddenly, they feel several drops of rain. Within seconds it turns into a heavy downpour. "Here we go again." The Marines stop to put on their ponchos, but they are already soaked.

The elderly villagers squatting down in the rice paddy pay no heed to the Marines or the rain. Dennis had once heard that Buddhists consider rice to be sacred and believe that each crop contains its own spirit essence which must be cultivated carefully keeping its divinity in mind. He watches now as the villagers hunched over in the paddy, tend fastidiously to their godly grains.

The Marines walk down the muddy road to the village, carefully screening each hut they pass, looking for suspicious activity. Several yards away, a door to one of the huts flies open. There's no cause for alarm; it is Lilly's hut. Dennis smiles as he sees his favorite little girl standing in the doorway wearing her fancy red plumed hat. She calls out to them and waves. "Maries numbah one!" Dennis waves back. Her parents stand behind her in the doorway and bow their heads. The Marines bow theirs in return. Dennis thinks that maybe the pacification program is working well. After all, the village hasn't been uncooperative or otherwise blown off the map.

The platoon returns from patrol later that evening. It is still raining and Dennis' gun is slung low over his shoulder. He is exhausted. He hasn't slept or eaten much lately, and it's taking a toll. Harry walks over from the battery.

"Hey, how was it today?" Harry asks.

"Fine. I'm just so friggin tired and hungry right now."

Harry looks down at the ground pensively. "I wanted to talk to you about something." Dennis isn't sure he's in the mood to talk, but doesn't say anything. Harry continues, "I extended my tour for six months."

What? Dennis' head snaps up, not fully believing what he just heard. He is suddenly infuriated. *Why?* "What the hell is going on with you, Harry?"

"I want to take the Forward Observer classes next week. I want to get off the guns and find out what it's really like out there." Harry points to the valley. Then, he looks down at his boots and says quietly, "I want to go out as an FO."

Dennis is furious. "What do you mean: 'Go out as an FO'?" Questions swirl in Dennis' mind. "Is that why you gave me that letter?"

Harry is silent.

"What are you trying to prove, Harry?" Dennis starts pacing. "You want to be an FO? Yeah? Well, let me tell you something. It sucks out there. It's wet. You've got no tent. You lie in mud, sleep in water, hump twenty miles a day, and have little guys running around in black pajamas trying to kill you. Now why in the hell would you want to do that?"

"Same damn reason you do."

Dennis doesn't say anything; he doesn't have to. He likes the responsibility of being a forward observer, likes calling in the fire missions, supporting the grunts, and having people rely on him for support. He looks at Harry suspiciously. Forward observers and radio operators are, in general, prime targets for the NVA because the radio antenna sticking out is a dead giveaway, and a sure way of knocking out the platoon's direct contact to artillery. But deep down, Dennis knows that Harry only wants to be a FO for the single reason of proving he has guts enough to do it.

"This is just something I've got to do, Denny. Of all people, can't you understand that?"

Dennis is still silent.

There is something else. Harry is right—something that only Dennis would understand. The position of FO, or scout, is not part of the platoon *per se*, but rather an attachment to the platoon from the battery. Forward observers don't share in the platoon camaraderie; they are outsiders. But calling in the fire missions, and being the battery's extension, especially when the shit hits the fan, is what makes the position satisfying. They are outsiders. And that is something that both Dennis and Harry, growing up, had in common. Yes, Dennis understands.

He remembers back to one of his first conversations with Harry. Harry had asked him why he joined the Marines. Dennis told him he'd wanted to be a Marine since he was six years old. Then he asked Harry the same question. Harry's response: "I figured if the Marines can't make a man out of me, no one can."

Dennis looks up and sees the earnest look in Harry's eyes. *There's nothing I can say that will stop him.* Shaking his head, he brushes by Harry mumbling something under his breath. Harry can barely make it out, but he thinks Dennis said, "If you're gonna do it, you're gonna friggin' do it."

Practice Nine

March 13, 1967

A MEMO FROM the Deputy Assistant Secretary of State for East Asian and Pacific Affairs to the Deputy Under Secretary of State for Political Affairs, which would later be recorded in the State Department archives, reads: "General Starbird and his associates briefed you on a strong point-obstacle system designed to inhibit infiltration into the northern portion of South Vietnam. The unclassified code name of this project is 'Practice Nine.' As you will recall, the initial phase calls for construction of a series of strong points just south of the DMZ extending inland a distance of approximately 30 KM. Secretary McNamara has given the go-ahead for the preliminary work on this portion of the system. Plans for a westward extension using air-dropped mines and sensors are still in a preliminary stage."

The conversation marked a turn-about in the inner workings of Pentagon politics. Less than a month ago, the Joint Chiefs of Staff had rejected the defense secretary's plan, objecting that "the diversion of forces and funding for the scheme could not be arranged in the time called for." The project would have remained unimplemented had it not been for Joint Chief General Wheeler, who later reversed his opinion and dissented with his four colleagues. On February 22nd, General Wheeler recommended the implementation of the Practice Nine plan.

It was the go-ahead McNamara needed. On March 6, he directed the JCS to prepare for the execution of the strong-point obstacle system, and gave them a deadline of November 1, 1967 for completion of the first phase. The port city of Hue would become important strategically, as it would receive most of the Project Nine materials. Improvements to the port, as well as to Route 1 north of the city would be required.

The barrier was to entail a static system of bases between areas of ground obstacles. Air operations in support of the line would later be termed "Muscle Shoals," the technology for it would fall under the alias "Igloo White," and the troop-supported components of the barrier came under the code name "Dye Marker." The initial development of the barrier was to occur in northeastern Quang Tri Province between the DMZ and Route 9.

The Marines were given orders for their next steps: acquire the necessary right of way for the strong point system and make arrangements for relocating civilians displaced by the construction work. The ancestral homes that had been passed down for generations would now be located in no-man's land.

They were expendable.

Whispering Pines

DENNIS AND HARRY LISTEN to the radio inside the tent, both still quiet and pensive about their earlier conversation. Chet, Pete, and several other gunners from Delta Battery enter just as the radio plays "Whispering Pines," one of Dennis' favorite songs. He perks up a bit as he recognizes the Johnny Horton classic:

> *Whispering pines, whispering pines tell me is it so*
> *Whispering pines, whispering pines you're the one who knows*
> *My darling's gone, oh she's gone and I need your sympathy*
> *Whispering pines send my baby back to me*

Chet rolls his eyes. "Jesus! Not again Denny! I'm gonna get that friggin' song in my head again. Why don't you listen to something good for a change?"

"This is good!" Dennis says defensively.

"Yeah, whatever," Chet retorts.

The Marines sit around in a circle and eat their c-rations. Pete throws his half-empty can down in disgust. "This stuff sucks. They feed guys in prison better food than this shit."

"No they don't," Chet says, looking down. "Trust me."

Everyone looks up.

"What, you've been to the slammer?" Pete asks, astonished.

"How you boys think I got here?"

Silence.

Chet continues nonchalantly. "Uncle Sam gave me a choice—either go to 'Nam or go to jail for life. I figured I liked my chances over here better."

"What'd you do? Pete asks.

"Killed a guy." Chet's response is indifferent and chilling.

"What? Are you serious?" Pete stares at Chet incredulously.

"He was a rival. A Pagan."

"You're a Hell's Angel?" Pete nearly falls backward.

Chet looks down at the ground, obviously uncomfortable. "Shit, it's no big deal. We kill guys out here all the time who are trying to kill us. Don't act like it's no different." He pauses to look each of them in the eye. "Killing is killing. It's all the same."

No one dares to speak. The song finishes playing. The tent is filled with awkward silence until Dennis tries to break the tension, "It's alright Chet, you're just another one of 'Uncle Sam's Misguided Children!'" He points to the USMC acronym on Chet's fatigues.

Chet snickers and playfully punches Dennis' hand away. The next song plays on the radio. *Over the Mountain*. Another of Dennis' favorites. Chet groans in disgust, "Ugh Denny! Now you're really killing me!"

Dennis smiles and leans back. "This song reminds me of my first girl-friend, Sarah Conroy. I was twelve. She was fourteen. We went to a party. This song came on and we danced." He pauses. "It was the first time I ever danced with a girl, and I still remember the smell of her sweater."

"Whatever," Pete interrupts him, "Get to the good stuff. Did you feel her up?"

"Naw, I kissed her though."

"What? You pansy!" Pete yells out. "I would've at least felt her up! I was twelve when I felt my first girl up. I had sex when I was thirteen."

Chet laughs at him. "You can't even get laid now without paying some-one, and you're trying to tell us you got laid when you were thirteen? What was she? Fat or ugly?"

Pete smiles good-naturedly. "Both!"

They all roar with laughter, except Harry. Chet notices. "Harry, you're always so quiet. What do you think man?

"Good one," Harry replies quietly. He and Dennis exchange a quick glance.

Dennis stands up. "Harry's got some news for us," Dennis announces. "He's going to FO School."

"That's right," Harry confirms, rising to his feet. "I'm going next week." Everyone is silent. They don't know what to say. They're not used to seeing Harry so assertive.

"Well, isn't that nice?" Chet breaks the silence. "You wanna go out and get some kills now, Harry?" He turns to another young grunt, "Hey, you, how many kills you got?"

"Twenty-three."

Chet turns back to Harry. "Think you can do that Harry? Think you can kill twenty-three gooks? McNamara only cares about numbers. You know that, don't you?"

"I can do it," Harry says defiantly.

"Well boys! Guess we gotta teach Harry here how to go out and get some kills!"

A proud smile crosses Harry's face.

Dennis sits back down in silence.

Phu Bai

HARRY STRIDES INSIDE the tent confidently. He appears to be taller, more robust, and seems to possess more self-assurance than Dennis has ever before seen in him. It is a transition that has happened over the last two weeks, ever since he began his forward observer training. Usually reserved for non-commissioned officers, forward observers are in short supply right now, and Harry has excelled at reading maps, marking grids, sending in fire missions and commanding radio operations during the informal field training sessions. While Dennis always thought of Harry as a good Marine, Harry didn't know it yet for himself. Until now.

"They're taking me off the guns. I'm now a certified FO." His voice is filled with pride, like the straight-A student who just brought home an exemplary report card and is eager for the anticipated approval. Harry smiles before taking a deep breath, he has another announcement he needs to make. "I've been re-assigned. To Bravo Company." Dennis is startled. *Bravo Company?* "My new orders are to guard the airfield down in Phu Bai. I move out tomorrow."

Reassigned? Phu Bai? Dennis is taken by surprise.

"Phu Bai? Ha!" One of the grunts scoffs. "You went through all that trouble to be an FO and you're going to Phu Bai? You're going to be the only FO in Nam without a kill!"

The reaction stings Harry. His face reddens with humiliation, but he swiftly takes control of his emotions, "I'll get my kills, don't you worry about me," he says through clenched teeth. His eyes are set with steely resolve; and even though he doesn't know how, where, or when, he will get his kills—he guarantees it.

But everyone knows that Phu Bai is the schoolyard of I Corps. Recently built up by the Seabees, the U.S. Naval Construction Force, and located just miles south of the ancient imperial capital of Hue, Phu Bai is an important advance base along the coast of the South China Sea that has seen little action in the war thus far and is considered to be a relatively safe place. What the Marines don't know is just how drastically the status of Phu Bai will change in the coming year.

"Anyone care to place a wager on how many kills you think Harry will get in Phu Bai?" A nearby grunt makes a crack.

"Enough!" Dennis yells, pushing the grunt hard in the chest. He storms out of the tent, not wanting to hear another word.

Homecoming

HARRY LEFT THE NEXT DAY, taking with him his sole possession, a Yashica camera he had bought in Japan. Neatly placed on Dennis' cot was a picture of the two of them, standing arm in arm. It had been snapped somewhere in Okinawa. It always surprised Dennis how much those things meant to Harry, and how much they meant to him, too, which is what made it so bad when Harry left.

Now back at his home in Ashburn, Virginia, Dennis checks his voice messages and reads the email Don Leary sent regarding the Marine's funeral arrangements on Saturday. He is to pick up the boys' mother at 10 a.m. and escort her to the funeral. He wonders how she is coping with the stress of losing a child.

Less than one hundred miles away, the body of the fallen Marine arrives at Dover Air Force Base under the auspices of night. Cloaked under the American flag, his coffin is stacked neatly in a row with the others, shielded away from media scrutiny.

He is home.

Lilly

LILLY IS PLAYING ALONE in the field next to her hut. Wearing her red hat, she is hunched over two primitive dolls made out of bamboo that she has wrapped in small swatches of cloth. She talks to them lovingly as she pretends to serve them tea, the child-mother innate in every little girl.

Hearing the sound of the Marines' boots, she leaves her dolls on the ground as she sprints over to greet Dennis, her favorite. He is the one with bright blue eyes and a funny ball nose who always gives her candy, the one she overheard her parents say has a good heart. They can just tell, and she can too. She reaches out and grabs Dennis by the hand and looks up at him, even though she has to squint from the sunlight streaming in her eyes. Dennis laughs at her scrunched face. "How's my girl doing today?" he asks.

She walks into the village with him and points over to her hut. There, her mother and father greet them with a bow of their heads. They motion for Dennis and Mills, the other forward observer, to come inside their hut.

"What are they doing?" Mills is somewhat bewildered. "I don't know." Dennis is cautious. He looks around the hut for suspicious activity, and peeks inside to make sure there will be no surprises. Lilly's parents smile, patiently allowing the Marines to examine their home. Satisfied with their inspection, the two enter.

The hut is bare, with mud walls and a dirt floor and virtually no furniture. In the center of the hut is a large hole dug into the floor that serves as the cooking area. The beds—cots, rather—are pushed up against the mud walls to make more living space available during the day.

Lilly's parents smile and gesture for the Marines to sit. Communicating through body language, nods of the head, smiles and a few words in English, Lilly's father points to a spot on the floor and motions for the men to sit.

Dennis assumes he knows rudimentary English from the American military presence much the same as the Vietnamese adopted the French language during the long years spent under colonial occupation. During that time, the French exported rice, developed rubber plantations, built churches, and taught the impoverished farmers the French language as part of their mission to "civilize" Vietnam, a country that had already been civilized by the native Viets for two thousand years.

Dennis sits cross-legged on the dirt floor. Lilly quickly sits next to him. Mills follows Dennis' lead and sits directly across from him.

Lilly's mother places fragrant plates of rice and fish heads in front of them, a delicacy for their family. Dennis bows his head in a gesture of gratitude.

They eat in the silence of smiles until nothing is left. Then her father places down his chopsticks and takes a deep breath. He puts his hand on Lilly's shoulder and looks at the Marines earnestly.

"America, yes? America. She go."

An awkward silence ensues. Mills stares at Dennis in complete bewilderment and says under his breath, "What is going on here?"

Dennis puts down his chopsticks and clears his throat. "You want us to take her to America?" He asks.

Her father smiles broadly, as her mother clasps her hands together and covers her mouth. He repeats, "America, she go America."

Dennis turns to Mills, whose jaw has dropped wide open. Dennis turns back to her parents and smiles. "Yes, we'll take her to America."

An astonished gasp escapes from Mills, but Dennis pays him no attention. Lilly's mother sighs and clasps Dennis' hand while her father just smiles and bows his head. For her part, Lilly pushes her red-plumed hat back, her eyes filled with excitement. Mills sits back uncomfortably. *What the hell is he doing?* He looks to Dennis for answers but Dennis just looks back at him and winks.

"We have to go now," Dennis explains to her parents. "Thank you for dinner."

Her father bows his head and says, "Thank you."

Outside, the Marines light up their cigarettes and resume their patrol. Mills looks at Dennis skeptically. "How the hell are we gonna get that little girl outta here? You know damn well the commander's not going to let some little Vietnamese girl hitch a ride home with us. I know you like her, but c'mon! Be reasonable, Denny!"

"I am being reasonable," Dennis says calmly. "I have an idea. What if we all put in a month's worth of pay and adopt the kid? We could send her back to stay with one of our families."

"You're crazy! How the hell are we gonna adopt her? Are you out of your friggin' mind?"

"I promised her I'm going to get her out of here, and that's all there is to it." Dennis is steadfast. "Do you hear me?"

Mills is silent for a moment. "You're serious about this?"

"Dead serious." He can't explain it to Mills, and knows it will be hard to explain to others, but to Dennis, she is the reason they are here. She is the reason they are trying to stop the NVA from invading the South and reuniting it with North Vietnam. In Dennis' mind it is very simple. She is his noble cause.

Mills sighs. "I just don't think it's going to be that easy is all."

"Just let me figure it out. I'll work something out," Dennis says, heading over toward a dirt mound. He wants to rearrange his gear; something is sticking out jabbing him in the back. Suddenly, they hear loud a scream.

It is Lilly.

"What the hell is wrong with that kid?" Mills shouts.

Just like the last time, Lilly frantically points to the mound. Dennis whirls around and stares hard at the ground just inches in front of him. The corner of an olive-drab box, mostly covered by grass, is exposed. It is a pressure type land mine, freshly planted, that would have killed Dennis, Mills, and anyone else standing within several feet of it. Dennis' heart races; he can barely catch his breath. The reality sinks in that he came within seconds of being blown to pieces. *She just saved my life.* Denis turns to Lilly and hugs her tightly.

"I'm going to get you out of here, little girl, if it's the last thing I do." Dennis looks up at the sky and gives her a grateful squeeze. "That's twice you saved my ass."

That night, Dennis lay awake, unable to sleep, replaying in his mind how close he came to dying, and mulling over different ways he could get a little girl out of Vietnam.

The next morning, he received the news; they were heading back to the "Street of No Joy" in the Thua Thien province for Operation Big Horn. Dennis knew the Street, and knew how dangerous it was. The Street was where Bernard Fall had been killed just a few weeks earlier.

Part III

Olongapo
November 4, 2004

Don't walk behind me, I may not lead. Don't walk in front of me, I may not follow. Just walk beside me and be my friend.

(Unknown, often attributed to Albert Camus)

Maybe Someday

DENNIS FINDS ANDY DOING exercises in his bed the following afternoon. Using the gurney for support, Andy flexes his broad shoulders and hoists his entire weight up and down repeatedly. Beads of sweat drip down his face. "Hey," Andy says without looking up. He is out of breath but resolved not to break his concentration. Finally, he exhales a loud, Whoooshhhhh, and lowers himself back down. "Trying to build . . . my strength back up," he explains, trying to catch his breath. Every second counts, and Andy knows all too well that in the physical therapy room on the third floor, progress is measured in inches and seconds. "I got your note yesterday. Thanks for coming by, sorry I wasn't here."

"No problem." Dennis wants to know how his appointment went with the surgeons. *Should I ask?* He doesn't have to.

"I met with the orthopedic team yesterday. They don't need to do anymore suction, thank God." Andy has waited to hear those words for a long time. Here since April, he has gone through several frustrating months of waiting for his wounds to heal, not knowing if a piece of unseen shrapnel would rear its ugly head, if further amputation was need, if the infection was gone or the stumps were still inflamed and swollen. Each setback had been met with the dreaded words, "Wait and see." *Wait.* One of the worst words in the English language, Andy has since surmised.

"You're doing a great job," Dennis reassures him.

"Thanks."

Dennis doesn't know what to say next. He feels relief when Andy takes the lead. "Dennis . . . . I'm not ready to talk about what happened to me," he begins slowly. "Mostly because I honestly just don't know, I have a hard time remembering." Andy pauses, his eyes suddenly flicker, and he looks off to the distance as if he's been distracted by something invisible.

Dennis knows that look. *He just had a memory.* Regaining his composure, Andy continues. "But what I do remember," he says, "I'm not ready to talk about."

"That's okay Andy, that's not why I'm here."

"I'm not ready to think about my future yet, either, Dennis," he says emphatically, referring to his upcoming appointment with the medical review board. *Should he request staying on active duty, and take a desk job, or request medical discharge and retire, seeking disability benefits, and roll under the Department of Veterans Affairs?* The board will have the final say.

"Truth is, I don't know. And I end up ticked off when I think about it. Maybe someday things will be different, maybe someday when . . . . " He trails off.

Dennis knows the end to the sentence. *When he gets his prosthetic limbs. Maybe someday when he can walk again.*

"Maybe someday" is a Pandora's Box. And while for Andy, that day appears to be closer on the horizon than ever before, it could still be a long way off, and he doesn't want to jinx it, or worse, find that it's just a mirage in the desert sand.

"You don't need to explain yourself Andy. Not to me anyway."

"Thanks Dennis." Andy relaxes, slowly letting down his guard. He is beginning to trust Dennis. "I've been thinking an awful lot about what you said about being conceived in war. About the change . . ."

Dennis inhales deeply. "Well, I've been thinking a lot about that myself. I wasn't sure what I should tell you, or how much you wanted me to get into it."

"Tell me everything. I've got some time to kill." Andy laughs as he hears himself say those words. Just six months ago, he was a warrior out in the front lines killing insurgents, and now he's an amputee in a hospital killing time.

"Alright."

Dennis sits back into his chair and thinks about where to begin. "The Street of No Joy. In a period of three days, everything I once knew, and believed in—everything I once was, changed." Dennis pauses. *No, start at the beginning.* He checks himself. "But I guess for you to understand the change, you should first know who I was."

The Greatest Christmas

December, 1966

A MARINE CLERK carrying a large brown package walks in the crowded squad bay quarters. "Private First Class Dennis Michaels! Package for you!" The Marine heaves the heavy box on Dennis' lap. Dennis is confused at first. *What is this?* "Must be from one of my girls," he says with a sly wink. Whoops and hollers fill the squad bay as the Marines crowd around to watch as he opens the large box. He digs down deep, tossing out all the white stuffing, and finally pulls out a green oblong stick.

"What the hell is that, Denny?" Pete asks.

"I don't know. I think it's a . . . Holy hell! It's a Christmas tree!"

The men whoop and holler even louder upon seeing the artificial tree as Dennis unfolds it and stands it upright. There is a card attached to one of the artificial pine needles.

"We wanted you to have a nice Christmas. Love, Mom and Aunt Vesta."

"How in the hell did they get this thing here?" Dennis wonders aloud. He digs back into the package and pulls up a smaller box. It is filled with miniature decorations and silver balls for the tree. He pulls up yet another box. Chocolate chip cookies and assorted cakes. He takes a big bite out of a cookie and throws the box over to Harry.

"Here you go! Merry friggin' Christmas!"

Harry manages to grab a few cookies before being tackled by the rest of the guys. A loud cheer erupts in the far corner. Dennis wipes the crumbs away from his mouth. "What'd I miss?"

Pete jumps to his feet with a Johnny rebel shout. "Did you hear that, boys? They're giving us shore leave in Subic Bay while we load up! Anyone here ever been to Olongapo?"

"No, but I hear those Filipino girls are cute as hell!" Dennis laughs.

"They are, and most hospitable, if you know what I mean!" Pete says with a wink.

"I most certainly do," Chet chimes in, giving Harry a big wallop on the back, "And that's just what Harry needs!"

Harry's face turns red. "No, I don't." He says quietly. "Dennis introduced me to a nice girl back in Okie." Immediately, Harry realizes how silly that sounds, and blushes.

"Ooh! Denny introduced me to a nice girl in Okie!" Chet mimics him. Harry's blush turns a deeper shade of crimson red. "What? And you didn't tell us?" He turns to Dennis. "You didn't tell me that Harry finally got laid? Shame on you!"

"Well, I couldn't have him going back to 'Nam for the second time still a friggin' virgin!"

"All right, all right," Harry cuts them off. "About Olongapo, you were saying . . .?"

Pete shakes his head with pride. "Our boy Harry is now a man." He sighs with a dramatic flair. " I was saying . . . ." He tries to recollect his thoughts. "Ah, yes! Well, boys, since this may be our last Christmas, and our last New Year. Hell, maybe even our Last Supper . . . . I propose we take this opportunity to make our mothers proud and show the Filipinos that the Marines have a little bit of class. A little bit of sophistication," Pete drawls with his southern charm and a flare for the dramatic. "I propose we show them that the United States Marines can maintain!"

"Pete, I believe you have a point." Dennis stands up and puts his arms around Pete. Then, throwing his hand up in the air to gesture a salute with an invisible beer, he shouts out, "Gentlemen, to maintaining!"

Maintaining

TWELVE PRESSED AND CLEAN-SHAVEN Marines stand on the dock at Subic Bay early the next morning. The group includes Dennis, Harry, Chet, Pete, and Dave, as well as Jim Roberts—an American Indian—and Gomez. The men jokingly eye each other up and down with approval. Dennis sucks his stomach in, sticks his chest out, and takes a deep, deliberate breath, drawing up the finest airs he can muster. The group follows suit. It is time to go.

The streets of Olongapo flash in neon pink, in a New York City meets Miami in the Philippines kind of way. The group stops in front of a restaurant; a sign in the window flashes "E Club." Dennis peers in the window. It appears to be quite the upscale establishment.

"This will do nicely."

"Shall we?" Pete mocks.

"We shall," Dennis replies.

A gracious Filipino host greets them and seats them at a large round table. The Marines file in and sit down as if they are Knights at the Round Table; finely dressed Filipino patrons fall silent. A waiter approaches them and Dennis orders a round of drinks. "Twelve whiskey sours, please."

The waiter nods and returns shortly with the drinks. The group holds their glasses up high for a toast. "To maintaining!" The waiter passes out the menus. Harry looks at it strangely; he is unfamiliar with anything on the list. Pointing to an item, he leans over to Dennis, and whispers, "What's this?"

"I don't know, looks expensive though. Let's get it!"

The waiter overhears, and responds to Harry in broken English, "Pheasant under glass."

"Huh?" Harry asks quizzically.

"What, don't you speak English?" Dennis whispers, teasing him.

But Pete approves of the selection, "Mmmm, yes, exquisite. We'll take twelve orders of the pheasant under glass, and . . ." He points to another item. "What is this?" he asks.

"Sherry duck," the waiter smiles.

"Excellent. And twelve orders of sherried duck . . . . And another round of drinks, please!"

A well-dressed couple at a nearby table is staring at them. Dennis catches them from the corner of his eye, and raising his glass, he politely smiles. Embarrassed, the couple looks away.

An hour later, the table is littered with empty plates and glasses. The men sit back in their chairs, lazily smoking cigarettes, and holding their full stomachs. An attractive Filipino girl walks by. Gomez stares at her derrière and sighs.

"Oh, how I'd like to sherry her duck!"

They giggle.

Pete motions with his hands, "Like I was telling you guys. This here is one of the greatest bar towns in the world! Nothin' but bars and girls, and more girls! It's been that way since WWII."

Chet leans over to Harry. "Whaddaya say, Harry? You gonna go to that place Pete was talking about earlier?"

"Nah, I'm going to go with Dennis. We're gonna visit his friend over at MP Barracks.

"Boy, that sounds like a load of fun. C'mon Harry! You don't know what you're missing. Even Dave's going!

"Like hell I am! Are you kidding me?" Dave yells down the table, playfully indignant. "I'm engaged! There's no way in hell I'm going with you drunkards!"

Pete waves the dissenters off, "Aw, let 'em go. That just means more girls for us."

Jim Roberts raises his hand to get the waiters' attention. The waiter nods and hurries over to the table.

"Another round of twelve whiskey . . . ," Roberts begins. A loud thunk rattles the table. A glass rolls off the table and breaks. Roberts glances over at Gomez sitting next to him, and quickly does a double take. Gomez' head is planted face down in his empty plate. Without missing a beat, Roberts coolly turns back to the waiter, "Make that eleven, please."

Everyone giggles. The "maintaining" is officially over.

Pete yells down to Roberts, "Someone wake that jerk up and tell him it's time to get drunk!"

Roberts smacks Gomez on the head. He lets out a load groan.

Dennis calls out to the waiter. "Check please!"

Subic Bay

THE BARS ON THE MAIN DRAG pump loud American music; inside, they are packed with military personal and Filipino girls. Dennis and Harry decide on one bar in particular and begin to scope out the scene. They order a round of drinks just as another attractive girl sashays past them and sits on a Marine's lap next to them.

"Damn, that was fast!" Harry remarks.

"Yeah, I'll say. Hope they have more of 'em like that around here!"

The "lucky" Marine rubs the girl's bare leg. She wriggles and coos on his lap, then leans over to whisper something in his ear. He gives her leg a squeeze. Dennis and Harry look away.

Dennis places money down on the bar for another drink. Suddenly, a loud blood-curling scream echoes throughout the bar. Music and conversation come to a grinding halt as everyone turns toward the direction of the scream. Dennis and Harry whirl around.

The Filipino girl is sprawled on the floor, dress hiked up to her hips, screaming for her life. The lucky Marine towers over her. His eyes are wild with anger as he lunges for her, hissing, "You son of a bitch!" She screams again as he raises his fist to strike her.

Dennis quickly reacts, jumping in to wrestle the Marine's arms behind his back. "What the hell is wrong with you? You don't hit a woman."

The Marine struggling to break his arms free, growls viciously, "God damn it, that ain't no woman!"

Stunned, Dennis releases the Marine's arm. The "girl" runs off like a scared rabbit as the bar bursts out laughing. The dam holding back the flood of the Marine's anger and embarrassment breaks; enraged, he punches the nearest man next to him. Dennis barely missing a sucker punch to the jaw. Fists fly, beer bottles break, and a bona fide brawl ensues. Through the fracas, Dennis grabs Harry's arm and yells, "C'mon, let's get outta here!"

They make it outside relatively unscathed. Outside, Dennis lights up a cigarette, and offers one to Harry. Inhaling deeply, they can still hear the shouts from inside the bar.

"That got ugly fast." Dennis remarks. He is always amazed how he seems to avoid trouble when he is with Harry, which is precisely why they became friends in Okinawa. Harry is his perfect balance.

Harry nods.

"Have you always been able to stay out of trouble, Harry?"

"Oh, I don't know. Depends on what you mean by trouble," he says with a wave of the hand. "What about you?"

"My dad's job was always moving us around. We never really stayed in one place much longer than two years. So it was hard; I always had to make new groups of friends. My brother was the straight-A student and always stayed out of trouble. But I was always in a fight. I figured if I beat up the biggest kid in school as soon as I got there, then I wouldn't have much trouble the rest of the year because they'd think I was crazy. Get 'em off my back before they could even start. Know what I mean?"

Harry nods; he knows. "There was a house bully in one of the foster homes I lived at for awhile." Harry drags on his cigarette. "He'd steal our stuff, take our food, crap like that. One day I got sick of it, so I fought him. I took a pretty good lick. At the time, I thought, 'It's worth it. Now they'll finally kick this kid out for fighting.' But they kicked me out instead." Dennis takes a puff and studies Harry as he continues his story. "After that, I was sent to live with Mr. Nelson. He was part of the reason I didn't get out much in high school. He's pretty old. That and he's a real Christian type of man, prays a lot and stuff. So I never wanted to give him any trouble, I didn't want the old man to think he wasn't doing a good job."

Dennis thinks about this for a moment and concludes he likes Harry even more. Harry is real. They walk in silence as Dennis tries to imagine what it must have been like to grow up as a foster kid like Harry, a stranger in your own home.

Sensing the deeper mood, Harry clears his throat, and throws down his cigarette. "Dennis? Have you ever seen a guy dressed up like a girl before?"

"Nope, can't say I have. You?"

"No, we didn't have any of those back in Trenton."

Dennis chuckles. "Don't be so sure about that, Harry."

Ducky

"HEY GUYS! OVER HERE!" a gunner from the battery calls out to Dennis and Harry, excitedly pointing to a bar at the end of street. The gunner is a short, affable fellow who walks with his feet pointing out, much like a duck. Dennis and Harry don't know him well, but they look at each other and shrug. They accept the detour. The three enter the dimly lit bar. It appears to be empty. Dennis turns around to walk back out to the street, but the short Marine grabs him by the arm. "No, back here," he says, pointing toward the empty kitchen.

Walking closer toward the rear exit, they hear voices then suddenly a load mix of groans and cheers erupts. The noise is coming from outside. Dennis is curious, Harry, apprehensive, and the short Marine, excited. "Wait til you guys see this!"

Outside, in the alleyway behind the bar, Marines and soldiers loiter around in a large circle. Cigarettes dangle from their mouths, beers spill out of their hands as they make a special effort not to step within the boundaries of a primitively formed circle.

Directly behind the men, against the concrete wall of the bar, are stacks of wooden crates. Inside them, hundreds of yellow ducklings are chirping loudly, flapping their half-formed wings within their limited wooden confines. A young Filipino boy, no more than eight years old, holds his hand up in the air, making a deliberate "high five" sign. He cocks his head back, and projects his child's voice above the adult fray. "Fitty cent! Fitty cent! Who wanna buy?"

Harry strains to see what's inside the circled pit. "Jesus Christ!" He exclaims, his eyes nearly popping out of his head as he stumbles back. Inside the pit, an eight-foot alligator snaps its angry snout, coming dangerously close to infringing the circle's non-existent boundary. The men holler, and drunkenly jump backward as best they can.

One drunken soldier hands the boy a dollar bill; he receives two ducklings in return. He holds the loudly chirping ducklings high up in the air for all to see, as if presiding over a sacrificial ceremony, and hurls them over the pit. They flutter down helplessly, one after the other, into the jaws of death.

The men holler and cheer. Dennis shakes his head in disbelief and looks at Harry, who is equally disturbed. "I'll be damned if I waste my shore leave watching some gator eat ducks for dinner. I've got a buddy who's stationed with the military police over here I wanted to visit. You wanna go?"

"Sounds good. Let's get the hell out of here."

On the other side of Main Street—or the street that they refer to as Main Street because it's the only street—a military police officer is sitting on the veranda of the barracks, smoking a cigarette. A lone shout from the street interrupts his cigarette break. "Hello there! Anybody home?"

He recognizes the voice instantly. "Denny Michaels? Is that you?" The officer tries to make out the two figures in the dark.

"No, it's the Easter Bunny."

"Ha! Denny! How the hell are you?"

The two men shake hands and warmly embrace. "Hey Lou, this is my friend Harry Williams," Dennis says, motioning to Harry. "He's from Jersey too."

"Nice to meet you Harry. Where abouts in Jersey are you from?"

"Trenton." Harry quietly replies.

"Oh sure, I used to run around there a long time ago."

Then Lou turns to Dennis, slapping him heartily on the shoulder. "So Denny, what the hell are you doing here? I thought you were laid up back in Pendleton with a broken neck?"

"I was. After my car accident I was laid up for six months, but that's over and I'm here now."

"Same ole Denny, crazy as ever!" Lou laughs.

"Well, on the bright side, I had a chance to talk to some of the guys who were already here and figure out what 'Nam was all about, seeing as how I missed my first tour."

"Yeah, well, hope they informed you well. Casualties have been up. This oven's starting to heat up."

"Well, you know what they say. 'If you can't stand the heat, get out of the kitchen.' And you know me. I just love the kitchen!" He winks again.

Lou chuckles and shakes his head.

Suddenly, loud yelling coming from the direction of the street interrupts them. Turning around and squinting, Dennis is able to make out the short, duck-footed Marine stumbling down the street, flailing his arms wildly in the air.

"Denny!" He cries out at the top of his lungs. "Denny! Where are you? I saved them! I saved them, Denny!" Something is moving inside the Marine's shirt. Dennis covers his eyes and laughs. Lou looks cock-eyed at Dennis. "You know him?"

"Yeah, he's with us."

"What the hell's in his shirt?"

The Marine stops to tuck four chirping ducks back in his shirt, patting them lovingly. Lou elbows Dennis. "Jesus, you better get him outta here before my guys do."

The men shake hands and say their good-byes. Dennis yanks the drunkard by the arm, "C'mon, 'Ducky!'"

"I saved them!" He slurs heavily, "I saved them from being eaten alive!"

He pulls back his arm, and tucks the ducklings in once more, "Good little duckies, it's alright," he coos as if talking to a baby. "I've got you now."

Harry rolls his eyes. "Oh, for God's sake!"

Dennis grabs his arm again, "C'mon, hurry up, we gotta get back to the dock."

"Wait, I gotta take a piss first," Ducky whines, as he locks his eyes down the road on his destination—the "E-Club."

"Take a piss out here."

"No, I want to go in there," Ducky slurs, and points to the club, its flashing neon sign is attracting inebriates like moths to a flame. Within seconds of walking in, Dennis realizes this foray into the E-Club is going to be *much* different than the first one.

The bar is crowded with Navy servicemen, with not a Marine in sight. "Jesus," Harry mutters, "this place is crawling with squids!"

As if on cue, the music stops and the all eyes fall on the three Marines who just walked in the door. "I'll be right back," Ducky whispers over to them, making his way to the restroom.

"Jerk," Dennis whispers back.

"Might as well grab another drink while we're here," Harry offers. Finding their way to the bar is not easy, but they finally make it and quickly chug two beers each while they wait for Ducky to return. Before ordering a third, Dennis hears a commotion halfway between the bar and the bathroom.

Ducky is crawling around on the floor on all fours, reaching out his hands like those of a blind man feeling his way around, parting the Navy garrison around him like the waters of the Red Sea. "Stand back! Move!" He shouts frantically.

"Hey, watch it!" one growls. "What the hell do you think you're doing?"

"Crap." Dennis slams down his empty glass and pushes his way over to him. "What the hell are you doing?"

"I lost one of the ducks!"

Ducky sees a yellow flutter of wing. Scrambling to his knees, he knocks a guy over as he dives for the loose duck like a fumbled football, thereby breaking the spirit of whatever feigned congeniality had existed. But Ducky, oblivious to the mayhem above waist-level, gently tucks the stray duckling back in his shirt.

Dennis breaks free, grabs Harry in mid-throw, yanks Ducky by the back of his collar, and makes a run for the door. "You couldn't take a piss outside?"

"I . . . I . . . But my duck, I lost my duck."

"Never mind your friggin' duck, we're going to be late for the launch."

Several minutes later, they reach the dock area. Dennis' worst fear is confirmed. The naval officer on duty glares at them. "Good evening gentlemen. It is my pleasure to inform you the launch has already left," he says smugly. "You Marines are AWOL."

Dennis looks down at his watch. "Oh crap."

"Crap is right, Marine. And that's exactly what you'll be shoveling soon."

"Look," Dennis says as coolly and reasonably as possible. "We got to get out to the Thomasson. We're heading in-country."

"I don't care where you *were* heading, you guys are AWOL now." The ducks chirp loudly. The naval officer scowls at the sight of them, and turns his back on the three Marines. Defeated and dejected, the trio walks to the end of the dirty dock, and together they plop down.

"So what the hell are we gonna do now?" Harry wonders nervously.

"I don't know, but I'll think of something," Dennis says soberly. Whatever buzz he had earlier in the night has quickly dissipated.

Ducky looks behind his shoulder, and nudges Dennis and Harry. "Hey, guys, look!"

A Naval commander in his pressed whites is stumbling down the dock, extremely drunk. The officer on duty salutes the commander, but the commander brushes past him, and staggers toward the three Marines. The Marines quickly stand to their feet and muster all the energy they have to keep their backs straight at attention.

"Howdy, Marines! No, sit," the commander orders. And with that, he plops down on the dock, instantly ruining his white uniform. The Marines follow suit.

"How you boys doing tonight?" he slurs.

"Sir. Not good, sir. We missed our launch," Dennis informs him.

"Aww, no sweat!" He swipes his hand. "The launch has got to come back and get me—my guys will take you out. What ship are you boys on?

"The LSD Thomasson, sir."

"No problem, we'll find the Thomasson."

Ducky pulls out a can of Coke from his shirt pocket, and holds it out for the commander. "You want some, Commander?"

"Yeah, I'm thirsty."

Ducky turns to Dennis. "Got your knife on ya?" Dennis shakes his head no. The can of Coke has no opening and requires a knife or sharp object to open. Ducky looks around and sees a loose plank with a nail sticking out of the board. He grabs the board and hands it to Dennis.

"Here. I'll hold it, you hit it."

Dennis raises the board and comes down with it hard—the nail pierces the can but pierces Ducky's hand too.

"Aaaaghhhhh! That was my hand . . . . Owwwwwww!"

The commander looks over. Ducky sucks it up, and holds out the can of Coke, "Here you go, Commander." The blood and Coke spray all over the commanders' whites. Dennis and Harry hold their breath. The commander looks down at his shirt, then at Ducky, and laughs heartily. Dennis cannot believe their luck.

Moments later the launch pulls up to the dock. The commander and the Marines stand to their feet. The officers on the launch salute the commander.

"Take these men out to the Thomasson."

"Do they know what number the Thomasson is, sir?"

The Marines shake their heads, no.

An hour later, the exasperated launch crew pulls up to yet another docked ship. Dennis crosses his fingers and looks over at Harry. "This has gotta to be it."

The commander hollers up to the officer on deck. "Is this the Thomasson?"

"It is, sir."

"Good! You forgot some of your men. I brought them here for you."

"Thank you, sir. But they're AWOL. And they're not coming up in that condition."

"AWOL?" The commander's face turns red. The veins in his neck look like they're about to pop out as he reaches out for the Thomasson's ladder. He deftly scurries up the ladder and within seconds, stands inches away from the officers' face, hollering belligerently. The officer quickly gives in. Looking down at the Marines, he is barely able to contain his frustration. "Get your asses up here and get below deck! Now!"

Scrambling up the ladder, the Marines stand at attention as the officer looks at them in disgust. He takes one glance at Ducky, and angrily yanks the ducklings out of his shirt. In one swift motion, he hurls them overboard. Ducky lurches for the ducks fluttering into the bay, crying out, "Noo-o-o!"

The commander, wiping tears of laughter from his eyes, climbs back down the ladder to his launch. "See ya, Marines!"

Home

ANDY LAUGHS HEARTILY. He thinks back to the guys in his own squad. They had their own bag of similar stories, their own "Remember that night, when . . . ." It was exactly those stories that kept their morale up, particularly after winding down from a house raid, or changing shifts at the check points, or after recovering bodies from a suicide attack—the times when they needed it most.

"So," Dennis says, "I guess you could say we were just your typical bunch of nineteen-year olds. Give us some booze, some girls, a gun, and a one-way ticket to a foreign country, and, well, that's what you come up with."

Andy shakes his head in agreement. "I know. I was just thinking back to some of the stupid shit we did before we left." Andy looks at Dennis differently now. He admits he didn't quite know what to think of him when they first met on Monday. He wasn't sure if he needed a mentor, whatever that entailed. But he's concluded that he likes Dennis—likes him for the same reason Dennis described liking Harry. *He's real.* He has an innate sense that Dennis truly understands something that very few people do.

Do you still stay in touch with everybody?"

"Nah, a lot of them were short-timers at that point. They had already been in-country and were just getting resupplied in Okinawa to finish their last ops by the time I got there. I never saw that guy Ducky again. Gomez was done end of January, Jim Roberts was out in February, and Pete left the

1st of April, before we went to the Street. Dave would later extend his tour, and Chet . . . well, Chet was a lifer."

Andy nods. Many of the men in his squad were on their second and third tours as well. Rumor had it there would be even more rotations.

"Well, listen, I have to head on out. But I'll be back tomorrow."

"I'll be here. I'm not going anywhere anytime soon."

"Hey Andy, one question. Where's the first place you want to go—I mean, when you get out of here?

"Oh, I don't know. Disney World? Ha! No, I don't know. Probably home."

Home. Home was the last place Dennis wanted to go when he got back from Vietnam. He remembers a speech he gave several years ago at one of the VAs, telling the audience of veterans, "I could deal with dying, and thought I would die over there. But I had a hell of a time coming home. I was afraid of home, afraid of the notion of it. And I resisted it." Dennis then told them that, upon returning to the States, he went so far as to fly into New York City instead of the Newark airport, just to give himself some extra time before seeing his family.

"I wasn't ready. I didn't know myself or even trust myself. I was afraid of the things I might do, things I might say. I was a stranger. And there's not many feelings worse than feeling like a stranger in your own skin."

Several veterans in the audience had nodded their heads. What he said resonated with them; he had spoken true. Later a middle-aged veteran pulled him aside and said, "Maybe the great parable for all veterans is this: If it is true for you, then it is true." He further explained his philosophy. "If you feel it, if you experience it, if you've seen it—then that is what your truth becomes."

Dennis liked that veteran's definition of truth. He knew first hand that the hard part, for many, was reconciling the old truth with the new. It was a daily struggle, a constant fight that often left him wondering if he really saw the things he saw; if he really did the things he did; if things happened the way he remembered; or if his experiences were such a violent break from reality that it distorted his perception and his memory. But what he has found is that truth does not and cannot exist in bold-faced lies. It can however, exist in different perspectives—which at its core means that truth depends on the trinity of viewer, space, and time. That viewpoint, however, did not reduce the hardship of finding the proper place—or home—for the internal changes that resulted from old and new realities, or, rather, his past and present truths from colliding. But right now, home is a place Dennis merely frequents for brief spells in the morning and at night, and sometimes the occasional dinner, usually frozen chicken or a potato thrown in the microwave. More often than not, he'll fall asleep on the couch watching TV.

And that's exactly where he finds himself the next morning.

Part IV

The Street of No Joy
November 5th, 2004

"The dead soldier takes his misery with him, but the man who killed him must forever live and die with him. The lesson becomes increasingly clear: Killing is what war is all about, and killing in combat, by its very nature, causes deep wounds of pain and guilt."

—Lt. Col. Dave Grossman, *On Killing, The Psychological Cost of Learning to Kill in War and Society*

Hate

AT 6:00AM, THE ALARM clock radio blares full blast, but Dennis is already awake; in fact, he is walking out the door when he hears the news.

"Good morning, it is Friday, November 5th, 2004. And the top headlines this morning: News correspondents from Reuters report that the US military sealed off Fallujah Friday and launched a night of air strikes on the rebel city ahead of an assault seen as critical to the interim government's attempt to pacify Iraq before January polls.

"In other news, the Associated Press reports that the brutal beheadings in Iraq appear to have inspired militants in other parts of the world who are drawn to the shock value of the horrifying attacks and the intense publicity they attract."

Dennis slams the door shut.

He wishes he could also slam the door shut on the cruelty and horror taking place in Iraq and around the world. Many people, including those in the media, have been wondering: Where does that kind of evil come from? Dennis, at one time, was like most people. He too, didn't understand the origins of evil. Until the day in Vietnam he found the source. *Hate. Deep, unadulterated hate.* He has seen that kind of hate before.

Bernard Fall

THE FRENCH CALLED IT 'La Rue sans Joie,' or 'The Street Without Joy,' because there wasn't a damn thing good about it," Dennis tells Andy over breakfast. He had stopped at Krispy Kreme on his way to the hospital and brought doughnuts and coffee, Andy's favorite. "It was Bernard Fall who first wrote about The Street, a section of Colonial Route 1 that was a favorite location for NVA ambushes."

Dennis recalls how the ambiguity of small villages, rivers, canals, rice paddies, hedges, bamboo groves, and elephant grass three feet tall made it the perfect location for Ho Chi Minh's sympathizers to set up shop. During the height of the Indo-China conflict in 1953, French surveillance there was nearly impossible, and they tried many times, unsuccessfully, to clean up the street.

A French-born, naturalized American citizen, Bernard Fall, had documented their military effort and subsequent failure in his book, *The Street Without Joy*. He also wrote a detailed account of one of the most decisive battles in military history in *Hell in a Very Small Place: The Siege of Dien Bien Phu*. That battle, and its attendant defeat of French forces, ended that country's occupation of Vietnam.

"Those two books," Dennis tells Andy, "were practically pre-requisite courses on Vietnam, and I read them cover to cover at Camp Pendleton."

At the time he read them, however, Dennis knew little about the political implications of the French defeat at Dien Bien Phu. The battle had set the stage for the Geneva accords to recognize the Viet Minh victory and to partition the country into two zones, Communist North Vietnam and French-administered South Vietnam at the 17th parallel. The fear of communism spreading into Southeast Asia, coupled with the increasing US involvement to sustain the South Vietnamese government—which grew ever more dependent on that support for its own survival—percolated for ten years and finally escalated into the second Indo-China conflict: The Vietnam War.

"The danger of the Street was that it was completely NVA held," Dennis tells Andy. "In late February, Bernard accompanied a patrol unit from 1/9 on Operation Chinook, a typical search and destroy mission. He was there to document the Marines' return to Vietnam—more specifically, our return to the Street. When they got there, Bernard and a combat photographer, Gunny Sergeant Byron Highland, were walking behind a patrol group down the path of a wide rice-paddy dyke alongside the sand dunes. Bernard was talking into his tape recorder, narrating what he was observing, when suddenly a land mine—a 'bouncing Betty'— detonated, killing him and Highland instantly. Bernard was forty years old. Damn good writer too."

Dennis pauses to let the information sink in. "So when I heard we were going back to the Street for Operation Big Horn, I had no illusions. I knew how dangerous the operation would be. What I didn't know was how drastically it would change me for the rest of my life."

The Big Leagues

LACKING A FORMAL PLAN, the 11th engineers begin to clear the "Trace," a four kilometer swath of land between Gio Linh and Con Thien, under the guise of clearing fields of fire and building modest field fortifications.

Back at Camp Czzowitz, four platoons leave the base under the cover of darkness and head east for the operation. Everyone is silent and anxious, wondering what the day will bring. The heavy monsoon rains have returned, making visibility poor. One of the grunts causes a commotion when, sleep deprived and somewhat delusional, he mistakes a firefly for a flashlight and falls into a rice paddy. Furious for making noise and possibly foiling their attempt to surprise the enemy, the lieutenant scolds him for taking a "friggin' Roman Bath." But they reach the Street of No Joy without further incident.

Standing in the pouring rain, they overlook the group of villages three to four miles long that line the Street. The South China Sea is barely visible a thousand yards away. Dennis can make out the sand dunes to the left. The center of the street is raised as if designed for a railroad track, but no tracks exist. To the side of the hill, an informal command post is established.

The battalion commander briefs the 1/9 officers, reviewing maps and discussing their strategy. Dennis awaits the operation plans, assured that they are the professionals. Soon, the lieutenant meets with the forward observer teams. Dennis huddles next to Mills as they try to keep the maps as dry as possible. "Okay men," the lieutenant begins, "Alpha and Bravo Companies are going to set up on the sand flats, here." He points to his map, but the rain pelting down makes it hard to read. "Delta will set up on the other side of the villages, by the South China Sea. That will allow Charlie Company to come up and carry out the sweep." He looks up to make sure everyone understands the directions. "We'll be re-supplied the following day—food, water, ammo."

The squad leader inspects the men for readiness. "Ammo?"

"Check."

"Frags?"

"Check."

He instructs one Marine to jump up and down, which causes something inside the Marine's backpack to clank loudly.

"Move it or lose it," the squad leader barks. The Marine begins to protest. He's already down to the essentials with nothing left to toss. Another Marine taps a magazine of ammo against his helmet—once to make sure the round is set, and twice for luck.

The squad leader continues down the line. "FO's, check your maps, compasses, and your frequencies."

Dennis checks his radio batteries and goes down the list of networks, turning the knob to click on the frequencies assigned for the battalion, artillery, air, medical and company networks.

"Check," Dennis replies, pushing down his radio antennae.

"All right, men . . . . Saddle up! Move out!"

Dennis is dispatched to Delta Company, and the units begin to take their position on the other side of the villages. They walk past Alpha and Charlie Companies. Visibility is worsening; it is getting darker and raining harder. Dennis can barely see anything in front of him, but he is able to make out two figures standing in the rain. Up a little closer, he recognizes one of the Marines. It is the sergeant, John Malloy. Dennis is confused. *I thought his tour was up?* Approaching the seasoned veteran, he slowly begins to make out the other figure. Dennis stops dead in his tracks. *Harry.* Dennis' heart sinks. What is he doing here?

Harry is oblivious to Dennis' approach; he is busy studying his maps, shielding them from the rain with his poncho.

"What the hell are you doing here?" Dennis glares at him menacingly.

Harry is caught by surprise. He starts to smile, happy to see his friend, but the scowl on Dennis' face causes his excitement to fade. Harry stands up taller. "They brought me up from Phu Bai today for the op. I'm going out with Sgt. Malloy."

Dennis turns to Malloy, "I thought your tour was over."

John Malloy looks at Harry reassuringly. He has a mature, composed air about him, and Dennis can see that Harry clearly looks up to him. "I turned down my flight to take Harry out, make sure nothing happens to him. This is my last op. I'm going home after this."

Dennis can see the pride and excitement in Harry's eyes; he has the look of a career ballplayer called up to the big leagues after spending half a lifetime in the minors. Harry wants Dennis to say something, anything. *Aren't you happy I'm here?* But Dennis doesn't say another word.

Only two thoughts are going through Dennis' mind: *You're not supposed to be here* and *that stupid letter*, the one that pisses him off every time he remembers it's in his pocket.

Another Marine walks up between Harry and Sgt. Malloy. Harry begins to introduce the Marine to Dennis. "Dennis, this is Cole, another FO on my team." Cole reaches out to shake hands.

Dennis' eyes narrow. He ignores the introduction, brushing past them without returning the gesture.

"What's with him?" Cole asks.

Harry shrugs. "I don't know. Something's up his butt, though." Then, just to tease to Dennis, Harry calls out to him. "Hey Denny! Make sure they send my body home!"

Dennis bristles and stops abruptly. *What did he just say?* Filled with rage, he turns to Harry. "God damned it! Do you have any friggin' idea how bad the Street is? I've got enough shit to worry about without having to worry about you."

He stares at Harry with contempt. Seconds go by before they break the deadlock and Dennis finally turns to walk away. Harry just shrugs it off. *He'll get over it.*

Jonesy Takes a Hit

BY DAWN, ALL OF 1/9 is in position; guns are locked and loaded. The early morning sun is rising above the eastern horizon. Suddenly, loud explosions fill the air. Smoke trails form arches across the sky ending their nefarious rainbow with black clouds of destruction, ruining the innocent dawn. The Street Without Joy is under mortar attack.

"Incoming!"

The Marines jump in their holes and cover their heads. Dennis dives for cover and immediately reaches for his radio, but traffic is heavy. Dennis crawls on his belly toward the platoon leader, who is already communicating with the command post.

"Point squad made contact. We need arty in here," he tells Dennis.

Dennis pulls out his map and points to an area that he estimates is the position of the NVA in the tree line one hundred and fifty yards in front of them and calls in for a strike.

"Bay Way Delta, Bay Way Delta, this is Birmingham 6-4, do you read? This is Birmingham 6-4, copy? Request fire mission, I repeat, request fire mission. Do you read?"

"Birmingham 6-4, this is Bay Way Delta. Over. Request your mission."

Dennis bellows into the radio. "Two, five, niner . . . . Niner, six five. Direction, two, four hundred. One round. Whiskey Pappan. Battery Six. Hotel Echo for effect. PD Fuse. Roger?"

The battery methodically repeats Dennis' request for confirmation. It is correct.

"Roger."

Moments later, a 105mm round whizzes overhead and strikes the tree line with deadly accuracy.

"Good effect on target," Dennis reports. But the traffic is too heavy. Fire Direction Control is communicating with the forward observer nicknamed "Sasquatch," from Alpha Company. Dennis listens to the report over the radio.

"Mercury 3-3, Mercury 3-3, this is Bay Way Delta. Is Alpha in position?"

"Affirmative."

The platoon leader who instructs his squad to stay close. "We're going back toward the Street to push the NVA into the flats where Alpha's in position."

Dennis and the platoon move in closer to the street. The narrow dirt road is eerily quiet; the villages appear to be evacuated, as all of the huts are empty. A point team goes out in front of the squad, walking briskly, but cautiously, eyes darting, trying to anticipate any snipers that may be hiding in the harmless looking huts.

Everyone is silent with eyes locked into the thousand-yard stare. They pass Charlie Company set up in position. Dennis sees Harry again. He is sitting on a paddy dike. Harry calls out to Dennis.

"Hey Denny! Make sure they send my body home!" Harry is showboating now. Dennis flinches slightly, but dismisses him, refusing to make eye contact. *Don't pay attention, just stay focused.*

"Yeah, yeah, sure. No sweat," Dennis mutters to himself.

The platoon continues onward to their position. Dennis looks down at his watch. It is noon. The rain has stopped, and a suffocating heat replaces it. Dennis stops to take his poncho off. He starts removing his pack. The tall elephant grass and hedgerows provide cover as Dennis crouches low and peers out over the street. A Marine next to him scans the locale and talks softly under his breath.

"Can't prep the street with artillery or air strikes," the Marine says, talking more to himself than anyone else. "That's the friggin' problem with this place; it's technically a no-fly zone because of that Catholic church and monastery that sit over there. Part of the pacification bull shit. Pacify the villagers. Keep the NVA away."

Suddenly, two North Vietnamese soldiers jump up out of the high grass and run into the village. They disappear before anyone in the platoon can take a clean shot.

"This area is pacified all right," Dennis says sarcastically. "They breed NVA gooks faster than rabbits on this street."

Dennis overhears the commander update the lieutenant on the supply situation. "The otters are coming in to re-supply us," the commander informs them. "I gave them orders to come through the area we already swept."

"So the otters are coming from the south?" The lieutenant asks.

"Correct. They should be here in an hour," the commander confirms.

Dennis relays the news to Mills who looks relieved, "Good, I can hear my stomach growling."

An hour later, the rumbling sound of heavily armored trucks is heard in the distance. Dennis ears perk up. It is the sound of the Marine trek vehicles, the Otters, driving down the street. But something is wrong. They are coming from the north end of the street.

Dennis starts turning the knobs to the different network frequencies to get clarification. He picks up garbled conversations. "Map said we were . . ." a voice transmits over the radio. He has picked up the otters' communications. "Must have read the map wrong. Haul ass! Get out of here. This place is crawling with NVA!"

Suddenly, a thundering clap of gunfire is heard, and a brilliant flash lights the entire sky.

"Jesus!"

The radio falls silent.

The platoon leader runs up, "First Platoon! Provide cover! Now!

The platoon, including Dennis, sprints toward the decimated Otters' position. They can see where the NVA has opened up on the other side of a rice paddy by the telltale smoke.

Forty Marines jump in the rice paddy. Dennis has waded half way across when more loud cracks surround them. Machine guns have opened fire on them and red tracer rounds whiz past their bodies.

For Dennis, time has stopped.

Nineteen Marines are cut down with the first volley.

Dennis watches them fall, in what seems like slow motion. Blood flies, bodies writhe, and men splash face first into the paddy. He cannot believe what he is seeing. He drops to his knees and calls in for a fire mission.

"Negative. Too many friendlies in the area," Fire Direction Control responds.

Dennis yells, exasperated. They're right in friggin' front of us!

Not sure what to do next, he acts on instinct. *Get the guys out.* He looks over and sees Jonesy, the tall black Marine, running next to him, "C'mon, we gotta get them outta here!"

Together, they sprint toward the fallen Marines. Suddenly, Dennis hears a loud thud. The first thought that goes through his head is, *I'm hit, oh Jesus, I'm hit.* He looks down at his jacket. There are no holes. It's not him. He looks over at Jonesy who has a queer look on his face.

Dennis' eyes immediately lock in on Jones's chest. Tiny plumes of smoke are emanating from two black holes that have punctured his green canvas vest as he realizes that the sound that was heard was the bullet going through the fiberglass in Jones' flak jacket.

"Shit, ah shit, I'm hit!" Jonesy cries out. He staggers forward. His boots feel heavy in the muddy paddy, but remarkably he stays afoot.

Dennis reaches out and feels the blood gushing from the left side of his chest just under the clavicle. "Wait here. I'll be right back."

Out in front of them, dead Marines lay face down in the paddy. Dennis tries to move forward to reach them, but he is stopped in his tracks. The fire is too thick. Red and green tracer rounds fly over his head, as the enemy fire interlaces with the Marine fire and ricochets in all directions. Dennis pulls out his radio, resolved to try another mission. "Bay Way Delta, Bay Way Delta. Request fire mission."

"Hold all fire missions."

"Jesus, we gotta get 'em off our backs." He changes frequency. He can hear another voice calling in for a mission. It is Harry's voice.

"Heavy enemy contact. Request fire mission." Dennis hears Harry via radio.

"Hold all fire missions. We don't know where our guys are out there."

After what seems like hours, the enemy fire begins to subside. Marines line up along the rice paddy to provide cover for the retreating first platoon. Dennis crawls out of the paddy, dragging Jones along with him. Standing on firm ground, he realizes his legs are shaking. Taking a deep gulp of air, he stares in disbelief at what just happened. *Get a grip*, he tells himself. He looks over at Jones, who is struggling to breathe, and immediately snaps out of self-awareness.

He rushes Jones toward the village, where a hut has been converted into a makeshift triage area. Inside the hut, a corpsman is frantically attending to dozens of wounded Marines, some half-dead, and others in shock. Dennis grabs a wad of bandages from the corpsman's medical kit and applies pressure to Jones's chest. The big Marine reaches out, grabs Dennis by the hand, and squeezes hard.

"Thank you."

The corpsman rushes over to assess the wound, but Jones waves him off. With as steady a voice as possible, he tells the corpsman, "I'm fine Doc, go help those guys first," pointing to the other casualties.

The Street of No Joy

ALPHA AND CHARLIE COMPANY are in position along the hedgerows that line the village. They are preparing to move in for the sweep. Sgt. Malloy's voice comes over the radio.

"Fire Direction Control. We're getting ready to make the sweep. We're moving out. Charlie 2-2. Moving out!

Dennis is alarmed. They can't make the sweep. The NVA position hasn't been cleared out! He frantically keys his radio.

"Charlie 2-2, Charlie 2-2! Do not sweep! I repeat do not sweep! Heavy NVA in position!"

The radio traffic is too heavy and his dispatch does not go through. He tries again.

"Charlie 2-2! Do not sweep! Roger?"

"Move out!" Sgt. Malloy orders.

Charlie Company stands up from their position. Malloy taps Harry on the shoulder. "Let's go!" Harry jumps to his feet.

The NVA open fire point blank from the hedgerow. Charlie Company is mowed down on sight, caught completely off guard. The gunfire is quick and thunderous. Within seconds, it is over. No one is left standing.

Harry is laying face down in the dirt next to Cole and Malloy. Malloy is motionless.

Dennis hears the explosive gunfire. It is brief. *Oh my god.* He cradles his head in his hands. "Oh, please no, please Jesus, no!" He pushes his ear hard against his radio as if that alone with somehow help. He listens in as command tries to contact the Charlie Company lieutenants, sergeants, platoon leaders, and forward observers.

They radio Malloy's call sign. "This is Bay Way Delta. Click if you can respond."

No clicks.

The call Harry's call sign, "Click once, over."

No clicks.

Finally, after several minutes a crackle comes over the frequency. Dennis hears someone whispering over the radio.

"C'mon Harry, we can get outta here . . . ."

Dennis' head snaps back and his eyes light up. *Harry is alive.*

At the spot where Charlie Company once stood, Harry Williams lies face down in the dirt. His eyes are wide with fear. His breathing is heavy, but quiet. He looks up and sees Cole a few feet away. Cole is trying to get his attention. "Harry . . . !" Cole whispers urgently.

Harry doesn't respond. Instead, he looks over to his other side and sees Malloy. He is dead.

"C'mon, Harry! They don't know we're alive. Let's get the hell out of here!"

Harry looks around. Images pass by in slow motion. He looks at Malloy again. He sees the others; they are all dead. He looks back to Cole. His breath quickens as his heart beats faster and faster. Cole is looking at him earnestly.

"Williams! C'mon, let's go! Malloy's dead. C'mon, we can make it!"

Harry's body shakes. He pulses back and forth. A look of wild abandon sweeps over his face as he gathers his strength and jumps to his feet.

"Ahhhhhhhhhhhhh!" Harry shouts, spraying bullets into the hedgerow.

An NVA soldier screams at the sight of the American. He fires at Harry point blank. Four shots to the face. Harry falls like a tree.

Characters Whiskey and Moby

DENNIS HAS HEARD the second burst of fire from his position overlooking the street, and his heart sinks to the pit of his stomach. He radios Charlie Company directly. "This is Birmingham 6-4. What is the status of characters Whiskey and Moby?" He asks, using code for Harry and John's last names.

No response.

He tries again. "This is Birmingham 6-4. What is the status of Characters Whiskey and Moby, damn it?" Dennis shouts into his radio.

This time, he is reprimanded. "Clear the frequency."

Several minutes pass. Finally, someone comes over Charlie Company's network. It is Cole.

Cole clears his throat and whispers softly. "Both Character Whiskey and Character Moby . . . KIA."

Dennis' legs feel weak and as his heart feels like it is being ripped outside his chest. Falling to his knees, he heaves but no vomit comes out. He drops his head down to the ground and begins to shake uncontrollably. "No, no, no," echoes in his mind, over and over. With clenched fists, he looks up at the sky and shouts at the top of his lungs, "You son of a bitch! You stupid son of a bitch!

He cradles his head and silently weeps.

When he looks up, a flicker of cognizance breaks through the void of time and perception. Reaching into his jacket pocket, he pulls out Harry's letter. Shaking, his vision blurred with welled tears, he tries to read it again but can't. Instead, he folds it and tries to tuck it back into his pocket. Placing his hand over his chest, he feels as listless as the letter he's holding. "Harry."

Why?

But instead of answers, a sickening feeling sweeps over him, a feeling that is unrecognizable. He's never felt anything so thick, black, and vile churn in his stomach before, and he can physically feel his heart harden as his grief first turns into rage and then into pure, unremitting hate.

When he finally rises to his feet, the tears are gone. His eyes look cold and deadened. Hatred, deep and profound, has seeped into his heart and galvanized his soul. He shakes his fists in the air again and screams for all to hear, "I swear to God, I hate you! And I'm going to kill every last one of you! I hate you! Do you hear me? *I hate you!*"

Dennis and the war have become inextricably and forever linked. It's personal now. The war is real.

Aftershock

ANDY IS PENSIVE. He's been keenly aware of Dennis' changing emotions, but despite the anger that is still there, he sees something that he saw in the eyes of many from his own platoon. "Dennis, I'm really sorry about Harry. I don't know what to say."

"You don't have to say anything. It's just something that happened," Dennis says solemnly. He still remembers the bodies of the dead—it was the first time Dennis had ever seen that many dead Marines at one time—thirty, forty men stacked along the side of the road, with their boots sticking out ominously from under the ponchos covering them. He can still clearly visualize the 782 gear of canteens, flak jackets, and helmets piled up next to the bodies.

Dennis remembers the face of one wounded Marine who was propped up against his gear, off to the side of the landing zone, smoking a cigarette. His leg had been blown off and blood saturated the earth under his mutilated stump. His hands were shaking, his face was white, and his piercing blue eyes were glazed over; Dennis knew he was in shock. The choppers flew in low, and, anticipating their arrival, Dennis ran over and picked the Marine up. He loaded the wounded Marine into the chopper without saying a word. Just before take off, the Marine reached out for Dennis' hand.

Dennis didn't know the Marine's name, nor would he, until many years later.

He thinks about him now for a moment, silently, not wanting to tell Andy about the Marine who had lost his leg, although he's not sure why. Then he remembers Jonesy.

"Jonesy had refused to be loaded into the first round of choppers, insisting that the more critically wounded Marines be taken first. It was the last time I would ever see Jonesy. But I always admired him for that."

Dennis stops talking but the mental reel continues playing as he remembers the choppers buzzing along the Street, carrying the dead and wounded off to Da Nang. He remembers loading the dead bodies into the choppers while knowing they were doing the exact same thing on the other side of the street with Harry. *Take his gear off, put a poncho over him and throw him in the chopper… Get him out of here as if he didn't exist, as if he never did.*

The Price of Hate

THERE'S A REINFORCEMENT OF South Vietnamese troops a couple of miles down from the Street," the lieutenant informs them. "Our orders are to move out and push the NVA right into a trap. Pinch them between us and the ARVN forces."

The Marines follow the NVA along the narrow, marshy length of the Street of No Joy. Although they cannot see the NVA, aerial reconnaissance reports coming in from battalion headquarters help them stay in hot pursuit. The heat is sweltering; sweat drips from Dennis' face as he stops to knife off a sleeve of his undershirt, using the cloth as a rag to wipe the dripping sweat.

The Marines approach a village, passing by a series of deserted rice paddies. In one paddy, a lone teenage boy wearing a customary hat is hunched over, toiling in the hot sun. The platoons stop.

"What's that dumb gook doing in the middle of the paddy?"

"Aww, just some villager kid," another grunt dismisses.

"Like hell he is, there ain't no village kids left to work in these paddies. Not kids his age."

The platoon leader instructs two Marines to retrieve the village boy for questioning. "Find out who he's with."

Wading into the paddy, two Marines surround the teenager. Startled, the boy looks up at the Marines confused and points down to the paddy. They grab him by the arm. He resists. They grab his other arm and forcefully lead him to the open field.

"Take off his shirt," the platoon leader instructs.

The boy's shirt is whisked off. His shoulders and back are marked with deep, red swollen welts.

"See, I told you," sneered one of the Marines. "He's a pack mule—hauls gear down from the north. Well boys, looks like we found ourselves an NVA caddy."

The boy lowers his eyes.

The platoon leader instructs two Marines to hold him for questioning and walks away.

"Who are you with?" one of the Marines snarls at him. The boy looks at him in utter confusion; he does not understand or speak English. They bind his hands and feet with rope as the boy talks to himself in Vietnamese, whispering something over and over, rocking his body back and forth, as if in a trance.

"What the hell is he saying?"

"No friggin' clue."

One of the Marines takes out his pistol. The boys' eyes grow wide with fear. The Marine holds the pistol against the boys' temple. "Who are you with?" He shouts.

The boy squeezes his eyes tight. He continues to rock back and forth, faster and faster. The Marine pushes the pistol harder into the boy's skin, his voice raising. "Where are the rest of them?"

Tears stream down the boys' face. The Marine pulls the trigger. The boy holds his breath.

Click.

No fire. It is Russian roulette.

"You think I'm friggin' joking?" The Marine hollers. "Tell me who you're with, cause I know you can understand me now."

The boy rocks himself faster still, mumbling even louder. The Marine, exasperated, hollers again, inches from the boy's face.

Dennis has been watching from afar. He is disturbed by what he sees. Turning his back, he walks as far away as possible. He realizes that there is nothing sicker in the world than the hatred he feels inside, and he is confused by the conflicting emotions swirling inside of him. On one hand he feels sorry for this kid; on the other hand, for all he knows, this could be the same guy that shot Harry in the face four times. He tries to rationalize the strange phenomenon that he can kill people, but yet, he always wants to be the first to go in and patch them up. And that's exactly what he wants to do now. Go over there, and help that kid. *Patch him up.*

Suddenly, a gunshot rings out.

Dennis doesn't turn around. He doesn't want to know.

The Porcelain Man

BY THE TIME THE MARINES reach the church and monastery atop a hill overlooking a mile-long stretch of the Street, they are tired, hungry, and thirsty. A priest and two nuns still occupy the church, a leftover French attempt to spread Christianity among the Buddhist villagers. They had been friendly to the Marines in the past by offering to share their well for drinking water. But the priest and nuns are nowhere to be found.

Dennis feels strange standing in front of the ornate church; but then again, he's never been comfortable in or around Catholic churches. When he was a young boy, his mother used to call nuns, "witches." He still isn't sure why. Maybe it was their black frocks, or maybe their ways seemed mysterious to her, a strong Protestant. He doesn't know. All he knows is that she distrusted them and that, as a result, he distrusted them and has since felt uneasy around nuns and Catholic churches.

One of the grunts walks inside the church, but returns several minutes later bewildered. "They're not in there. Maybe they evacuated?" he reports to the platoon leader.

"Just fill up the canteens. We have to keep humping. I'll make a note of it in my report."

The Marines walk behind the church to the well and pull out their canteens. They throw the bucket down, dipping it into the depths, and pull it back up. They groan in disgust upon seeing the water. It is murky and reddish brown.

"What the hell is this?"

The platoon leader looks down the well. Confusion, then disgust, follows.

"Jesus. They dumped their bodies down there." He turns around and calls for two grunts. "Thompson . . . Andrews . . . Get the bodies out of there," he orders, shaking his head as he walks away.

The grunts retrieve the priest first. Dressed in a black frock, his body is barely decayed. Then they pull up the two nuns. All three have been shot in the back of the head, execution style. Seeing their dead bodies, Dennis instantly feels bad that his mother ever called them witches.

He feels dizzy. Images of the last twenty-four hours play out in his mind in slow motion. He conjures the image of Harry; he imagines standing next to him and witnessing Harry jump up and getting shot in the face. Next, he sees the image of the frightened Vietnamese pack mule with the deep red welts in his back and the fear in his eyes. He remembers the sound of the gun. Now, the priest and two nuns. Dennis grabs his head, fearing it might explode.

He looks back down at the dead priest, and wonders what he is supposed to think, what he is supposed to feel. He doesn't know anymore. But he knows one thing: *I don't want to see or feel another goddamned thing.* He looks into the others' eyes; he can see it in them too. A change.

The platoon leader tries to rally them forward, "C'mon. We'll call for a chopper and have them pick up the bodies."

The tired, dirty, and emotionally drained Marines continue trailing the NVA. They reach the outskirts of the village where the South Vietnamese Army of the Republic of Vietnam, ARVN, await with reinforcements. But no sign of their forces exist. The platoon leader immediately senses that something is wrong. *Shit, where the hell are they?*

The Marines scan the village. Suddenly, from across the paddy, they see the ARVN. They are not in position. Instead, they are loading into trucks.

"Why aren't they firing? What the hell is going on?" Someone yells.

The platoon leader spits on the ground in disgust. "Damn them, it's Friday." He looks down at his watch. "Four O'clock."

Every Marine in the platoon is seething with anger. "You've got to be friggin' kidding me? We humped for twenty miles and those assholes are taking liberty call?" someone shouts out.

Isn't it their freaking liberty that we're fighting for in the friggin' first place? Dennis wants to shout, but instead, he holds his tongue.

"Pull back men," the platoon leader replies coolly. "We're heading back to the base."

In bitter silence, the Marines hump back to Camp Czzowitz as the last remnants of NVA melt back into the landscape and the South Vietnamese rumble down the road in their jeeps, relieved for the weekend. The Marines walk in silence; hungry, dejected, and pissed.

Dennis looks back over toward the South China Sea. Something catches his attention. It is an elderly Vietnamese man wearing a mint green shirt, lying face down in the sand flats. Dennis walks over and stands above him, noting that the man's head is tilted unnaturally to one side and his eyes are wide open. The back of his head is completely gone, blown off, most likely from a piece of shrapnel. Even the lobes of his brain are gone, leaving nothing but his face intact. Looking at him, Dennis feels a morbid fascination with how the human body comes apart, and yet, a palpable, persistent thought underlies it all—*this could be me*. Strangely, he thinks of the dolls the girls back home used to play with, the ones made of fragile porcelain. This man reminds him of one of those dolls—a porcelain head with nothing inside.

The Shadowed Valley of Death

DENNIS REJOINS THE PLATOON. The only thing that makes him feel better is the thought of seeing Lilly again. Maybe it is her innocence, maybe it is what she stands for. He doesn't know. All he knows is that she is his noble cause, the only good thing he has left.

The platoon reaches the base by morning. Dennis immediately heads toward Lilly's village. He is surprised to find several gunners from Delta Battery stationed at the base already standing outside Lilly's hut, including Chet. They are smoking cigarettes and talking softly to one another.

He knows immediately something is very wrong.

Chet sees Dennis approaching and elbows the others. They block the entrance to the doorway. "You don't want to go in there."

Not Lilly. Dennis feels a lump form in his throat, but externally maintains an icy composure. "Move," he growls at his friends blocking the doorway.

"Dennis . . . Really, you don't want to go in there," Chet implores him.

"I said, move," he snarls.

"Denny, just go back."

Dennis brusquely walks past them and enters the hut. The stench of death fills the air. His heart sinks to his stomach. *No, this can't be happening.* Flies swarm around two lifeless bodies. Lilly's mother and father lay on the dirt floor in a pool of blood, their hands and feet hogtied behind their backs. They are dead.

Hanging from the ceiling in the back of the hut is a small body. Dennis closes his eyes. *Lilly.* Bound by her ankles and hung upside down from the ceiling, her throat is slashed. A pool of brown, dried blood stains the dirt floor beneath her body. Her eyes, reflecting the last seconds of her life, are frozen with a horrified look of fear. Dennis quivers with emotion as he unbinds her feet and cradles her small body in his arms. He lays her down next to her parents and looks for blankets to cover their bodies. There, sitting in the corner of the room, is Lilly's red-plumed hat.

Why would anyone do this to a little girl? But he knows why, and the cold hard reality sinks heavily into his heart. They killed her to send a message to the other villagers—she was helping the Marines. *They were watching her, and I wasn't here to save her.* And with that, Dennis breaks his composure and cries. He cries for Harry, he cries for Lilly, and he cries for himself, the person he once was. Each of them now gone forever.

The Casualties

THIRTY-SEVEN YEARS and thousands of miles away from the Street of No Joy, Dennis falls silent. The room is so quiet Andy can hear the clock on the wall ticking. When Dennis speaks again, his voice is different, almost hollow.

"We left the base on April 3rd, Harry died on the fifth, and I found Lilly on the seventh." Dennis clears his throat. "In that very short period of time, ninety percent of who I was, or who I *thought* I was, changed. And I was left with only a fraction of myself—like the porcelain man with nothing inside."

Andy lets that image seep in. It's strange to listen to the innermost feelings of another, to watch how a soul is deconstructed, layer after layer, until the very core of a human being is revealed. He too, remembers the moment when something deep inside of him changed, and he will never forget the Iraqi man who lost his entire family before his very eyes.

It was just after sunrise, at a checkpoint outside of Tikrit. The man had packed up his wife, two small children, and all of their belongings in a dingy black Oldsmobile. Andy had ordered the man out of the car so they could inspect him for explosive devices. Suddenly, another Marine guarding the checkpoint started yelling. A vehicle, careening wildly, was speeding directly toward them, showing no signs of slowing down. Instant dread swept over Andy. *Suicide bomber*. Andy shoved the man out of the vehicle's path and fell on top of him, shielding him from the coming danger. The last thing Andy heard before the explosion were the man's children screaming in the back seat of the car. Then, *Boooooom!* The Oldsmobile exploded on impact. Heat from the flames seared Andy's arms as he wrestled to keep the Iraqi from flinging himself onto the burning heap of mangled steel and flesh.

Later, after the sirens waned and the remains of the car were towed away, the man walked around in circles, pacing back and forth, holding a remnant of cloth from his wife's dress, wringing it in his hands. Andy did not understand the man's words, but he understood the anguish in the man's voice. Andy had never seen pain like that before. Real pain. That night, back at the barracks, he called his mother to tell her how much he loved her, and to thank her for everything she had done for him growing up. And he went to bed that night silently crying for the man who had lost everything. Or maybe he was silently crying for himself, for realizing that out there, not a trace of grand or glory was to be found. *Only pain exists.*

Arlington

DENNIS LEFT THAT EVENING deciding against telling Andy about the funeral for the fallen Marine, instead saying, "I've got something that came up this weekend, so I'll see you on Monday." He's not sure why he didn't say anything. Maybe he didn't want to make Andy feel guilty. Or was that just a projection of his own fear? Would *he* feel guilty tomorrow?

Dennis remembers the last time he walked the hillsides of Arlington cemetery. It was mid-November, 1954; just two weeks shy of Dennis' seventh birthday. His father, Hunter, a retired commercial pilot, had just moved his family from Martinsburg, West Virginia to Frederick, Maryland. An avid history buff and former War World II pilot, Hunter wanted to take his two young sons to Washington D.C. to tour the memorials and visit Arlington National Cemetery to pay respect to his friends who were buried there.

Dennis recalls the surge of excitement he felt that day sitting in the back seat of the car. Looking at the brilliant autumnal trees lining the George Washington Memorial Parkway, he remembers his father pointing out the Memorial Bridge, telling his two sons, "Do you boys know that bridge was built as a symbolic link to reunite the North and the South? It crosses the river right between the Lincoln Memorial and Robert E. Lee's Arlington House."

No, they didn't know. Dennis stared at the bridge with a newfound appreciation. The majestic marble and gold equestrian statues caught his eye, and he let his imagination pretend he was standing in ancient Rome or Greece. It would be many years before he would understand the significance of those sculptures: Valor, Sacrifice, and the Arts of Peace. Just outside of the bronze cemetery gates, Hunter told the boys another story.

"When Virginia seceded from the Union, Lee accepted the post of Major General for the Confederate Army. His Arlington House was confiscated. The Union general wanted to stick it to him by making Arlington unlivable. So General Meigs started burying dead Union soldiers in the backyard." Hunter laughed. He had an infectious, almost devilish laugh, and he finished the story with a twinkle in his eye. "Meigs went so far as to bury eighteen hundred Bull Run casualties right in Mrs. Lee's rose garden. That did the trick, the Lees never returned to their home again. And that's how Arlington became a military cemetery."

Dennis marveled at his father's storytelling. Like most sons, he revered his father. A decorated pilot in War World II, Hunter was awarded the Distinguished Flying Cross—the highest medal given to pilots, for his bravery flying the "hump," the air supply route over the Himalayan mountain ranges. At the time, no other C-47 pilot had ever flown the hump; the altitude was thought too high, and oxygen too scarce. But Hunter accomplished that feat, and flew missions over China, Burma, and India, providing transport and supplies to the troops.

Like their father, the two sons grew up loving all things military. They loved reading about great battles, listening to war stories, and of course, loved all things "Ike"—who just one week earlier had presided over the ceremony dedicating the Iwo Jima Memorial. It was the 179th anniversary of the Marine Corps. Dennis had heard older people talk about the "good war," but it was not until Hunter explained that "out of those six men whose faces you see, only three made it home alive," did Dennis understand its magnitude. Looking up into the giant thirty-two foot high likeness of Ira Hayes, Franklin Sousley, John Bradley, Harlon Block, Michael Strank, and René Gagnon, it was hard to imagine any of them not being alive. They all looked so strong, so young and vibrant.

"Roosevelt wanted the survivors to come home, to help boost morale and raise money for the 7th Bond Tour," Hunter told them. But when Ira Hayes came home, it was Truman who greeted him at the White House and told him 'You're an American hero, son!' But Hayes didn't feel that way. He said, 'How could I feel like a hero when only five men in my platoon of forty-five survived, when only twenty-seven men in my company of two hundred and fifty managed to escape death or injury?'" Hunter recited from memory.

Then, he read aloud the inscription at the base of the sculpture: "Uncommon Valor was a Common Virtue," the tribute given by Fleet Admiral Chester Nimitz to the men who fought on that island. Hunter shook his head. "That was Iwo Jima, Some of the craziest sons of bitches I ever . . ."

He caught himself mid-sentence. "Well, let's just say, some of the bravest men I ever met in my life were Marines."

It was the moment Dennis knew: *I want to be a Marine.* Later that afternoon, standing in front of the white marble headstones that marked that graves of Hunters' lost friends, Dennis witnessed for the first time in his life what it meant to honor someone. And in the way a young boy makes a wish, be it for a Christmas, or a birthday, or for just a special gift, Dennis wished that someday, he too, would be buried in Arlington.

That was almost fifty years ago. And now, on the eve of the funeral for one of America's fallen sons, a National Park Service grounds keeper walks by a mound of freshly dug dirt in Section 60. For him, tomorrow is just another day.

Part V

The Funeral
November 6, 2004

"In peace the sons bury their fathers, but in war the fathers bury their sons."

—*Croesus*

The Ocean's Tides

THE WINDSHIELD WIPERS SLOSH through the pouring rain, beating back and forth in rhythm like the pendulum of a grandfather clock, tick tock, tick tock. Just twenty minutes ago, the mother of Lance Corporal Ryan Haydon met Dennis in the Fisher House lobby. "My condolences, ma'am." Margaret Haydon had feigned a smile, and taken his arm. Now, driving across the Memorial Bridge approaching the entrance to Arlington National Cemetery, Margaret mindlessly stares out the passenger side window at the gray, choppy waters of the Potomac River below. She does not notice the ornate marble statues, and she surely does not contemplate the significance of the bridge itself, or the divide it crosses.

The only thing divided right now is her emotions, and she is focusing all of her energy on keeping those emotions restrained and bridled. It has been a daily struggle to bridge the gap in her life since that day the Department of Defense called. *It can't be, it just can't be,* she had repeated over and over again. But it was true. The overwhelming feeling of grief had crippled her and blocked out all sense of time, space, and reality; the world around her collapsed and she became nauseous, vomiting on the kitchen floor.

After the initial shock, anger set in. She was angry that Ryan had died so young. Angry that he died with so much future left ahead of him. But most of all, angry that he was taken away from her forever. *I have no right,* she told herself. Her mind told her to be proud of the boy she raised and the man he became. Her pastor told her to find solace in the fact that Ryan died honorably, doing something he loved. And she tried. But at night, those feelings of grief and anger and solace waged a war inside of her, with each opposing side equal in strength and ferocity, beating and bruising her psyche, until only her mind was left as the casualty in the morning.

Now, grief for Margaret Haydon comes in waves. Like the ocean's tide pulled by the moon's invisible string, emotions surge within her, then ebb and flow back out to sea, leaving crystallized sands of sorrow in their wake. Her son chose to be a Marine, accepted the consequences, and died for what he believed in. *That's all there is to it*, she tells herself. But her heart aches with every breath she takes. And it is that acute sense of loss that troubles her the most. He was a piece of her, once a physical entity of her own flesh, and now he is gone. She commands herself to stay disciplined, to keep the emotional cancer at bay. If she allows the one nagging question to enter her mind, it will eternally eat her alive: *Did my son die in vain?*

Margaret sucks in a deep breath, and reclines her head back against the headrest. She closes her eyes as they pass by the granite pillars of the cemetery entrance and she tries to mentally prepare herself for what is to come. *But how does a mother prepare herself to bury her child?* Dennis parks the car and walks around the back of his Ford, grabs an umbrella from the trunk, and opens the door for Margaret. She places her foot firmly on solid ground and takes Dennis' outstretched hand. She seems light and frail to Dennis, liable to be blown over by a strong gust of wind at any second. They walk toward the cement-colored administration building through the pouring rain. Dennis looks down at his watch; it is 10:30 am, the service starts at eleven.

Inside, they are greeted graciously and shown downstairs to the room where Ryan's body lies in repose. Ryan's casket is in the center of the room, closed. Margaret cries out upon entering the room. She rushes over to the casket and buries her head in her hands as she quietly sobs. Ryan's father solemnly consoles his ex-wife as the other guests, three Marines in dress blue uniforms, and a young girl wearing an Army ROTC uniform, bow their heads in reverence. Margaret cries for several minutes, then composes herself and speaks quietly with Ryan's father, John.

Dennis stands against the back wall. With his hands folded and his head bowed in silence, he wonders if this is what it was like at Harry's funeral. *Did Harry's broken family mourn over his broken body the same way?*

It is time to bury Ryan, and his casket is taken out of the room. Dennis steadies Margaret as he escorts her back to the car and follows the procession. It is still raining heavily. The Marine honor guard removes the casket from the silver hearse and gently lays it down at its final interment. Margaret and John stand directly center. John's second wife, Patrice, flanks him. The three Marines stand at attention behind them. The girl in the ROTC uniform, Ryan's girlfriend, is crying loudly now and bursts of sobs cascade over the soothing words of the chaplain.

"Ryan is with the Lord, our God and Maker. May he rest in peace for all eternity. Amen,"

"Amen." Moments later, the chaplain ends his eulogy, and seven Marine riflemen point their guns in the air to commence a gun salute. The first volley is fired. Ryan's family flinches at the sound of the rifles, unprepared for the loud reverberating clap. The second volley is fired; again, they flinch.

The third volley is fired. This one finalizes the harsh reality for Margaret Haydon. *This is it. My son is dead.*

The military bugler begins the first melancholy strains of Taps. It echoes over the Arlington hills as the flag draping the casket is carefully folded and presented to Margaret.

"On behalf of a grateful nation and a proud Marine Corps, this flag is presented as a token of our appreciation for the honorable and faithful service rendered by Lance Corporal Ryan Haydon to his country." The Marines salute her.

Margaret looks down at the flag now neatly folded in her lap. The last vestige of her composure breaks. She closes her eyes and weeps. The sound of a mother's grief is the most heartbreaking lamentation in the world.

The Angels Are Crying

DENNIS WATCHES THE COLD RAIN crush the autumn leaves into the soggy earth as the service ends. *Today is the perfect day for a funeral.* He remembers what his mother used to tell him as a boy, that when it rains it means the angels are crying; and he wonders if the guys from 1/9 are up there crying now.

One of the Marines in attendance at the service, a lance corporal, walks up to Mrs. Haydon. "I operated with Ryan in Iraq," he tells her, then explains his tour is over and he's now stationed at Quantico. Margaret clasps his hands and gives him a hug. "Ryan was a good Marine," he tells her. "One of the best. He and I were close friends." Tears streak down her face as she hugs him even more tightly.

"Thank you," she whispers.

Dennis feels like he's an intruder standing in another world that is being superimposed on his own. *Another Harry being buried.* It has hit him hard today—the guilt, that is. The same strain he felt when Harry died; the same pit in his stomach when he held Dave in his arms, the same sickness that came over him at Con Thien when he looked down out of that chopper and saw the guys still under siege. Dennis wonders if this Marine standing stoically before him with Margaret Haydon's face buried in his chest feels the same way. *Does he ask himself everyday why he made it, too?*

Dennis didn't accompany Harry's body home, nor did he take a short leave and go to the funeral as was customary. It just wasn't something he was capable of doing at the time. Shortly after Harry's death, his foster father, Mr. Nelson, sent Dennis a package containing Harry's camera. Dennis knew that Mr. Nelson had also sent a letter addressed to his mother, Mrs. Michaels, thanking her for her condolences and asking that she encourage Dennis to come visit when he returned home. The nightmares of standing over Harry's grave began the night he received the package.

Years later, he would come to understand that the nightmare really represented his survivor's guilt. Harry was his best friend—his right arm, gone forever—and the camera, the albatross of survivors' guilt. Mr. Nelson wanted to know how Harry died. Dennis recoiled at the thought then, as he does now. *What was he going to tell the old man, that Harry died because he was trying to prove he was brave?* He never did visit Mr. Nelson, and to this day, has never been to Harry's grave in Trenton—something that weighs on his conscience today just as heavily as the camera always did in his dream.

Dennis takes a last look at the picture of Ryan. He was a good-looking Marine, with soft brown eyes and a determined face. *Too young. Too friggin young.* He looks out at the headstones next to Ryan's, all neatly lined and newly white, five rows deep. Dennis estimates that at least a hundred servicemen and women are buried in this section already. All casualties from Iraq and Afghanistan; their headstones read "Operation Iraqi Freedom" and "Operation Enduring Freedom." But it is the dates on the headstones that catch Dennis' attention. Born 1982 – Died 2003. Born 1985 – Died 2004. Dennis pans over to the left side of Ryan's site and notices the open fields that are conspicuously empty, inviting almost, as if anticipating the arrival of even more sons and daughters, like an expectant mother who yearns for the day she can finally cradle her child in her arms. Dennis shakes his head. *Not again.*

John Haydon walks up to greet Dennis. "I've heard all about you. Thank you for driving Margaret, and coming to honor my son today. It means a lot to us."

Dennis shakes his hand. "The guys from 1/9 know he's reporting in. He'll be in good hands up there."

John smiles, and tries hard to fight back the tears. "We knew he'd come home, we just didn't know he'd bypass us and go straight to Arlington," John tells him, trying to make a light joke through the tears. But Dennis knows it is just his way of dealing with his son's death. Different people cope in different ways.

The lance corporal finishes consoling Margaret, giving her one last hug goodbye. His face is drawn and sad, his eyes red and swollen. The Marine looks Dennis directly in the eye and nods his head. Dennis nods back. He reaches out to shake the young man's hand. "Ooh-rah," Dennis says softly.

"Ooh-rah," the Marine replies.

The fact of the matter is Dennis feels sorrier for this Marine than he does for Ryan. In a strange way, he almost envies Ryan. Ryan made it. He paid his dues. He doesn't owe anybody anything. It is a paradox that is difficult to explain, but the way Dennis sees it, death for people like them is probably the best thing that could happen. It keeps them complete—it keeps them whole. Ryan will never experience survivor's guilt or the body bag syndrome; he'll never damage relationships over fears of intimacy, or wake up with nightmares. Death is freedom. But for those who make it home, life is a price and dues must be paid. And Dennis has been paying his dues for thirty-seven years. He takes one last look at Ryan's casket and whispers, "Semper Fi, Marine." *Always Faithful.*

Part VI

Gio Linh
November 7, 2004

The mind is its own place, and in itself
Can make a Heav'n of Hell, a Hell of Heav'n.

—*John Milton*

The Dawn

Fallujah, Iraq

SUNDAY EVENING. TEN O'CLOCK. Two companies of the Iraqi 36th Battalion jump off seven-ton trucks and storm into Fallujah General Hospital. Ten thousand coalition forces comprised of units from the Marines, Army, British Black Watch, and Iraqi forces begin their full scale campaign to stamp out the estimated two to three thousand insurgents embedded throughout Fallajuh. The siege follows a week-long bombardment campaign that has already leveled parts of the city, including Nazal Emergency Hospital and a nearby medical center.

The Prime Minister, Ayad Allawi, a Shi'ite, has declared a state of emergency for sixty days. At a news conference in Baghdad he explains to the Iraqi citizens, "I have given my authorization to the multinational force. We are determined to clean Fallujah of terrorists." In political terms it is critical for the upcoming Iraqi elections to rid Fallujah of insurgents and smoke out Abu Musab al-Zarqawi, at that time the leader of the al-Qaeda in Iraq.

Inside Fallujah General Hospital, bewildered patients, doctors, and staff are told to lie on the floor, hands tied behind their backs while the Special Forces look for persons of interest. Four or five foreign fighters, including two Moroccans, are captured inside the compound. Pictures of flag-draped American coffins and derogatory comments that translators said encouraged jihad are reportedly found in one examination room. Also found are two cellular phones atop the roof, presumably used by insurgents for roof spotting.

Taking the hospital is a tactical decision, as its location on the eastside of the peninsula on the Euphrates River is of strategic importance to the Allies and is believed to be the most logical area for insurgents to fall back if driven from Fallujah. Blocking access means restricting the insurgents' mobility. Seventy to ninety percent of the city's population of three hundred thousand has already evacuated. Women and children have been allowed to leave the city freely.

Rumors circulate throughout alternate media outlets that the purported reason for storming the hospital is indeed "tactical"—speculating that the hospital needs to be secured in order for the Allied forces to win the propaganda war. By cordoning off access to doctors and medical staff, the Allies can thereby control information regarding casualties, especially civilian casualties. The hospital had earned a reputation for being a refuge for insurgents and a center for propaganda against allied forces since the last standoff in April, when the Pentagon blamed the doctors and staff for inflating the number of civilian casualties.

Contradictory reports of six hundred women, children, and innocent civilians killed or wounded—coupled with the images of mass graves being dug at the nearby soccer stadium—had incited hotbeds of insurgents and increased the number and intensity of other terrorist attacks. Suicide bombings, beheadings, and assassinations increased and had the potential of derailing the Iraqi's confidence in their country's ability to hold the upcoming free election. The Coalition will not make the same mistake twice.

The hospital is taken in less than an hour. Reportedly, not a shot is fired. The first part of Operation Phantom Fury, or al-Fajr, "The Dawn," has begun.

Letters

ANDY FLIPS THROUGH the cable news channels. He reads the snippets of information crawling across the bottom of the television screen. CNN, Fox News, MSNBC, are all detailing the same news: "US Storms Fallujah. Operation Phantom Fury underway."

This is it, the big one.

Talking head pundits across the country are scrutinizing every angle of the conflict, offering opinions and back-seat analysis. But the unspoken question no one is asking: *How do you wage a war within a country while doing so on behalf of that country?* It is a question to which Andy does not know the answer.

There is a knock at the door. "Come in," Andy calls out, expecting Dennis. But it is Francis, one of the assistants at the front desk. She is carrying a white rectangular box. She hands it to him with a friendly smile, "Special delivery for you."

Andy opens it up and finds a large manila folder. A typed cover letter is clipped to it.

Dear Andrew Taylor,
    Enclosed are several letters from our seventh-grade students. Thank you for all that you have done. You are a true American hero.

        Sincerely,
        Margaret Crimshaw,
        Principal, Fairfield Junior High School

Andy smiles, Fairfield Junior High is his alma mater. Andy leafs through the packet of handwritten letters bound together. He counts at least two dozen letters, each with distinctive youthful writing; some cursive, some block letters, some hard to read, others very girly with heart-dotted i's.

Dear Andrew,
    Our teacher told us you used to be a student here, and that you got hurt real bad in Iraq. I'm sorry to hear about what happened to your legs, but I'm glad you're OK. Thank you for being so brave.

        Your friend,
        Jackie

He is about to read another letter, but his attention is drawn to an announcement on the television. The Defense Department briefing is starting. Voices fall to hushed tones and background murmurs fade as Secretary Rumsfeld walks to the podium and begins his address. Andy is half-listening. He used to like watching Rummy on TV, liked his style; his answers were always deft, clever, and vague, and Andy enjoyed the efficiency of his question and answer sessions. But after experiencing Iraq first hand and seeing what was really going on, he knows the pictures being painted here at home don't always correspond to reality.

And it troubles him that it is getting harder to know the truth. Yet in his heart, he feels it would be almost a conflict of interest to criticize the government or call out all the "bullshits," because at the end of the day he is still rooting for the home team. Besides, he has never been one to vocalize his political opinions, a philosophy he learned early on from his father, whose favorite maxim was, "Never talk about politics, religion, or sex—you never know who the person is sitting next to you."

His father had always spoken such words of wisdom, especially at critical times in Andy's young life. He remembers one incident in particular when he was in junior high school. Coming home from the Fairfield baseball team practice, he had stormed through the back door and threw his glove in the kitchen trash can. "I'm quitting the baseball team," Andy announced to his parents.

"But why, Andy? You love baseball," his mother asked, shocked.

"Coach benched me and is starting his son instead. Everyone knows Bobby stinks. It's not fair," Andy huffed. "I'm quitting, that's all there is to it."

He remembers stomping up the stairs to his bedroom, slamming the door shut, and staring at his Bo Jackson poster. Bo had retired many years earlier, but his father had somehow managed to obtain an autographed poster for his son, so it stayed pinned up on his wall for years. "Bo Knows," the poster proclaimed. *Yeah? If Bo knows, what the heck would Bo do?* Andy wondered.

Just then, his father knocked on the door and sat down at the foot of the bed. His father hadn't really said anything down in the kitchen when Andy made his announcement. He was always a man of few words; but when he spoke, people listened. "Son," he began contemplatively, "you are not a quitter. You cannot let what others say or do dictate what you believe."

Andy wasn't convinced, but his father continued. "For every left there is a right, and for every right there is a wrong. *You must be the master of your own emotions.*" His father paused to look him in the eye. "Do you understand that, Andy?"

Andy nodded yes, but he did not understand.

"Good," his father said, rising up to his feet. He leaned over to rumple Andy's hair in his fingers. "Remember son, that is your one and only true domain. If you can understand that, then no man can ever control you."

Andy was fourteen at the time. The next day he quit the baseball team. His father unexpectedly passed away from cancer six months later.

Andy looks down at the stack of letters in his hand. He wonders if these thirteen- and fourteen-year-old kids really understand what's going on in Iraq and Afghanistan.

Andy begins reading a letter from a youngster named Lauren when he is interrupted by a knock at the door. This time, it is Dennis.

"Hey, come on in, have a seat."

Dennis sits down. The first thing Andy notices is Dennis' appearance. He looks tired, his face appears to be weighted down, and his demeanor seems heavy, almost sullen. "Here, take a look at these." Andy hands him a few letters. "Some kids from my hometown wrote these."

Dennis leafs through them as Andy turns his attention back to the television. A news reporter is summarizing Rumsfeld's main talking points.

"Have you been watching the news?" Andy interrupts the silence.

Dennis nods; he has heard. He knew they went into Fallujah and secured that hospital and two bridges. In fact, he has been thinking about it all day. It struck Dennis as odd to publicly acknowledge storming a hospital. *Wouldn't the outside world look at that as a violation of the Fourth Geneva Convention?*

"Yeah, I heard. Funny, how things change. We always called targets like that supply centers."

Supply centers? Andy flashes back to something Dennis had said last week, about the Deckhouse mission. *Did he mean . . . ?* But just as Dennis did not turn around to see if that Vietnamese boy was shot in the head, Andy doesn't ask Dennis to clarify. He doesn't want to know.

An awkward silence ensues. It is clear Dennis doesn't want to discuss Fallujah anymore. He has been in a foul mood all day. Between the memories from the funeral and the news this morning, a nagging feeling has formed in the pit of his stomach. *This is just like Vietnam.* It has been seeping into his consciousness for some time now, but was reinforced this morning after hearing reports the Fallujah attack was expected to become the biggest urban engagement since Hue in '68. And he was reminded of something said over thirty years ago. A quote from an American officer on why he felt it necessary to destroy the Vietnamese village of Ben Tre: "We had to destroy the town in order to save it."

Destroy it in order to save it. Dennis has been replaying that phrase over and over again in his mind all morning long. *Isn't that what he had to do? Destroy himself in order to save himself? Murder his emotions, feelings and humanity in order to survive? Isn't that what he had to do at Gio Linh?*

Boots

THREE "BOOTS," FRESH-FACED ROOKIES, stand in the artillery pit waiting for direction from the lieutenant. Their fatigues are crisp and clean, their
boots shiny, and faces clean-shaven; they stand in stark contrast to
the dirty and hardened veterans. The lieutenant is crouched down low; the
trenches are only three-feet high, and at this location snipers take easy pot-
shots at Marines who carelessly stand even a fraction above the line.

"Gentlemen, welcome to Gio Linh, or 'A-2.' As you can see by these
half-assed trenches, they were built by short Europeans . . . the French."

The boots look around at their new surroundings. The base is cramped
and dirty. There is no grass on the hill, only dirt. The style of the trenches is
reminiscent of those built during WWII, obviously still fresh in the minds
of those who constructed the fort. It is often said that militaries build their
armies to fight the previous war. In the open DMZ, where guerilla warfare
prevails, the WWII-inspired forts and trenches are, without question, useless.

"Here's a breakdown of the area." The lieutenant points over to the
bridge. "There's Freedom Bridge straddling the Ben Hai. Over to our right
is the South China Sea. And over there," he points to another hill in the distance, "is Con Thien, our sister base on Leatherneck Square."

The quadrilateral of land anchoring the Dye-Marker bases called Leatherneck Square refers to an old nickname for the leather stock or neck piece

that was part of the Marine uniform that ensured nineteenth century Marines kept their heads erect. Standing now with no concern for his neck—other than keeping it low enough to avoid being shot off—one of the rookies asks the lieutenant, "How close are we to North Vietnam?"

"Close enough to kiss Big Ho on the mouth. Approximately fifteen hundred meters away."

The rookie whistles under his breath. "Jesus."

"You won't find him up here," the lieutenant deadpans.

The lieutenant's frustration is palpable. His platoon, and the others of the III Marine Force stationed along the DMZ, have been confined to fixed defensive positions while following orders to construct and man the Strongpoint Obstacle System. They have been told, more or less, to "make do." After all, they have been using the same uniforms, equipment, and rations since War World II and Korea. It's common knowledge that the Army gets all the money. And the Navy would rather spend theirs on its ships and fighter jets than on the Marines merely used for beach assaults and quick land strikes. Usually, the Marines are pulled back just as quickly as they are sent in, so the Army, the real occupying force, can run the show. But up here on the DMZ, the "in and out, quit screwing about" mentality has been thrown out the window. Now saddled down and forced to stay defensive, it goes without saying that building and manning Dye-Marker is not the lieutenant's cup of tea.

Dennis knocks back a swig of two-day-old coffee and heads down to the artillery parapet for some water from the blister bag. There he finds himself face to face with the three rookies. *Great, more FNGs. Friggin' New Guys that don't have a clue.* Dennis' mood is in large part a reflection of the base as a whole; they are sitting ducks, and every one of them is filled with tension, anxiety, and numbness as a result of the heavy artillery and mortar fire they've taken incessantly for the past several weeks.

"Are you Dennis Michaels?"

"Yeah?"

"We were told to find you. The lieutenant said you can show us around," one of the rookies tells him. Dennis can see he is the extroverted one of the group. The other two are shorter and more timid. None of their features stand out, but it doesn't matter. To Dennis, they are all faceless.

Suddenly, a sound echoes in the distance. Gio Linh is so close to North

Vietnam that enemy rounds can clearly be heard when fired from their artillery. *Shhhhooooomb.* This one is a rocket. Shouts fill the air.

"Incoming!"

The rookies hit the deck with a loud thump and cover their heads with their hands. Dennis rolls his eyes at them and merely bends over at his waist. The rocket whizzes overhead, exploding well off target. The rookies stand up and dust themselves off, looking sheepish. Dennis raises a suspicious brow,

"How long have you boots been in-country?"

The extroverted rookie volunteers, "I've been on a couple of patrols. These guys just got here today."

"Have you ever been under heavy artillery before?

They shake their heads no.

"Well then, I've got a couple pieces of advice for you. First of all, learn the sound of incoming. If you can hear 'em, they're going over you. If you can't hear 'em, you're screwed. Remember that. And two—don't bunch up. One round'll get you all," Dennis says sternly, walking away from them before they have a chance to speak.

The veteran Marines are no strangers to the perils of artillery fire. A direct hit can kill instantly, blow a person apart or the shrapnel will tear them up. Sometimes the concussion from the incoming blast will jar the brain so badly it will kill them. Worse yet is the fabled "White Butterfly" in which the concussion of the blast will turn insides into liquid. From the outside, one may look perfectly fine; but inside, everything has turned to liquid, the heart, lungs—everything.

"Jesus, what's up his ass?" one of the rookies asks sarcastically within earshot.

Dennis whirls furiously around. "You're boots! You don't know what the hell you're doing. You're bad luck." The words have a stinging, biting effect.

The extroverted rookie tries to shake it off, holding his hand out to introduce himself properly to Dennis. "Hi, let's start over. My name's Sam. I'm from . . . ."

Dennis snaps, "I don't care who you are, or where you're from. I don't want to know what you're about. I don't want to know you. *Period.*"

Sam's jaw drops. Dennis immediately wishes he hadn't sounded so harsh, but the truth is, he's a veteran now, and veterans want nothing to do with rookies. They're too green, too inexperienced and it's too hard to see friends die. The last thing Dennis needs is another friend. But he can't help feeling guilty when he sees the confusion and disappointment in their eyes. Dennis takes a deep breath; his face softens slightly. *Oh, all right.* He motions for the three to follow him.

Crouching below the trench-lines, Dennis guides the three rookies to the vicinity of a large hole dug in the ground. "Over there is the ammo dump. There's forty thousand pounds of high explosives in there including the white phosphorous rounds."

"That's mean shit," Sam whistles, "I hear if you get hit with a phosphorous round, it'll burn right through your skin, eat a hole through your muscle, right down to the bone."

"That's right," Dennis confirms. "Only thing you can do is pack mud on it. If there's anything that scares you, it's that shit. Worst way to friggin' die."

The three rookies shake their head just from the thought of it.

"Here, see these? These are the beehive rounds." Dennis points to an ammo box of hard 105s filled with steel flechettes. "If we ever get overrun— and we *will* get overrun, you can count on it—fire these right into the enemy. If worse comes to worst, and you know nothing can be saved, make sure you put an incendiary grenade into the gun barrel. That way they can't turn our own guns on us."

The rookies nod their heads.

Twenty minutes later, Dennis finishes giving them the tour and leads them back to the artillery parapet. "Good luck," Dennis says, allowing himself a half-smile, as he shakes each of their hands. The three rookies make their way over to the blister bag for some water.

Suddenly, Dennis hears a round being fired from the north side of the river. His head shoots up; he listens closely, and waits to hear the telltale whistle. He does not hear it. *Shit!*

"Incoming!"

Dennis dives over the parapet and throws himself up against the sandbags, bracing for the explosion.

The round explodes just yards away. The ground shakes from the impact, the concussion of air slams against the sandbags. A dark cloud of smoke, dirt, and debris fill the air. Sticky, grimy, red stuff rains down on Dennis, covering his helmet, his face, and his hands. He looks down at himself in disgust. *What the hell is this?*

Suddenly, a sick realization sweeps over him. *This is someone's blood and bones.* It is thick and gooey, and it is everywhere. Dennis looks over the sandbags to where the three rookies had been standing. They are gone.

Jesus Christ, they took a direct hit. Dennis jumps to his feet and runs over to help them. Other Marines are running over too. Shouts fill the air.

"Corpsman, up!"

Dennis kneels over their bodies. He checks for pulses. They are all dead. One of the rookies is lying in a very natural looking prone position, with his legs seemingly lying straight out. Dennis begins to pick him up. It is then he realizes. *These aren't his legs.* They belong to one of the other rookies. Another Marine assists Dennis in picking up the bodies, but there are only two bodies left.

"Where did the other one go?" the Marine asks.

"That's it. He's gone." Dennis' voice trails off.

He then grabs a metal meal tray and begins combing the ground for little pieces of body parts, a grisly duty he undertakes somberly. Scouring the impact site by the blister bag, he finds a piece of skull. He picks it up and places it on the tray. It still has a tuft of hair on it. He places the tray next to the corpsman to be tagged. The corpsman looks at the contents in the tray and shakes his head. "I'm okay with guys getting shot and dying. But this? This is just gross," the corpsman says sadly.

Dennis doesn't say anything. He knows what the corpsman is saying—there are clean kills, and then there's this. No one ever really talks after a direct hit; it's almost as if they pretend it didn't just happen. Only the survival mantra is repeated over and over again: *It's just a thing. Ain't nothin' but a thing.*

The corpsman places the bodies and the remains in body bags. Dennis takes one last look at them. He sees their boots sticking out from the bag. It is a sight that will be forged in Dennis' memory forever, as he notes with sadistic irony: *Boots. The last thing you ever see on a guy. You never take off a guy's boots.*

The Trace

Dear Mom and Dad,
This is just a short note to let you know that everything is OK. I'm up
at Gio Linh with the BTRY now. Everything up here is underground.
We are sitting right on the edge of the D.M.Z., as far north as you can
go. I'll write tomorrow when I'm on radio watch. I'm just too tired to
think right now.

Love,
Denny

DENNIS IS EXHAUSTED FROM having humped at least nine miles today on patrol. But it was worth it. He personally called in the artillery that killed four of the enemy combatants they chased the length of the Trace. However, all has not been quiet back at the base as Dennis and the grunts find upon their return. Gio Linh has taken intermittent incoming all day, evidenced by the pockmarked landing zone, and it is clear the enemy is becoming increasingly more disruptive and the Trace increasingly more expensive.

It has been three weeks since the Marines learned they were the official beneficiaries of Practice Nine and their inheritance included clearing the Trace—a swath of land parallel to the DMZ between Con Thien and Gio Linh, where the strong point posts are to be set up to better see enemy movement.

Tired of the seeming merry-go-round, the Marines find it absurd that the military geniuses back home actually believe that pulling a strip of land across the DMZ will enable them to see enemy movement and thwart penetration into South Vietnam. After all, for the NVA, just fifteen hundred meters away, to fire artillery at them is like skipping stones across a pond.

Lt. General Lew Walt, the III MAF commander, had initially protested the assignment, fearing it would siphon off focus, materials, and more importantly, manpower. He argued that he would have to commit his entire 3rd Division to the barrier, essentially confining his Marines to fixed positions. Unless reinforcements in the northern I-Corps tactical region could be provided, his division would not be able to conduct offensive operations while burdened with constructing and defending the strongpoint system.

General Westmoreland had assured General Walt that the Marines would be reinforced as soon as resources and units became available. Despite deep misgivings, General Walt committed his resources on the presumption they would later be compensated.

With their enemy lurking in the shadows of the forests and hedgerows, the Marines build McNamara's Line, fixing themselves to a static location with no intention of penetrating the northern shores of the Ben Hai River.

And the NVA watch, wait, and bait.

Leatherneck Square

A LOUD, BOOMING CLAP of thunder startles Dennis awake. *What time is it?* It is just before three AM. *Oh hell.* His first instinct is to roll over and try to fall back to sleep. Suddenly, he hears the sound of heavy drumming. *That's not thunder.* He jumps off his makeshift bed—an air mattress thrown across empty ammo boxes—and runs out of his bunker. *Stay below the trench line,* he cautions himself as he runs to the command post.

A green flare light illuminates the sky over the south hill of Gio Linh's sister firebase, Con Thien. A savage mortar and artillery attack follows immediately. Suddenly, a rocket streaks across the sky, accompanied by an ominous, whistling sound as it careens toward Gio Linh. The round explodes with such a fierce concussion that Dennis feels the earth shake beneath him.

Today is the 13th anniversary of Dien Bien Phu, and the outposts within the quadrilateral of Leatherneck Square are under simultaneous attack, with Con Thien taking the brunt of the barrage. Coveted for its terrain features, Con Thien is a hill 158 meters high, located less than two miles from the southern DMZ boundary. Perched in the middle of the red, mud plains, it affords the best observation capabilities in the area, overlooking the DMZ to the north and west, Dong Ha to the southeast, and the South China Sea to the east.

Currently defended by the 1st Battalion, 4th Marines and a small South Vietnamese Civilian Irregular Defense Group, who are there to help provide security for the 11th engineers and the Seabees building Dye-Marker, Con Thien is now fighting for its life.

NVA units maneuver under the cover of a heavy barrage, and breach Con Thien's concertina wire with bangalore torpedoes. At 0400, two enemy battalions armed with flame-throwers, RPG's, and automatic weapons attack through the breach. The Marines engage the enemy force in brutal hand-to-hand combat as an engineer platoon moves in to reinforce the embattled Marines. Despite the lack of 81mm mortar illumination rounds, reinforcements are finally able to assist the beleaguered base.

By daylight the Marines halt further enemy penetration and seal the break in the wire. By 0900, the last remaining enemy soldiers within the perimeter are dead or captured.

The battle for the DMZ has begun.

Hawks in the Sky

A DOUGLAS A-4 SKYHAWK was flying a radar-controlled mission nearby when three SAM's were fired north of the Ben Hai River," Dennis tells Andy. "The A-4E went down. It was the first reported use of a communist surface-to-air missile over South Vietnam, and yet we still weren't allowed to go into offensive mode," he finishes, shaking his head.

"We just had to continue patrolling the Trace, destroying any sniper, arty, and mortar positions we could find. And every morning we'd go back out on patrol and find the exact same positions we'd destroyed the day before, fortified even stronger."

Andy is familiar with the frustration Dennis is describing. Over in Iraq, they called the strategy of sweeping and re-sweeping the same positions "whack-a-mole."

"In Vietnam, we never took a position to hold that position. We took a position to kill. Wipe out the NVA positions, and kill. The whiz kids inside the Pentagon figured that if we killed enough of them, eventually they'd run out of men and resources to replenish their losses and lose their will to fight. It was a war of attrition. But the NVA had the same tactic."

Dennis remembers how Gio Linh, Con Thien, and Khe Sanh were under constant bombardment from the spring of '67 through the fall. *Constant.* The daily barrage of bombardments had literally drove the Marines to the brink of insanity as they waited, wondering—*When is the next round coming? Where will it hit?*

"More than 4,200 mortar, rocket, and arty rounds were fired at us that May. We thought they were trying to squash the obstacle system. It wasn't until many years later that we would come to understand that those bombardments were really the start of the NVA build-up for the Tet Offensive, and that we were just being baited into the DMZ."

Dennis sits back in his chair and looks out the window.

"But at the time, we were just rabbits in the grass. Not like the hawks in the sky who could see for miles."

First Heart

ARTILLERY AND MORTARS streak across the sky, leaving deadly smoke trails in their wake. Explosions from the heavy bombardment form craters in the blackened earth. At Gio Linh, Delta Battery is furiously returning the fire from the battery parapet, and gun chiefs are frantically barking out orders to their crews.

The six guns in the battery are positioned in a star formation. Standing in the battery parapets out in open with artillery raining down on them, the six crews furiously ready the fuses, cut powder charges, and load heavy round after round, each weighing ninety pounds. The crews deftly hoist the rounds and slam them into the guns.

Even though Dennis went through artillery training at Pendleton and knows the difficulty of their job, he's developed a newfound appreciation for the battery guys. Out here, in the open, they take whatever comes in, hell be damned, and the saying around Gio Linh is "hard work and guts is all they've got." It is ironic, Dennis thinks, that Harry was so desperate to get off the gun crews and get out in the field to prove he was a man. Watching them now, he concludes that the artillery guys are some of the bravest men up here.

"Gun One . . . Fire! Gun Two . . . Fire!"

Dennis quickly runs out of his bunker over to Fire Direction Control to get maps. Inside the FDC bunker, officers and radio operators frantically man the incoming and outgoing radio communications for fire missions.

"Charge 4, Shot out!"

Dennis can hear Delta Battery systematically fire out rounds as Fire Direction Control provides them with the coordinates and powder charges.

More radio missions call in.

"Bay Way Delta, Bay Way Delta. Request for fire mission."

It is borderline chaos. One of the radio operators looks to Dennis for help. Dennis takes the cue and rushes over to the table and grabs a radio.

"This is Bay Way Delta." Dennis answers the radio and takes the fire mission. He repeats back the mission for verification and plots down the coordinates on the grids of a map with pins. Then he takes another call.

The FDC bunker shakes from the force of outside explosions as more and more calls come in and more and more missions go out. But for some reason, the guns are suddenly and eerily quiet.

"Can someone find out what the hell is going on out there?" An exasperated FDC operator shouts out. The operator looks over in Dennis' direction. Dennis nods and runs outside.

Smoke and ashes fill the sky. The base is mangled with debris and craters. Dennis covers his head, crouches low, and sprints over to the battery. Reaching the artillery parapet, he stops dead in his tracks. The battery is destroyed. Gunners are strewn around the blown guns, their bodies torn and lifeless. Only Guns One and Six remain intact, and only a handful of gunners remain standing. One gunner leans against his gun for support. Standing on one leg with the other mangled and shredded, he is still trying to fire.

To Dennis, the scene looks like what he'd imagine a Civil War battle to have been like. *It wasn't supposed to be this way.* He sprints back to FDC. "All the guns are hit! Only guns one and six are up!" He storms in the bunker, nearly out of breath.

The FDC operators look horrified. Dennis runs back out, sprinting across the base to help the decimated battery. Reaching the pit, he sees Captain Gunlatch trying to man Gun One, struggling to load a high explosive round by himself. Dennis rushes over and takes the canister as Gunlatch opens the breach. Dennis slams in the round, making sure his hand is clenched in a tight fist so the breach doesn't take off his fingers. The round is fired.

. . . Shhhhmmmmmmmbbbbb!

"Shot out!" Gunlatch hollers.

Dennis helps Gunlatch load a second round, then a third one with a PD fuse. Gunlatch looks down at his ammo supply.

Gunlatch curses. "We're outta rounds!"

"I'll go get more," Dennis yells, and races off toward the ammo dump. Crawling across bunkers he reaches the ammo cache and searches for a box of 05s. He finds them, grabs the heavy box, and drags it outside. Suddenly, he hears a loud whistle.

Shhhhhhhmmmmmmmmmmmmm!

Then silence.

He strains to hear the round. More silence. Then something hits Dennis with such heavy impact that it spins him completely around and drives his body with traumatic force against the ammo bunker.

His world fades to black. Motionless and unconscious, he hears and feels nothing.

In a blurry haze, with seconds passing like minutes and minutes passing like hours, Dennis finally twitches his hands. He doesn't know how long he has been there or what exactly has happened; blinded by smoke and debris, he has no perception of where he is. He tries to remember what he was doing before the round hit. *Gunlatch*. His memory begins to stir. *I'm getting ammo for the Battery.*

Dennis tries to take a deep breath, but he can't, it hurts too much. *Agh.* Dennis moans. But he's relieved in a perverse way. *Pain is good. Pain means I'm not dead.* He wiggles his fingers, then his toes. He can feel both his hands and his feet. *I'm okay*, he reassures himself.

He can hear the firefight outside now. Hearing the rounds whistling overhead and feeling the jolt of the explosions hitting the base, he regains even more clarity. Grimacing in pain, he rises to his feet. *Something is wrong with my back.* He shakes off the debris covering his body and bends down to grab the box of 05s.

He tries to run, but finds he can only limp. He hobbles as fast as he can over to the battery pit. Gunlatch looks at Dennis once, then twice.

"Jesus. I thought you were friggin' dead."

Dennis shakes his head no. He struggles to lift the heavy canisters.

"I can't hold up any more rounds. My back's all screwed up!" Dennis yells.

"It's no use. I can't hear shit from FDC anyway. And if I can't hear 'em, there's no way in hell Gun Six can hear 'em either." Dennis realizes he can be of more use retrieving the gun coordinates and elevation from FDC. He crawls over the top of the bunkers to Fire Direction Control and storms inside. "Guns One and Six are still firing. Give me their coordinates."

He rushes out and crawls back over the bunkers to Gunlatch and relays the coordinates. Gunlatch nods and looks through his sites. He adjusts the gun for windage by raising the barrel. Dennis turns around to head back to FDC. Again, he receives the information, this time for Gun Six, and relays the mission, then crawls back over the bunkers as quickly as he can toward FDC to get the next mission.

Suddenly another round careens toward the base.

Shhhmmmmmm!

The ammo dump takes a direct hit and explodes in a blinding flash of light. Dennis presses his body flat down against the bunker. Cracked white phosphorous rounds fly out everywhere. Steel flechettes from the bee-hive rounds rain down on Dennis, pricking his back, neck, face, and arms. He is cut and bleeding, but he continues to make his way back and forth between Fire Direction Control and Guns One and Six.

He loses track of time, and of everything going on around him. All that matters is getting the coordinates from FDC. He crawls back and forth over the tops of the bunkers, not noticing steel flechettes and cracked white phosphorous rounds strewn across the bunkers ripping the flesh on his hands and burning his knees.

A half dozen trips later, the incoming fire ceases, suddenly and completely, ending just as quickly as it had begun.

Dennis stops. He looks around. *Where am I?* Everything around him is so decimated it looks foreign. He is in the battery parapet, near Gun Six. He slinks down against the back of the sandbags and plops down on an ammo box. He feels lost in a fog. Sitting there with steel flechettes poking out of his skin, and blood dripping from his ears, nose, and mouth, he leans against the bags for support, and slowly becomes aware of the pain.

One of the grunts nicknamed "Groundhog,'" a mechanic from West Virginia, rushes up and takes one look at Dennis. "Do you have any idea how screwed up you are?"

"I don't feel shit," Dennis says, barely able to look up at him. He still feels like he's in a different level of consciousness.

"Medivac's on the way," Groundhog assures him.

Dennis closes his eyes.

When he wakes up he finds himself in a hospital. A nurse is leaning over him, assessing his wounds to a doctor. "His ribs are broken, there are some minor shrapnel wounds, and he's severely concussed," she tells the doctor.

"Okay. Keep him in the rear for a while and let his head settle back in." The doctor scribbles down some notes down and moves on to the next patient.

The nurse looks down at Dennis reassuringly. "You're going to be just fine."

Dennis looks up, straining to see her smiling face. Through his blurred vision, he thinks she looks like an angel.

"You rest now, get some sleep," she whispers.

But he is already asleep.

Dave

Hi Parents,

I guess you know by now that I got a purple heart the other day. Well, don't worry, all I got was a headache and concussion, and some bruises. There is no time to play hurt up here. We had guys hurt worse than me and they are still going. This is not the time to be scared or hide in a hole. You do what you have to do. That's being a man and a Marine. I won't ask to stay in the rear or leave. I hope you understand Mom. I know Dad does. I don't mean to worry you but I wanted to set the record straight. I'm FINE! So now forget it!

How is everything back there now? I tell you, every time I hear about those colleges, I get sick. I don't know. Things ain't what they used to be! I'm sending a flick of a handsome young Marine. Dirty, but handsome, ha ha.

Love,
Denny

DENNIS STANDS OUTSIDE his bunker and lights a cigarette. It has been a quiet morning, and he feels relatively well-rested and refreshed. The cuts on his face and body have healed nicely. He hears someone walking up behind him. He turns around and finds his old friend, Dave Keating. Dave gives him a hearty embrace.

"Denny, how are you? I heard you were hit?"

"Aw, I'm fine. Just a few broken ribs and some shrap." Dennis waves it off, dismissing it as nothing serious enough to discuss. "I just got back from Dong Ha."

"Glad to hear you're okay. I just got back myself. I was in Da Nang this morning and hitched a ride back here with the motor pool guys making an ammo run. And well, here I am, back in dear old 'Nam."

"Yeah, what the hell are you doing here anyway?" Dennis asks him quizzically. "I thought your tour was up?"

"It was. I extended so I could go home for a month and get married."

"Married?"

"I had to! I was afraid she'd get tired of waiting for me! They gave me twenty days leave for my honeymoon, and I took her to Hawaii. So here I am, back for another six months, then I'm done for good and can go back home to my wife and start having some kids."

Dennis smiles and slaps him on the back. "Congratulations, Dave. I'm really happy for you."

"Thanks, Denny. That really means a lot to me—the other guys have been giving me nothing but shit! Well, I gotta head back over to the battery and check on my new guys, but I'll see you around."

Dennis watches Dave walk away, but privately, he isn't as happy for Dave as he let on. *Married?* It's hard for guys to come back from the civilized world after being away for that long. They lose something, their basic instincts, *the edge.*

Moments later he hears someone call out to him, "Hey, Denny!"

He knows that voice. He turns around. It is Chet.

"Hey man! Good to have you back!" Chet slaps him on the back.

"Thanks, it's good to be back."

"How are you feeling. Did anything actually go through that thick head of yours?"

"Nah, close though," Dennis laughs.

"Humph, too bad. . . . You could'a gone home," Chet teases. "Hey, speakin' of home. Did you hear about Dave? Stupid bastard went home and got married!"

"Yeah, I just talked to him."

"Hell, there's nothing worse than going home to a soft woman. Everyone knows that's the quickest way to get your friggin' self killed. They make you forget the killing part of you." Chet spits on the ground.

"Dave knows what he's doing," Dennis reassures him.

"Yeah, let's hope so," Chet grumbles as he heads off to help refortify the battery parapet.

Dennis walks over toward the Fire Direction Control bunker. Inside, the lieutenant is having a heated conversation with some of the other officers.

"We need to change our gun positions. The NVA has the battery bracketed."

"Can't. There's nowhere else to put them on the hill."

"We sent a patrol out last night. They saw something from their position on the river. Someone was out there signaling with a flashlight. I think there's a spy signaling back our gun positions, and calling in fire missions using some sort of code with his flashlight. There's a patrol of grunts out there now scouting for him to see if he returns again tonight.

"Patrol what? They know we're patrolling, they'll just hide until we're done, then go right back out there and do their thing. I'm sick of taking pot shots up here! What's the point of holding this friggin' hill in the first place?"

"The point is it's your orders. McNamara wants this line held. Period. End of conversation."

The lieutenant's words are cut short by a report coming in over the radio. Dennis listens as one of the scouts out in the field provides a status report.

"We got him. Looks to be from the popular force. We got him, though."

The lieutenant smiles. "Good. Maybe we'll get some sleep tonight, eh?"

An hour later, a patrol leads the captured Vietnamese spy to the Army 175mm Battery. He appears to be in his mid-twenties, wearing a light green ARVN camouflage uniform worn overtop scrappy pants and typical villager shoes. He does not look any of his captors in the eye; yet, he does not appear to be afraid. One of his captors puts a rope around his neck and ties the rope to the barrel of a long 175mm round. They raise the elevation all the way to make the barrel lift up in the air, hanging the spy in plain view of North Vietnam. The spy hangs from the round, kicking furiously for several minutes, then his body goes limp and dangles in the air. The execution is meant to send a message: the NVA can no longer rely on their spy.

Dennis watches the execution from outside his bunker. His face is expressionless. It's early in the evening, still hot, and his head is pounding from one of his all too frequent headaches. Dave walks over to Dennis' bunker just as the battery fires off a few capricious rounds. They watch the smoke trails streak across the sky as the dead NVA spy hangs in the air.

"Head still hurt?"

"A little . . . . But I'm fine."

Dave understands; he knows that Dennis is still in pain, but just doesn't want to say it. It's an unspoken rule—no matter how bad it is, never complain. He changes the subject. "Hey. I wanted to show you this earlier, but didn't want to catch even more hell from the guys." Dave pulls out a picture and hands it to Dennis. It is his wedding picture. He's dressed in a black tuxedo and smiling proudly. His bride, dressed in white lace, is stunningly beautiful.

Dennis whistles. "Wow, Dave, you weren't kidding! She's cute as hell!"

"Yeah, that's my girl. We've been together since high school."

"Must be nice to have someone like that to go home to."

"Yeah." Dave puts the picture back in his pocket and pats it against his chest. Dave pauses for a minute; he wants to say something, but feels hesitant.

Dennis can tell there is something else on his mind.

"I'm sorry about Harry," Dave says quietly.

Dennis is caught off guard, unprepared to hear the sound of Harry's name. This is not a conversation he was prepared to have. He stares intently at the beautiful sunset, searching for the right words to say. Taking a deep breath, he finally responds, "I should have been there with him. I would have told him to stay down. I would have held him down. I wouldn't have let him done that stupid cowboy stuff..." Dennis' voice trails off.

"It's not your fault, you know... It's no one's fault."

"Yeah, I know," Dennis says looking down at his feet. But it is a lie.

Dave looks out at the sky. He changes gears again in his subtle Midwestern way. "It's been awfully quiet today. Too quiet."

Dennis looks out toward the lush hills north of the river. "Yeah, something's up, though. I can sense it."

"C'mon, let's go bug Chet for some coffee."

They begin walking toward Chet's bunker when suddenly they hear a round being fired in the near distance.

Shhhmmmmmmb!

"Here we go again," Dennis mutters, hitting the deck.

"Nice welcome back, huh?" Dave yells out as he runs to the bunker behind Dennis and dives in.

"Incoming!"

The round hurtles overhead. It is close. Dennis covers his head as the round whistles overhead, missing him. *Shhhmmmmmmmb!*

Another round is fired. But this one, he can't hear.

Boooooooommmmm!

The round hits the ground, squarely between Dennis' legs. Dennis can feel the immense initial impact, and immediately thinks *I'm dead.* But he's not dead. And the round hasn't exploded. He can hear people screaming. "Don't move!"

Dennis is paralyzed with fear. Between his legs is a round with a point-detonating fuse that hasn't exploded yet. High with adrenaline, he lurches his body away from the round. He can smell the pungent residue of the round's gun charge. There is no explosion. He stares at the dud round, hardly believing his luck. *Thank you, God. Oh Jesus, that was close.*

Out of the corner of his eye, he sees the bunker where Dave jumped in. It is smoldering. His heart drops to the pit of his stomach. Marines are running over to the burning bunker. It has taken a hit.

"Nooooo!" Dennis yells at the top of his lungs. He sprints over to the bunker. His legs feel like jelly. "Dear God, no, not Dave!"

He finds Dave lying in a pool of blood. His body is torn in half, and he is gulping for air. A Marine kneeling over Dave looks up at Dennis. "He's hit. He's hit bad."

Dennis drops to his knees and cradles Dave's head in his hands. The shouts for the corpsmen are inaudible to Dennis. Nothing is real to him except Dave lying on the ground. A piece of shrapnel has taken out the lower half of his chest. Without hesitation, Dennis gently scoops up the exposed organs and puts them back in Dave's abdomen. Then, he carefully picks him up and carries him down to the landing zone.

Dave, struggling for air, tries to speak. He forces the breath out. "I'm not gonna make it, am I?

Dennis lays him down by the LZ, gently steadying his head in his lap. "It's okay Dave, you're going to be alright, you hear me? You're going to make it; you're going to be alright."

"Make sure they send me home to my wife." Dave looks up with blood-stained eyes and gulps for air.

"Just hang in there, buddy. You're going to make it."

Dennis and several other men quickly hoist Dave into the chopper before they attract enemy fire.

"Go!" The gunner yells into his mike.

The chopper lifts off carrying Dave with it, leaving Dennis standing in its circular wake of whirling wind and deafening noise. He stands there for several minutes with his face buried in his blood-soaked hands. His chest heaves, but nothing comes out. Then he begins to walk slowly back up the hill; to him, the base and the world are surreal. By the time he reaches the top of the base, he has nothing but a blank stare on his face.

A young Marine walks up to him to give condolences. "Look, man, I'm sorry . . . ."

Dennis cuts him off. "He's gone. That's it. Go back and do your thing." His voice is flat. The young Marine doesn't know what to say. Dennis walks past him with eyes that are deadened to the world.

It's just a thing. Ain't nothin' but a thing.

I Am Dead

I FELT ABSOLUTE HATRED for the North Vietnamese when Harry died. But when Dave died, my emotions died with him. There was nothing left for me to feel. By the time I reached the top of Gio Linh, I had nothing left. And that scared me to death."

Andy adjusts himself with his arms and shifts his torso higher up on the bed. Dennis is oblivious to the movement or anything else in the room.

"I knew that would be the last time I would ever see Dave. I knew damn well that he wasn't going to make it. And I hated myself telling him that, for lying to him," Dennis tells Andy. He remembers feeling every last one of his emotions drain out of him with every step he took. It was then that he realized he didn't hate anymore. He no longer had the capacity. "But everyone knew the deal by then. You could see it on everyone's face. We had just seen everything we thought we could possibly see. But the worst part about it was—it got worse."

Old Friend

INSIDE HIS BUNKER, Dennis washes his face and arms down in a small mud puddle, studying the dirt and blood trickling off his body. He lights a candle and places it on an empty ammo box and lies back on his dirty mattress. Staring off into the distance, he watches the sun set over the hills, and thinks about the loss of life today, the loss of innocence. He hears something, a scratching sound. Small bits of dirt fall by the bunker entrance.

A large rat appears, as big as a household cat. Its beady eyes peer into Dennis' as it enters the bunker and perches itself atop an ammo box, as though it were a family pet. Dennis pays little attention to the grim reaping bearer of plague and disease, instead reaching for a can of rations but only crackers are left.

He takes a bite of the cracker and throws a piece to the rat. The rodent greedily eats it as Dennis takes another bite and throws another piece. He continues to share the last of his crackers until only crumbs are left. Then he rolls over, and stares straight ahead into the distance, not giving a damn about the rat—or anything else for that matter.

He knows that in two weeks, 1/9 and Delta Battery, or what's left of them, will be pulled back to Dong Ha to regroup, redo the guns, and do it all over again.

Part VII

Banana Wars
November 8th, 2004

Your experiences have changed you – they've shaped who you are
They've tattooed your beliefs, and left you with scars.
But the scars and wounds do not define you,
They simply tell some of what you've been through.

—Michelle McCloskey-Alicea

Master of the House

THROUGH THE WINDOW, Andy looks out at a sky painted in ruby and amethyst jewel-toned hues. It is dawn, but Andy can't stop thinking about the stories that Dennis shared, or the sound of his voice and the hollowness of his words . . . . "We were just rabbits in the grass, not like the hawks in the sky that could see for miles."

Which is better, to experience war from the top where you can see everything, or from the bottom, where you can only see what is in front of you, like a horse with blinders? Andy wonders. Most people would undoubtedly say, "from the top." And that's easy for him to put into perspective; the majority of what is heard or read is generated or filtered through the top. *But is that really better? Does the sniper firing from the rooftop become a casualty of his own actions in the end anyway?* Andy knows that when you're there, in the thick of a firefight, it's one thing; but he also knows that when you come home, it's another. Perspectives change.

He thinks about Fallujah. He knows what is likely to happen next. There will be discrepancies in the accounts of what happened, of how many people were killed, military and civilian. There will be reports of hitting unintended targets, of women and children dying. And of course, different opinions will surface from Monday-morning analysts of how the operation should have been carried out. The question dominating the airwaves will be, "What happens next?"

Then Andy thinks of Dennis, of how he has become two men, one born of this world, and one born of war. He finds it fascinating to observe Dennis' face as he talks about Vietnam—Andy has learned the visual cues that indicate when Dennis is about to go deeper into territories charted only once before. Dennis' face will contort and change its shape and color as if in a trance.

It's odd how accessible the warrior within this sixty-year old man is, and how, by the mere act of talking, the mask is removed to reveal the boy that was always there, hidden from normalcy so that he could survive, rather, exist again.

Andy then looks down. He, too, is like Dennis in many ways, and he ponders the fact that his own physical body has been literally cut in two. He examines the bandages wrapped around his stumps. He takes a deep breath and swallows the anger and resentment gurgling up in his throat. *Stay in control*, he tells himself. Soon, he will look down and see walking computers attached. He will be half flesh, half titanium, a modern-day chimera of man and machine.

Next he thinks of the Iraqi people he met and the look in their faces, some filled with hope and excitement, others with fear and disdain. He thinks of the Iraqi man who lost everything. And he thinks of the men he fought for, his father, his friends, the president, and Rummy. He thinks of the country he fought for, and how its political beliefs are twisting and pulling it in two directions, split right down the middle, equally divided.

All of these disparate thoughts swirl inside Andy's head, until finally they funnel down into a singular conclusion. War is always a paradox, a perpetual co-existing paradox of those who unleash it and those upon whom it is unleashed. The only people that will ever really know are the ones who were there. And what takes place will entirely depend on the physical or ideological vantage of each individual. How they see it, how they experience it, or how they hear of it, will create their truth. Like Einstein's theory of relativity.

Andy wonders if maybe, the veteran at Dennis' VA speech was right. "If it is true for you, then it is true." Those on the ground will always be horses wearing blinders. Those at the top will always be the chess players. And the people in the rubble, well, they'll always be the casualties. But in the end, they all fall casualty—one way or another, each looking to find the way back to good.

Andy is reminded of the seventh graders from his hometown. They represent everything that is virtuous and untarnished. They are blessed with innocence. He reaches for his envelope of letters and carefully places them inside a plain brown box. It is an ordinary box, filled with his keepsakes and personal belongings. He rummages through the postcards, the newspaper clippings, and pictures, and stumbles upon a picture of his ex-girlfriend, Katie. She is standing on a rock they climbed overlooking the Sandia Mountains in New Mexico. He remembers snapping this picture. They were on a cross-country road trip, just three weeks before he left for boot camp.

Staring at her smiling face, he is overwhelmed by a desire to call her, to reach out and tell her something that once seemed beyond his comprehension, yet somehow he has known all along. He wants to tell her that he finally understands. *There are always two faces of war, two views, two bodies, but only one master.* But he knows in his heart that he can't call her—not because she wouldn't listen, but because he's not able to invite her to be that close to him yet. It's too intimate, too personal. And he's just not ready.

Instead he feels an urge to do something he hasn't done in three years. He takes out a pen, flips over one of the letters, and begins writing on the back of it. Words spill out, free flowing out of his head onto the paper. Each word has its own perfect place and time, its own perfect match. Kind of like people.

He scratches a line, adds two more. This works. This doesn't. Until finally, he feels satisfied. Ten lines. Ten lines that say everything. He titles it: *Master of the House.* At the bottom he signs his name. He folds it in two, and places it inside the plain brown box.

No, wait. He's forgotten one thing. He takes it back out. At the top he writes the following words: Dad, I finally understand.

Master of the House

Two worlds colliding;
Both of them mine.
Unleash the corner winds,
The four horsemen ride.

Masquerades of lonely, despondent despair
Gather in strength, the warring air.
Forces diverge,
West and east,
To master the emotions—
Is to slay the beast.

—Andrew Cahill Taylor

Bleeding Out

"DO YOU WANT TO LIVE?" the doctor had asked.

In the fall of 1990, at age forty-three, Dennis couldn't answer that question. Staring up at the fluorescent light illuminating the cold, sterile emergency room with fear in his eyes, he heard the doctor repeat the question. Dennis didn't know the answer. Did he want to live?

The only thing he knew was that for twenty-three years the dull, aching pain of Vietnam still persisted. *What if I just ended it?* For years, he had often thought about suicide. But try as he might, he could never figure out a way to do it without embarrassing his kids. So he continued on, submerging himself in work, burying his guilt, masking his feelings, and isolating himself—or insulating himself—until the afternoon when a searing pain ripped through his chest and pierced his heart. His throat tightened up and he unbuttoned his shirt. *I'm having a heart attack.*

While that was almost fifteen years ago, he can still remember the feeling of not being able to breathe, as though the air had mysteriously thinned, and his heart no longer belonged inside his chest. His eyes had flickered darting back and forth, looking for signs, any sign. *Is this it?* It was the same feeling he had when he was buried alive at Con Thien when the full weight of the bunker was on top of him and he could smell the acrid, burning rubble as the voices outside shouted urgently, "Get him out of there!" He couldn't see, couldn't feel, but worst of all, couldn't breathe.

The reason he remembers it so vividly now is because it is the exact same feeling he is having at this very second. Every time he walks across the Walter Reed campus to Andy's room, that tightness in his throat, that shortness of breath, returns. *Why is this happening again?* He can only wonder. *Is it meeting with Andy that's taking a toll on him, was it the funeral on Sunday? Is something inside so submerged, so long forgotten, that it's only now being re-awakened?* Sure, he has been sharing many things with Andy, but he is only telling him what he is able to tell him. There is more that lies beneath the surface, things that he's not ready to share with anybody: the killing, the burning villages, the babies crying. *No, no need to go into those details. War is war,* Dennis reminds himself. *Andy has his own demons to deal with; no need to tell him mine.*

But for reasons unknown, it is getting harder and harder to make that drive to Walter Reed, to walk across that campus, and talk to Andy. Purging the past makes Dennis feel emotionally heavy, depressed, and drained, like a mental bloodletting. And it reminds him of the ill-fated Marine that bled to death at Operation Buffalo.

It was July 2nd, 1967, the first night after the NVA had ambushed three companies of 1/9 patrolling the DMZ on Highway 561. Dennis could not see the enemy, but he could hear their voices. They were close. Loud groans of pain from the wounded echoed through the jungle, cries for help were quickly met with metallic bursts of rifle and machine gun fire.

Dennis could hear one wounded Marine in particular scream for help. "Jesus, someone help me! For the love of God, please ... someone, help me!"

Maybe I can get to him. Dennis had tried to maneuver over to the wounded Marine's location. He saw the Marine sitting up against a tree, instantly recognizing him as one of the grunts in Delta Company. The Marine had been shot in several places and blood was spurting out from wounds in his arms, legs and chest. His eyes were panicked and his body jerked uncontrollably. He tried to claw himself closer to the tree, as if that alone would somehow provide cover. But it was futile; there was no cover.

Fear completely took over and his pleas for help became louder and more urgent. "For God's sake, someone, please help me!"

Dennis had scanned the area to see if it was safe to get up. He saw another Marine, hiding in the elephant grass, also trying to move closer to the wounded grunt. The Marine inched closer. Crawling on his belly, still fifteen feet away, a twig snapped under his weight. An NVA sniper, hiding in the elephant grass, shot not the rescuing Marine, but the grunt. Blood spurted out from his femoral artery and the grunt screamed out in pain.

"Ahhhh…!"

Again, the other Marine in the elephant grass tried to move closer to save him. Again, the NVA shot the wounded grunt hunched against the tree. That time in the arm.

"God help me!" Grimacing at his bullet-ridden body, the wounded Marine cried helplessly as he tried to stop the blood gushing from his body. Fear and panic filled his eyes. He knew that he was going to bleed out and die. He knew it—the NVA knew it—and they were torturing him.

The grunt whimpered as the life began to fade out of him. Pinned down, Dennis could stand it no longer. He covered his ears and closed his eyes and felt like he was going crazy. He wanted to get to that guy more than anything else in the entire world, but knew he couldn't. And he felt absolutely helpless. Watching that grunt die literally gagged him. *If I can't help this guy, what friggin' good am I?* The Marines prided themselves on never leaving anyone behind, and there Dennis was, pinned to his position while that grunt was pinned to the tree and forced to slowly die.

He tries to imagine how that Marine must have felt, watching himself die. It isn't hard for Dennis to do; in fact, he considers that old hat. He has so often embodied those he saw killed, and those he killed himself, that he often felt like he was a cohabitant in their deaths. He was their witness, their chronicle. And now, meeting with Andy, it feels as though he is chronicling his own death—the slow demise of his innocence and emotions.

Dennis remembers the moment he saw his parents at Newark Airport. They were huddled together, waiting patiently at the mouth of the arrivals terminal. But Dennis was not on the plane. He had taken a flight to La-Guardia Airport instead, and had taxied over to Newark to buy some extra time. And as he stood behind his parents, unnoticed, he panicked over-whelmed by one thought: *I'm not ready.* So he walked right past them, and prayed they wouldn't recognize him. They didn't. Averting his eyes, he headed straight for the bathroom. There, he stared at his reflection in the mirror. He was a stranger to himself. He rinsed the nervous sweat and clamminess off his skin, but he couldn't rinse off the dread of being home.

He took a deep breath and walked back out. *Jesus, what do I say?* Standing before his parents, he fumbled for words. His mother paid no attention. He'll never forget the first thing she said: "It's okay, you're home now. You're safe." Tears of joy streamed down her face as she hugged her son tightly and thanked God that her prayers for his safe return were answered.

But her words stung Dennis like nothing he had ever known. *No I'm not okay, damn it! Can't you see? Safe from the NVA maybe, but not from myself. Besides, don't you hate me? I wasn't even supposed to be in Vietnam. I lied to you; I hurt you.* Despite the red-hot anger coursing through him, he remained silent and his heart turned cold. He stood frigidly in his mother's arms as she hugged even tighter and continued to thank God. His arms hung limply around her warm body, and he stared icily past her, no longer willing to be recognized as part of her own flesh and blood.

His heartbeat quickens still, after all these years from his reaction to her words. *It doesn't matter anymore*, he tells himself. *She is dead now.* She passed away years ago. When he laid her to rest he laid to rest his anger too. Or did he? Did he really put aside his resentment, or was that merely an agent of the Body Bag Syndrome—that peculiar numbness, that strange void of emotions that he summons at will? Maybe he had no longer felt anger because in actuality he felt nothing—a shocking truth that still resonates within him.

For years, a lonely sentiment has echoed in the closed chambers of his mind: *If I can no longer feel hate, I can no longer feel love.* And day after day, that self perpetuated fear has played out in his life, repeating itself over and over, depriving him of intimacy. *Was his real tragedy of Vietnam the inability to feel close to anyone?*

Fifteen years ago, when the doctor had repeated the question "Do you want to live," Dennis paused for several minutes before answering. *Yes.* And now, walking across the campus of Walter Reed on this crisp fall morning of November 9th, 2004, the eve of the Marine Corps' birthday, Dennis reminds himself of life's ultimate paradox: *You begin to die the minute you are born.* He has long resigned himself to that universal truth—in fact it was the one and only reason he had agreed to seek treatment at the VA for Post Traumatic Stress Disorder. He didn't need to induce death; he was already dying.

Banana Wars

"HEY DENNIS," ANDY CALLS OUT as Dennis walks in the room. "Good news. They're fitting me for the molding for my left prosthetic tomorrow," Andy says, flushed with excitement. Dennis can see a sparkle in Andy's eyes. *What a strange course we're on*, Dennis thinks. He is losing energy, while Andy is gaining it. *It is as it should be.*

"That's great, Andy. I'm really happy for you." Dennis tries to project the same level of energy in his voice as Andy's, but falls woefully short. Andy picks up on it immediately. *Something's not right.*

Andy looks at Dennis suspiciously, trying to pinpoint what is wrong. He quickly locates the problem. Pain. Dennis is in pain. And Andy can sense pain a mile away.

He had sensed it in his father too, well before his parents admitted to him that his father was diagnosed with liver cancer. By that time it had already metastasized to his other organs. There was no cure, the doctors told Andy's mother.

"How long?" she had asked.

"A month—maybe two."

Andy watched helplessly as his Dad grew sicker and sicker every day. A week before he died, frail and thin—a shadow of his former self—his father still tried to hide the pain from his wife and son. But Andy could see it in his eyes. After he passed away, Andy abstained from food for nearly a week.

Food was a reminder of how his father's cancer had eaten away a once strong and vibrant body. The mere thought of putting sustenance to his lips had made Andy nauseous.

Because of that experience, Andy is acutely aware of what Dennis is trying to hide right now. He decides that maybe it is a good time to tell Dennis of his own pain, to share in his burden, and he searches for a way to begin. "I talked to a buddy of mine, Bob Wallace, this morning," he starts tentatively.

"Oh?"

"We were over in Iraq together. He just got home recently and looked me up—he wanted to see how I was doing." Andy continues. "He told me a story about getting pulled over the other night on I-95 outside of Quantico. He told the cop that he just got back from Iraq, hoping that would get him off the hook. But the cop had clocked him doing over a hundred, so that didn't happen. Bob had no idea he was going that fast. Then the cop told him that he had switched three lanes going under an overpass. And it dawned on him. He was so used to gunning the pedal going under overpasses, and making sure to be in a different lane coming out the other side than he was going in, that he forgot where he was. It was something we learned in Tikrit ... to avoid snipers and insurgents in RPG Alley. They used to sit up there and fire down on us . . . ." Andy pauses. "He said it's funny how differently things have been affecting him now that he's home."

Dennis nods his head empathetically. "Yeah, it takes a while to readjust. Your body might be out of the war zone, but your mind doesn't always remember that.

"Bob and I were stationed together outside of Tikrit, but I first met him at LeJeune. I remember how we were so excited to be a part of 1st Division. The Guadalcanal, The Old Breed. . . ."

Dennis can imagine the pride the boys must have felt being assigned to the legendary 1st Marine Expeditionary Force. Activated in 1913, the first MEF fought in the Banana Wars in Haiti and the Dominican Republic and later the Pacific Campaigns of WWII, Korea, and Vietnam. More recently, they fought in the first Gulf War, and are fighting now in Iraq on their second tour, battling in Fallujah, as he and Andy speak.

"We deployed last March, first to Nasariyah and Baghdad, then Tikrit," Andy tells him. "There were forty-five thousand of us that took part in the

Operation Iraqi Freedom." Just saying that aloud, Andy instantly remembers how gung-ho they were taking center stage in the Iraq arena. Every place was exciting to them—Baghdad, the epicenter, and Tikrit, the birthplace of Saddam Hussein and Saladin. And Andy had reveled in the idea that he was walking on earth that had been inhabited by civilizations for centuries. But the excitement soon faded. "We saw some real shit in Baghdad. But one raid I remember in particular was in Tikrit . . . ."

"We were raiding a house that a source told us belonged to Saddam's financial backers. The house was in a pretty affluent neighborhood. It was about three AM when we stormed in."

The camouflaged Marines, with rifles ready, kicked in the door. Immediately, they heard a woman scream. After a full sweep of the house, they found two families and ordered the women and children to kneel on the living room floor while they ransacked the house looking for suspicious activity or weapon caches. The children cried and held tightly onto their mothers' necks. The men shouted obscenities and shook their fists angrily. Andy was struck by how mundane the house seemed. If they had hoped to find anything, weapons or diamonds, their hopes were quickly dashed after finding nothing out of the ordinary.

"We always had to wonder. Were these people really who we thought they were? Or was this a local vendetta we played right into? Someone throwing us a bone to keep us occupied so the real financial backers could sneak away?"

Dennis nods his head. That's the often-cited dilemma of waging war within a country that you are also trying to defend. *Who are the real bad guys?*

"We decided to bring the men back to the base for questioning. We walked them out to the front courtyard. Before I knew what was happening, bullets started flying overhead. A sniper was taking pot shots at us from a rooftop. Next thing I knew, an RPG whizzed over my head and hit the side of the house. I dove back into the house and leaned against the doorway to return fire. That's when I realized how close that rocket really came to taking off my head."

Andy opens his arms to show Dennis approximately three feet of space.

"It was over as soon as it started," Andy said pensively. His thoughts still shadowed by the quandary of urban warfare—the perpetrators had the advantage of melting back into the scenery and walking amongst the civilians the next morning. "There were no KIA's; that is, except the two men from the house we were taking in for questioning. The snipers made sure those two were killed. I assumed it was for insurance purposes."

"I'm sure," Dennis says softly. He doesn't want to interrupt Andy's flow of thoughts. This is the first time Andy has really opened up and talked about his experience in Iraq.

"That was my first really close call. It's strange how when the shit hits, you feel like everything happens in slow motion, like its all 'Chariots of Fire' or something. My body, my brain—everything—felt like I was in an old-time black and white movie. Everything was grainy, deliberate, and slow."

Andy's description is a textbook example of a phenomenon Dennis had researched on PTSD regarding the body's response to trauma. And he's always been fascinated by the theory that during a traumatic experience, a person's brain activity actually speeds up so that the situation appears to unfold in slower motion. It is a trick the brain is hardwired to perform as the change in perception allows the mind to take stock of what's going on and act accordingly. But Dennis remains silent, not wanting to interrupt Andy now.

"We controlled Tikrit by April and the Pentagon declared it the 'end of major combat.' So we went to SASO mode, stability and support operations, and kept running raids. We were hot on Saddam's trail. Finally, by December we caught a break and captured him."

Without warning, Andy's mood turns suddenly dark.

"We thought it was our total victory. I mean, this is it. We got the bad guy, right? But it wasn't. Sure, some people cheered, and we knew that most felt relief. But it stung nonetheless when people in the streets chanted, 'Saddam is in our blood, Saddam is in our hearts.' I couldn't believe it. I had to stop myself from getting pissed. After all, it was an informant who led us to Saddam in the first place. I figured what Major General Mattis says of the Marines is also true of the Iraqis: 'No better friend, no worse enemy.'"

Dennis nods. *Well said.*

"When I came home after my first tour, I felt different. I felt like a man, even though I still wasn't old enough to get in the bars." Andy suddenly becomes sidetracked. "This country will give you a gun and say, 'Here son, go kill our enemies,' but they won't let you buy a friggin' beer?"

Andy quickly regains his thoughts. "When they deployed us the second time, they gave us this book called *The Small Wars Manual.*" Dennis was familiar with the SWM. A Marine who fought in the Central American Banana Wars during the 1920s and 30s, wrote the manual in 1940.

"I read it on the way over there. It talked about how to operate in MOOTW—Military Operations Other Than War. Guerilla warfare, insurgencies, nation rebuilding, you name it. Some of the stuff like how to pack mules and what not, was kind of stupid. But you'd be surprised by how much of it—how to cordon off insurgents, how to get the civilians to trust you—is still valid as hell. Everything finally made sense. The 'Three Street Strategy.' Everything. I felt like I had graduated from my rookie season and was coming back as a sophomore able to read the field and the defensive sets for the first time."

Dennis smiles at the analogy.

"I was back in Iraq a little over a month, operating in the Anbar province, when I was heading back to Fallujah from Ramadi. We'd been traveling back and forth all week, so we thought the road was free and clear. Then I heard the explosion."

Andy pauses for a minute. There is a long silence. He looks at Dennis and takes a deep breath before he continues. "I looked over at our driver. He was dead. His arm had blown off and was lying in my lap. I couldn't tell if all the blood was his or mine. I could smell the diesel fuel and feel the heat from the fire. The last thing I remember is some guy pulling me out of the truck. When I woke up, I was in Germany."

Dennis has been quietly taking in everything Andy has said. But now, he has the overwhelming urge to reach out and thank him. Thank him for opening up; thank him for putting his body on the line. But sometimes it's the little things that are hardest to say. Finally, Dennis clears his throat and looks Andy in the eye.

"Thank you . . . . For being a good Marine."

Andy feels a lump form in his throat and tears instantly begin to well up. He blinks fast. He has always wondered what his father would have said to him if he were still alive today. And for some reason, he feels he has just gotten the answer.

The two sit in shared silence for several minutes.

Andy looks down at his missing legs and says philosophically, "I figure for me to get back to normal, I've got to look at my rehab as my own Banana War. Focus on one area, make it stable and strong, then move on to the next.

Like how we'd conduct a MOOTW. Because that's what this is, right? An operation other than war?"

Dennis is taken aback; he doesn't know what to say at first. He is amazed how wise this kid is, but then again, isn't that what happens? *We go in as teenagers and come out as old men?*

"Exactly," Dennis says, but he is thinking of something else. PTSD is often called the second war, or the private war. That too, can be looked at as an operation other than war, yet there is no manual, no prescription for how to combat it. It is a personal Banana War that Dennis has waged for a long time.

He turns to Andy and says half-jokingly, "Did you know they actually had that thing—The Small Wars Manual—classified until 1972?"

No, Andy didn't know that.

"Glad they finally dusted it off for you boys. I know we sure could've used it during Operation Buffalo."

Part VIII

Operation Buffalo
November 9th, 2004

*"Courage is the art of being the only one who knows
you're scared to death."*

—Harold Wilson

Alpha, Can You Play?

•

"BIRMINGHAM, 6-4, COME IN Birmingham." Dennis' thousand-yard stare is broken as he pulls out his radio, and wipes the dripping sweat from his brow. 1/9 has been patrolling south of the DMZ since early morning, their concentration undeterred by the sweltering heat as they search every inch of the area with steely eyes.

"This is Birmingham 6-4, over."

"Be advised, Army Long Range recon has reported a small element of NVA pushing across the Ben Hai River heading toward Con Thien. Army 175mm Battery and Delta Battery in position one mile south of the DMZ. Be prepared to go in, we're sending Alpha, Bravo, and Delta Companies. Charlie Company will stay back at Dong Ha on Sparrow Hawk."

"Roger." Dennis decides it's best to radio Sasquatch, the forward observer dispatched to Alpha Company, and make sure their lines of communication are good.

"Sasquatch," Dennis inquires. "How do you read?"

"Five. Five. Five," Sasquatch confirms.

Dennis radios back, "Reports of NVA crossing the Ben Hai. Army Battery and Delta Battery in position one mile south of DMZ."

"Roger, I'm heading in with Alpha to the Marketplace to cut 'em off."

A nearby grunt looks at Dennis quizzically. "I thought the Marketplace didn't exist anymore."

"It doesn't," Dennis responds as he lights up a cigarette. "It's been burned down just like everything else on the DMZ."

The platoon quickly heads toward the river that runs parallel to the Trace. Alpha Company leads, followed by Bravo, then Delta. The platoons navigate Highway 561, a narrow dirt road heavily lined with hedges and elephant grass that runs north and south, joining the two Vietnams.

The Marines cautiously and quietly patrol the highway. A twig snaps. Dennis and several Marines wheel around only to find a bird rustling in the hedges. Up ahead, Alpha Company has nearly reached the Marketplace, a burned down village located between the firebreak and the river.

Suddenly a deafening roar of guns and explosions descend upon Alpha Company. Small arm, machine gun, and mortar fire rain down over their heads.

To Dennis, it sounds as if the world is ending. The Marines disperse like ants off the road, looking for cover in the hedges. From Delta Company's position, Dennis can tell by the smoke rising up that Alpha is receiving the brunt of the barrage as the incoming fire continues to thunder down. He quickly pulls out his radio and whispers into his handset "Sasquatch? This is Birmingham 6-4. Do you read?"

There is a long pause.

"Sasquatch? This is Birmingham 6-4. Over," Dennis repeats.

Finally he hears a muffled voice come in over the radio. "Birmingham, I read you."

Dennis looks at Mills, who dove into a nearby hedgerow for cover. The two look relieved that Sasquatch is still alive.

"How bad are they hit?" Mills asks.

Dennis gets on the radio. "Do you have enough guys to play football?" He asks Sasquatch in a code that only they would understand, in case the NVA intercepts the communication.

"No."

What?

"Can you play baseball?" Dennis whispers.

"No."

Dennis and Mills look at each other horrified. Dennis shakes his head in disbelief. He can't fathom what he is hearing. There are less than nine guys left in Alpha?

"Sasquatch, do you have enough to play basketball?"

Smoke and debris cover Alpha's position in the Marketplace. Lifeless bodies litter the ground. A Marine is hiding in a bomb crater, hidden from view under the foliage of dense elephant grass and dead bodies. It is Sasquatch. He is peering out from the crater looking for signs of life. There are none. He whispers in his radio to Dennis.

"No."

Bravo, Hold Your Fire

DENNIS PUTS DOWN his radio. His head slumps from the weight of the news. "Jesus Christ, Alpha's wiped out. They have fewer than five guys left."

Mills crosses his chest in the sign of a cross.

Dennis switches frequency to Bravo's network, and listens to their leader, Sergeant Stover, radio the command: "We're going in . . ."

The Delta platoon leader shouts out, "We're going in with Bravo! Move out!" Delta Company quickly scrambles to its feet. Covering their helmets and hunched over low, they sprint toward the Marketplace and the ominous smoke and fire. Bravo is also sprinting toward the Marketplace on the other side of the highway. Their goal is to meet up and reinforce what is left of Alpha, get the remaining guys out alive, and retrieve their dead and wounded.

As Delta approaches the Marketplace, Dennis hears Sasquatch come back over the radio. "We're gonna try to pull back! We're pulling back!"

Gunfire erupts again. This time it is so heavy and thick that the tracer rounds, every fifth bullet, can be easily seen flooding the sky. The Marines dig into their positions. Bravo Company is entrenched in an old rice paddy. The air is thick with smoke. Visibility is poor. Marines hide in the elephant grass in groupings of two and three. Sergeant Stover is among them, scanning the periphery of the paddy back and forth, looking for signs of the enemy.

It is eerily quiet.

Hazy figures appear through the smoke, like ghosts creeping through the elephant grass. Rifles ready, the Marines take aim. Straining his eyes, Sergeant Stover can clearly make out the helmets and flak jackets. *Our guys are pulling back.* He holds up his hand to restrain the men from firing.

"Hold your fire, men. It's Alpha. Hold your fire." Sergeant Stover radios back in to command, "We're holding fire, Alpha's pulling back. I repeat, Alpha's pulling back."

Stover and Bravo hold their fire. The figures flanking Bravo creep in closer. Disciplined, Bravo continues to hold its fire. Sergeant Stover watches as Alpha Company completes their retreat to Bravo.

"Oh my god . . . . *No!*" Sergeant Stover sucks in his breath. To his horror, he sees Vietnamese faces under the helmets. Khaki uniforms peak out from under the flak jackets. The guerilla NVA opens fire, spraying bullets on Bravo Company at near point-blank ranges, instantly decimating the Marines. The NVA are now positioned between the Marines retreating from Alpha Company, and the few remaining clusters of Marines from Bravo.

Across the highway trail from Bravo, Dennis and the rest of Delta Company hear the sudden fire. It is near, *very* near. Dennis lies in the elephant grass along the hedgerow, clutching his rifle. Visibility is becoming worse as the smoke mingles with the hazy dusk. He radios over to Bravo.

"Stover, come in, Stover. Over?"

"We're being flanked by little Marines!" Stover whispers into the radio, his voice both desperate and horrified.

"Stover, what is their position?" Dennis whispers back.

Silence.

Dennis tries again, but Stover's frequency remains silent. On his third try, Dennis hears voices over the radio. Voices speaking in Vietnamese.

The NVA have overrun Bravo's position. Sergeant Stover lays motionless, face down on the ground. He is staring blankly at his radio, clutching it with a death grip. Enemy NVA wearing Marine uniforms run over his dead body, screaming loudly.

Dennis can still hear the voices over the radio. He shuts it off, disgusted. They're everywhere. His heart sinks to the pit of his stomach, as he realizes how truly outnumbered they are out here in a burning jungle. They are trapped with no place to go forward, and no place to pull back to regroup. Dong Ha is visible, but unreachable. There's no way. Ironically, the only place he can conceive of offering them any protection, is the worst place in Vietnam: Con Thien. *What a cruel joke, our only safe haven is the worst place in the whole friggin' world.*

Dye-Marker

ON JUNE 18TH, the Operation Plan of the eastern Strongpoint Obstacle System, SPOS, was formally published. By this time, General Robert E. Cushman had assumed command of III MAF from General Lew Walt. Initially, Cushman believed the completion of the strong point system would free his forces along the DMZ for operations elsewhere. But soon the Marine command would come to view Dye-Marker, the new code-name for Practice Nine, as an albatross around its neck.

The formal plan outlined the establishment of six company strong points, labeled A-1 through A-6. Gio Linh was strongpoint A-2, and Con Thien, strong point A-4. Behind the strongpoint, three battalion base areas would be established and designated C-1 through C-3. ARVN regiments were to man A-1 and A-2, and Base Area C-3, while the Marines would be responsible for the strongpoint and base areas west of Route 1.

The goal was to complete the first phase of the obstacle system's mines, radar, towers, barbed wire, and sensors by November 1, 1967, before the onset of the monsoon season. The III MAF plan also outlined the requirements for improving the road networks, including Routes 1, 9, and 561. Highway 561 was to connect Con Thien to its combat support bases with Route 9. And the 3rd Marine Division base at Dong Ha was designated as the logistics center for the entire effort.

The project in its entirety was to be complete by July 1968. For the

Marines in the field, the published operational plan was merely a formality, as they had already accomplished many of the action items, including clearing the Trace. In addition, they had relocated eleven thousand civilians who lived in and around that firebreak to a resettlement village in Cam Lo during Operation Hickory. For 1/9 that was the hardest part of an otherwise gratifying operation, as they were finally given the order to wipe out the NVA SAM missile launcher that took down the A-4 Skyhawk in May.

From June to July the 11th Engineer Battalion continued to clear the terrain under the security of one or two grunt battalions. Along with the Seabees, they had secured the port of Hue and were now upgrading Highway 561.

But what looked innocuous on paper a month ago proved deadly during the Fourth of July's Operation Buffalo.

Operation Buffalo

SASQUATCH IS STILL LYING in the bomb crater, feeling worlds away from the closest Marine position. Lying on his back with his newly-issued M-16 rifle positioned between his knees, he shoots at any unsuspecting NVA that walks too close to the crater's edge—a tactic that has kept him alive so far, as several dead NVA are littered around the crater.

A machine gun positioned at the top of the hill fires down relentlessly at Delta's position. Every time a small, disbanded unit tries to get up, enemy fire rains down on them. Dennis cannot fire a shot without having fire returned tenfold. Exasperated, he tries to make his way up the road, staying as close to the hedgerow as possible. The NVA throw grenades at his position. Dennis stops. He is now trapped in position, crouched under the elephant grass, unable to move in any direction. Bullets fly over him, some uncomfortably close, spraying the dirt next to him.

No one moves as dusk quickly gives way to dark night. Dennis cannot see the NVA, but he can hear them. They are close. Loud moans of pain pierce the jungle, and these cries for help are met with quick bursts of rifle and machine gun fire.

Knowing what's going to happen is one thing, but not knowing is another; and Dennis soon begins to find himself increasingly consumed by fear of the unknown. Night shadows blanket the Marketplace as the NVA walk amongst the dead bodies of Marines. Entrenched in his position, Dennis freezes as a pair of NVA boots shuffle a few feet away from his head. He holds his breath and commands his body to be as still as possible. The enemy passes by without seeing Dennis under the dense foliage of the elephant grass. But Dennis' heart is racing from the encounter. *That was close, too close.*

After the longest night of Dennis' life, the sun begins its ascent into the eastern sky, enabling Dennis to fully take in with his eyes, what hours ago he could only hear. And he stares in disbelief at the small parcel of land that became the accidental battlefield. The elephant grass, once three feet high, is mowed in half; twigs, branches, and leaves all hang by threads, swaying limply in the air. Lingering smoke rises up from the earth in an eerie, smoky haze, revealing the scores of dead bodies littering the ground.

The grim task of retrieving the dead and wounded is done quietly and quickly as the survivors carry the casualties to the Marketplace. A corpsman is standing in the open center of the Marketplace, surrounded by hundreds of wounded men, moaning and crying out in pain. They reach up to commune with the good doctor, pleading with him to fix the unimaginable pain.

The corpsman reaches down and squeezes the Marine's hand. "Here, take this," he whispers. He reaches into his pocket and pulls out a package of M&M's. He tears it open and places the milk chocolates in their mouths, telling them it is chocolate-coated morphine. There is nothing else he can give him. He has no medicine, no morphine, no equipment, nothing to make them feel better other than lousy half-melted M&M's.

More and more casualties are brought in; cries for help to the corpsman mount.

"Please doc."

"Jesus, you got to do something."

"Help me, doc, please help me."

Very soon, the desperate corpsman breaks his composure. He looks up at the sky and yells at the top of his lungs, enraged, "I've got nothing to friggin' work with! I've got nothing to friggin' give them! What the hell am I supposed to do? Huh? Tell me. What the hell do you want me to do?" He shakes his fist in the air and yells at a cruel God.

"Help me doc, please help me," is still ringing in his ears when suddenly, the hedgerows lining the Marketplace are ablaze in a ring of fire.

The NVA, going for the jugular, have torched the hedgerows, hoping to finish off the wounded Marines by engulfing them in flames or shooting them down as they run for cover.

Chaos ensues. The Marines take cover in every direction, dragging, carrying, and hauling on their backs as many casualties as possible. Mortar fire pours into the Marketplace. In the distance, Con Thien is also being shelled. They can see the smoke-trails from the rockets and the return fire coming from the firebase Dennis drops off a wounded Marine in the brush, and furiously calls in a fire mission. "Delta Battery, this is Birmingham 6-4. Request a TOT."

Within moments, the destruction of the Time-on-Target provides the Marines with some cover as hundreds of rounds simultaneously hit the NVA mortar crews and machine gun positions.

The surviving Marines pull back to the firebreak, each cluster providing cover for the other. 2/9 meets them at the firebreak with tanks and reinforcements, and 1/9 is finally able to assess the extent of their casualties. Alpha is practically gone. Bravo's wiped out as well. Delta took heavy casualties, and Charlie was never able to get in. They load as many of the wounded as they can inside the tanks, and stack the dead on top. Those that are able to walk do so, semi-protected by the iron mass of the rumbling tanks as they make their way back to Con Thien. Reinforcements from 2/9 are already en route to the Marketplace.

At the Observation Post bunker atop Con Thien, a Marine stationed at OP-1 peers through his binoculars. Something catches his attention. He notices suspicious activity and rustling in the hedgerows off the road. Taking a closer look, he is able to see four gun positions. It is an ambush. The observer scrambles to find the right frequency on the radio.

"2/9 . . . Come in 2/9. This is OP-1. There is an ambush. 2/9! Do you read?

No response.

The observer tries a different frequency, radioing again, with the fear rising in his voice. "2/9? Ambush! Pull back! Pull back!"

No response.

The observer is screaming into the radio now, trying in vain to contact 2/9. He looks out in horror as 2/9 blindly walks straight toward the ambush. "2/9! Pull back! I repeat! Pull back!"

But it is too late. OP-1 sees and hears the fire, but can do nothing to stop it.

The Walking Dead

WHAT STARTED OUT AS a simple patrol around Con Thien turned out to be one of the biggest battles the Marines fought on the DMZ," Dennis recalls. "That 'small element of NVA', was in fact, the entire 324th NVA division. Fifteen thousand of 'em pushed across the river to try and take out Con Thien. But we held 'em. It was over by July 6th, but 1/9 was slaughtered, suffering on the first day alone eighty-four KIA. That's when whispers about 'The Walking Dead' started to resurface . . . ."

Andy's interest is piqued; he has heard of The Walking Dead.

"Just the year before, when 1/9 was fighting the NVA in the hills and valleys of the DMZ, Ho Chi Minh himself called the unit, 'Di Bo Chet'" Dennis tells Andy solemnly. "They were guys who were already dead, but didn't know it yet."

Andy is struck by an overpowering thought. The Walking Dead. *Walking.*

"That's kind of what we are now, isn't it?" Andy says evenly, catching Dennis off guard.

Dennis leans back in his chair and thinks about that for a moment. Then, with a far off look in his eyes, he answers faintly, "Yes."

For Andy, the word "walking" is a reminder that tomorrow, the scheduled fitting for his prosthetic molds will be a considered a significant step toward walking again. His new prosthetics will take the place of his former legs, which are gone, dead. And for the first time since coming home as a double amputee, he feels a surge of optimism swell up inside his chest. This is about renewal, regeneration.

What a strange juxtaposition, Andy thinks. *Part of me is dead. But I'll walk again; thanks in part to a man who is also half-dead.* Yet, Andy wonders how it is possible that Dennis contains so much life? He is reminded of something that his father told him once, long ago, when he was just a boy.

He had been walking along the beach with his father, combing for seashells, when his father told him that the shells, even the sand, were once living, breathing organisms. "You see the ocean, Andy?" His father pointed out to the vast expanse of water. "It covers dead mountains, continents, and even countries. Out there, death is what nourishes the sea of life. It creates; regenerates then dies again." Andy was confused, so his father further explained. "Everything has its own perfect balance, son. In nature, everything is alive and dead at the same time."

Now, looking at Dennis, he concludes that Dennis is like the ocean—the ultimate communion of living and dead. *Is this nature's way of balancing us out?* Maybe it unlocks the mystery of why they were brought together in the first place. Maybe they needed to learn how to peel back the layers of their existence, so that their physical and emotional winters could end, and spring could begin again. It makes sense to Andy now. But he still wonders about Dennis, often sensing that these meetings have been difficult for him. *Is this part of Dennis' growth, or is there a point of diminishing returns?*

"Dennis?" Andy pauses, unsure if he wants to go where he's about to go. "Why are you doing this? Why are you here helping me?"

Dennis sits up further in his seat; he doesn't know how to answer that question. After a long pause, he stands up; he is leaving now.

Andy senses that Dennis is not capable of giving him an answer at this time. He decides not to push the question again. Instead, he asks him another. "Dennis?"

"Yes?"

"I've decided to call my mom and ask her to stay with me for the rest of my rehabilitation. I'd like for you to meet her. Will you stop by again tomorrow?"

Dennis nods his head, yes. He is about to walk out the door when he sees Andy reach down for the phone on the night stand. He dials slowly, and then hangs up before anyone answers. Andy looks up at Dennis sheepishly. "I've been having a hard time making this call."

Dennis smiles, and assures him, "That's okay, she'll understand."

Andy exhales his reservations.

"See you tomorrow Dennis," Andy says abstractedly as he dials his home phone number again. Suddenly, he remembers something. "Hey, you know what? Tomorrow is the Corps' birthday." Then he looks down at his body covered in a white sheet. "Never thought I'd be celebrating it here at Walter Reed."

Neither did Dennis.

PTSD

ANNIVERSARY DATES WERE ALWAYS a funny concept to Dennis; you celebrate or pay deference to something that happened at one moment in time that can never be repeated. What's the point? But at the VA, anniversary dates were big on the list of diagnostic factors that help determine signs of post-traumatic stress disorder.

Dennis was uneasy when he went back to the VA in 1992. He had gone once before, in the early seventies upon his father's suggestion after Hunter had detected a change in his son. Dennis seemed different, more withdrawn, less social, and easy to anger. It was something Hunter experienced first-hand himself, having dealt with his own post-war demons. Hunter never said anything to Dennis directly, likely because he didn't think it appropriate for the pot to call the kettle black; instead he casually suggested that a trip to the VA might do some good.

Dennis had always thought of his father as a good man as well as a good father and provider. Yet emotionally, Hunter always kept his children at arm's length, and it would be many years before Dennis realized it was a reflection of PTSD. And son adopted the father's distant style of parenting, and the hell of constant reminders.

When Dennis visited the VA during the early seventies, PTSD was not yet defined. His symptoms were unknown. Terms such as "Soldier's Heart," and "Shell Shock" floated around. Dennis was offered psychological drugs to "help take the edge off," but he refused treatment and walked out. He saw the drugs as a sign of weakness.

So he was nervous about going back the second time around. But his doctor assured him that the VA had changed in the twenty years since Dennis had been there. He suggested that Dennis meet with Jerry Brentham, a veteran who was doing ground-breaking work on post-war related stress at the Veterans Affairs in Martinsburg.

Dennis was anxious to see what was in store for him, but soon laid his fears to rest when he walked in to Jerry's office. Jerry was a bull of a man, roughly one hundred eighty-five pounds or so on a five-foot, eight-inch frame. His office was filled with framed awards, certifications, and newspaper articles.

"I read your C-file."

Dennis didn't say anything. He knew Jerry had access to his military file and medical records.

"You're messed up.

What?

"I know you don't want to hear that, but tough shit."

What the hell is this? I don't need to hear this. Dennis wanted to get up out of the chair and walk out the door, but something inside told him to stay. *Maybe this guy is right.* Jerry must have noticed Dennis' body language; but he continued to let the moment linger, allowing his words to seep in before moving on, unhurried.

"You've seen a lot of fireworks," Jerry finally continued, putting Dennis' C-file down on the desk.

Fireworks. Dennis mentally flipped through his list of "anniversary dates," including April 5th, when Harry and John died. April 7th, Lilly. May 15th, Dave. July 4th, Operation Buffalo. September 4th, his second purple heart; and twenty days later, September 24th, his third purple heart.

But the mention of the word "fireworks" catapulted Dennis back to the bowels of the I-Corps war zone to exactly where he was lying on his belly under the cover of elephant grass outside the Marketplace.

He heard his call sign had come over the radio. It was dark, and Dennis had no idea what time it was, or how long he had been there.

"Birmingham 6-4, are you there? Key twice. Over."

The officers at the command post bunker in Con Thien were running through the calls signs desperately trying to initiate radio contact with the embattled companies at the Marketplace. First they tried to contact the officers in the field—the few that were left—then the forward observers.

Tired and war weary, the officers crowded around the table, pointing to maps and locating positions. So far, it seemed that Alpha, Bravo, and Delta companies had taken nearly fifty percent casualties. Charlie Company, deployed from Dong Ha to reinforce them, had thus far been unable to get in—an ominous sign.

The order was repeated. "Birmingham? Key twice. Over."

Click. Click.

Then Dennis heard command post radio Sergeant Stover's' call sign, "Lima Bean 2-2? Click twice."

No clicks.

Suddenly red and green tracer bullets illuminated the sky. Another firefight. Dennis paused; it looked like a fireworks show. *Fireworks.* Dennis was struck by the irony—it was almost the fourth of July, and he's in the middle of the jungle watching a fireworks show he wished wasn't real.

Dennis snaps back to attention. He is sitting in a brown leather chair in Jerry's office. Jerry is looking at him intently, knowing full well that Dennis has just experienced a flashback.

"Want to tell me about it?"

"Tell you about what?"

"What you were thinking about, just now."

Dennis is still reticent to confide in Jerry, but nevertheless, feels his mouth open and hears his own voice speaking, "I was thinking about Buffalo. How, during the firefight, I tried to remember my last Fourth of July before I went to 'Nam. And I couldn't remember it. The strange thing is that I still can't remember it. In fact, I can't remember any of my past holidays, not a single one. I know that every Fourth, my dad used to have BBQ, and we'd have fireworks, but I can't recall myself being actually there. It's as if I don't have access to those memories, as if those memories and that person aren't available to me anymore." Dennis' voice reveals no animosity, just matter-of-factness.

"Are you familiar with PTSD? Post Traumatic Stress Disorder?" Jerry asks.

Dennis made a so-so motion with his hands. At that time, PTSD was a relatively new field of study, having only been officially classified as a mental health disease a few years earlier in 1989. Dennis had heard about it, read about it—but wasn't sure if he believed in it. Like the drugs, he saw it as a sign of weakness.

"The clinical definition of PTSD is a psychiatric disorder that can occur following the experience or witnessing of life-threatening events such as military combat. People who suffer often relive their experience through nightmares and flashbacks. Often, they have difficulty sleeping, and feel detached or estranged."

Check.

"Symptoms can be severe enough and last long enough to significantly impair daily life."

Check.

"Clear biological changes can occur, frequently in conjunction with depression, substance abuse, problems of memory and cognition, other problems of physical and mental health.

Check.

"Others feel the inability to function in social or family life. For many, problems show up in their work, marital problems and divorces, family discord, and problems relating with or having good relationships with their children. Dennis, I'm talking about problems that pervade daily life."

Check.

"Now for the physical symptoms—headaches, GI complaints, immune system problems, dizziness, chest pains—all are common in people with PTSD."

Check.

"Well, how do you cure it? Dennis finally asks.

"You don't. It is your body's physiological survival mechanism to deal with events that your mind was forced to process. There is no known cure."

Well, what the hell good does that do me? Dennis wants to ask, but refrains.

Jerry smiles, as if he had just read Dennis' mind. "It can't be cured, but it can be treated. Right now, no treatment is definitive. But cognitive-behavior therapy, group therapy, exposure therapy, and a variety of forms of psychotherapy and drug therapy are all very promising."

Dennis liked Jerry. He was a straight shooter. He gave no run around or bullshit. Jerry was also a combat veteran, possessing two inherent traits—credibility and compassion—and because of that, Dennis trusted him.

"Look Dennis, it's not a matter of how you treat Post Traumatic Stress Disorder. Like I said, there is no cure. It's a matter of how you live your life with it."

That conversation proved to be a turning point in Dennis' life. Before that, hell was his own existence, in which he aimlessly wandered. He had no real sense of time, as most people know it, because he couldn't remember timeframes to reference.

Jerry referred him to a doctor for treatment, but Dennis never went to his appointment; instead, Jerry became a friend and confidant. Over the next few years, they expanded their informal group to include Sgt. Tom, and a young Army Airborne veteran who served in Grenada named John. They didn't meet at the VA; they met at restaurants and diners. They were each other's support group. They were all guys who made it, and each had their own form of survivors' guilt. Work was their anesthetic of choice to numb the pain. Compulsive work filled the void of time. *Go, go, go. Move, move, move. Don't stop.* Dinners, drinks, and conversations went well into the night. Exposing the dark corners of their minds, they talked about the things that never quite seemed to go away.

Never leave anyone behind.

Part IX

Con Thien
November 10, 2004

"Some psychiatric casualties have always been associated with war, but it is only in this century that our physical and logistical capability to sustain combat has completely outstripped our psychological capacity to endure it."

—Lt. Col. Dave Grossman,
On Killing, The Psychological Cost of Learning to Kill in War and Society

Piece of Cake

INSIDE ANDY'S DIMLY LIT room, a woman with light brown hair sits in a chair in the corner of the room, gently rocking back and forth, humming softly. Andy is sleeping deeply; he had been up all night, too excited to sleep, and now his chest rises and falls under the white linen sheets with each cadence of his breath. There is a knock at the door. It is early for visitors, only eight-thirty in the morning. Dennis enters the room carrying a large box. The woman smiles; her eyes shine brightly. She has the same blue eyes as Andy.

"Dennis?"

"Yes."

"Hi, I'm Sue Taylor. Please come in. Andy told me he was expecting you today. He's told me all about you," she says warmly. "Thank you. I wanted to see how he's is doing, and bring him this," he says, nodding to the box he is carrying. Inside is a frosted white cake with the words 'Happy Anniversary' written in red and gold frosting. "Where should I put it?"

Sue points over to the kitchenette.

Dennis has brought the cake to celebrate the Marine Corps' birthday. "It's a tradition for the oldest and youngest members of the platoon to cut the cake and eat the first piece," he explains.

Sue smiles broadly. She has a genuine smile, much like Andy's. But he sees the deep grooves in her face, and knows from Andy's depiction that she has led a hard, lonely life, full of worry and strife since her husband's early passing.

Dennis places the cake on the kitchenette table and sees her worn overnight bag stuffed haphazardly with clothes and toiletries.

Sue had packed her suitcase immediately after Andy's call and was on the I-70 heading east to Washington within the hour. She arrived late last night. "Oh, don't mind me," she says now with a wave of her hand. "Here, let me move that for you. Please, have a seat."

Dennis politely declines her offer. "Actually, I can't stay, something's come up, I have a meeting out of town, in Pennsylvania."

"Oh?"

"I just wanted to drop this off for Andy. How's he doing?

"Great. His team of doctors said his wounds look good. And they expect smooth sailing from here."

Dennis feels relieved. "Good." He looks down at his watch and knows it will be difficult to reach Pennsylvania by noon if he doesn't leave now. "Please tell Andy I'll stop back tomorrow."

"I'll tell him," Sue assures him. He turns to walk out of the room. Just as he is about to close the door, she calls out to him, "Dennis?" He turns around to face her. "Thank you."

Dennis nods his head and closes the door behind him. *You're welcome.*

R & R

DENNIS THINKS ABOUT ANDY as he navigates the District beltway. He wasn't surprised to see Andy's mother there. He would have done same thing himself—call his mother, that is. In fact, he did once, when he was taken out of the field and sent on "rest and recuperation" in Singapore. At first, he had resisted the urge, afraid it might re-humanize him, but he called anyway.

It was mid-August, 1967. Buffalo had been hard on Dennis and the Marines, especially The Walking Dead. That operation cost them 159 KIA and 345 WIA casualties, but it was even harder on the NVA, with an estimated 1,290 reportedly killed.

Dennis remembers the stories that came out of Dong Ha following Operation Buffalo. New recruits would report for duty and stand in line to receive their gear. The sergeants would bark out their names and their assignments, "Reynolds, 1st Battalion, 4th Marines . . . Johnson, 1/9." Hearing the words "1/9" would make everyone laugh. The rookies, of course, didn't know what was so funny; they didn't understand there really was no humor in it. The sergeants scoffed, "You'll get your first heart with your gear. Better yet, don't bother unpacking. You won't be staying long." As far as everyone was concerned, The Walking Dead was jinxed. Later that July, 1/9 was reassigned to Camp Carroll, and 2/9, 3/9 and 3/4 took over at Con Thien for their "time in the barrel." Dennis had stayed on the hill, operating as a battery forward observer with 2/9 and 3/9, continuing his daily patrols of Leatherneck Square. It wasn't long before the 1/9 torch was effectively passed to 2/9, and they soon had their own run-in with fate on Highway 606 in late July. What was intended to be a recon mission followed by a spoil attack was indeed spoiled—at 2/9's expense.

But throughout the beginning of August, the daily security mission operations around Dye-Marker had become a blur to Dennis. Battle-tested and weary, the exhaustion, heat, and malnourishment finally caught up to him in mid-August. He remembers he was near delirious, and sick with dysentery, out on a patrol near the Ben Hai River. When he returned back to the base later that evening, the command officer at Con Thien pulled him aside.

"Hey Michaels, about that fire mission you called in." The officer referred to a half-garbled and senseless fire mission Dennis called in earlier that day. "You're outta here for awhile. I'm sending you on R&R."

The words were not music to Dennis' ears. On the contrary, R&R was a death sentence. He had seen what happened to guys that came back to the field after vacations, he had seen what happened to Dave, and he didn't want the same thing to happen to him. He had an edge to maintain, and frankly, the thought of going back into civilization horrified him.

"You're outta here," the officer tersely repeated. And that was that; the conversation was over.

Dennis bought a few civilian clothes at the PX in Da Nang, where he caught a commercial flight to Singapore. Sitting on the plane amongst mostly Asian co-passengers, Dennis felt strange, as if he didn't belong in life outside of Vietnam. For eight months, his only reality had been war. And then he met Rose Choi.

Dennis walked into his hotel room. Re-entry into civilization felt stiff and strange. He dropped his bag against the bed and looked around the room. The linens were clean, the pillows plump with goose down, the bathroom and the shower glistened, and the windows were clear, reflecting the bustling world just outside the glass.

He took a shower. Standing under the hot water he watched eight months worth of dirt, blood, and sweat wash off, pooling at his feet in shades of dark brown as the red Con Thien clay washed down the drain. He brushed his teeth and shaved. He looked at himself in the mirror. His reflection had changed since the last time he saw it. He was thin and gaunt, and at least thirty pounds lighter. He got dressed and sat down on the bed.

He picked up the phone and listened to the dial tone. *Don't do it*, he told himself. But it was too late.

"Hi, Mom . . . ? Yeah, it's me."

His mother immediately broke down.

"No Mom, nothing's wrong. I'm in Singapore. They sent me on rest and recuperation for a week.

She was still sobbing. This was exactly what he didn't want to happen. He tried to assuage her fears.

"I'm fine Mom, you don't need to worry about me. It's not really that bad, I promise."

She felt a little better.

"Look, I have to go, okay? Is Dad there?"

"No, honey, he's over at your brother's house."

"Well, tell them I said hello. I've gotta go now."

"Denny, I love you."

"Bye."

He hung up the phone. "Damn it," he mumbled to himself. That was what he didn't want—to reconnect, re-humanize—which was *exactly* what happened when he heard his mother cry.

He stood up and began pacing, not knowing what to do with himself. He grabbed the hotel key and headed down to the hotel bar, unsure what to expect.

Two Australian officers were sitting at the bar, both with girls next to them. They greet Dennis. "Pull up a seat and join us."

Dennis ordered a beer.

The two girls smiled and giggled. Dennis wasn't sure he was ready for R&R—or "I and I," as the guys called it, "Intoxication and Intercourse." He took a long, slow sip of his beer, debating whether or not he should go back to his room. Making up his mind, he turned around, only to find a woman standing behind him. She was a round, pudgy woman with twinkling eyes and a big smile. A mama-san. "You want girl, Marine?" she asked him in broken English.

Dennis hesitated. "I don't know . . . I don't think so . . . not right now."

"Ah! You wait here. I be back!" She bowed her head and scurried off.

Minutes later she returned, this time with a beautiful Asian girl. Bashfully standing behind Mama-san, the girl kept her head bowed and averted her eyes. Mama-san took her by the hand. "This is Rose Choi. She new girl. She stay with you."

Rose Choi picked up her face. She looked up, her eyes meeting Dennis' for the first time. She was beautiful, and Dennis couldn't take his eyes off her.

"Good!" Mama-san laughed, and clasped her hands in joy, pleased with her own selection.

Dennis didn't quite know what to do, or how to start a conversation. He stuck his hand out awkwardly. "Hi, I'm Dennis."

Rose blushed. She bowed her head, and repeated his name.

Rose Choi

DENNIS CAN STILL REMEMBER the warmth of Rose's skin and the scent of her hair. Rose Choi was Cantonese, all of sixteen, and beautiful. And she stayed with him the entire week. They dined at different restaurants, went bowling, shopped downtown; he even met her parents for dinner one night. He remembers there were times when he needed to be alone, and he'd tell her, "Rose, I want to be alone right now," and she'd understand. Somehow she always knew exactly what he needed.

At the end of the week he took Rose back to Mama-san. Then he walked outside and hailed a taxi. He called Rose over and they kissed good-bye. He cupped her hands and emptied out his pockets, giving her all the money he owned: one hundred and seventy-five dollars. Her eyes brimmed with tears of joy; he had just given her more money than most families in her village earned in a year. They hugged for the last time.

On the flight back to Vietnam he tried his damnedest to pretend the whole thing never happened, but he couldn't stop thinking about Rose and how good she felt, or the hotel room and what it was like to sleep in a soft bed holding somebody, to feel human again—everything that he wanted to avoid like the plague.

The War's Womb

"WHEN I SAY, 'JUMP!' I mean *jump*! Cause you've got a better chance of surviving than you would in this damn thing," the crew chief yells back. The Da Nang airfield is under mortar attack, with one plane already burning on the runway. Bullets bounce off the small airplane carrying Dennis, two Marines from a recon team, and their dog. The crew chief informs them it may be too dangerous to land, yet somehow the plane manages to land safely, without incident. Dennis jumps out and sprints over to a chopper that takes him back to Con Thien, back to the Hill of Angels.

Setting foot on the red Con Thien soil, he feels strange. He is clean, very clean. Everyone else is filthy dirty. He has eaten; everyone else is sallow and sunken in. He's had sex three times a day for a week. No one else can even look him in the eye; it is if they had forgotten how to be human.

Rockets fire overhead, and just like that, Dennis is welcomed back. NVA snipers in the tree lines just two to three hundred yards away are picking off Marines openly. The rows of concertina wire offer no protection or solace; the Marines are targets, brutally exposed. The NVA continue opening fire on both sides of the hill with fifty caliber machine guns, trying to catch the Marines in a cross-fire.

Dennis' vision seems blurry, he feels lightheaded. The sudden rush of sheer adrenaline intoxicates his brain. In a perverse way, he's happy. He's missed this feeling. It's a feeling that can only be described as a sort of passion, a passion for life and death so intense that it doesn't exist outside of war—hence the reason it is hard to explain and even harder to name. He's back in the bosom of war.

Minutes later it is over. Dennis looks around the base. Everyone appears to be relatively unscathed. He looks down at himself; he's okay. He is a filthy, hardened killer again. If Rose Choi was his heaven, Con Thien is his hell.

Brother John

WHEN JOHN HEARD DENNIS' voice over the phone last night it sounded hollow, almost monotone, and John immediately knew that Dennis was in trouble.

"Can you meet tomorrow?" Dennis had asked.

"Sure, what's up."

"I wanted to talk to you about a business opportunity—a project—for the guys."

John wasn't sure which "guys" Dennis was referring to—the guys on the wall, or the guys who came home—the veterans. "Yeah, sure. Same time, same place?" John asked, referring to Angie's Diner located just on the outskirts of Altoona, Pennsylvania.

"Yeah."

End of conversation.

Now, sitting at the corner booth, the same corner booth where they always sit, Dennis faces John and regrets having made the call. But he's the one who asked John to meet him here, just as he was the one who asked John to take care of his mother to make sure she was eating adequately and help her around the house. Brother John obliged.

"So, how are you doing?" John asks.

Dennis gives a little shrug.

"That bad, huh?"

"Yeah," Dennis replies, avoiding eye contact. Instead, he immediately reaches across the table for a laminated menu and begins studying it intently. He reads over each item, never pausing long enough to look up and make eye contact with John, who watches him in silence. Dennis leans on one elbow and places his hand over his forehead, shielding his eyes from John's concern and rubs his temple.

John can't get over how tired Dennis looks. He hasn't seen Dennis look so haggard since Mrs. Michaels passed away. But that's not a topic of conversation John intends to bring up. Not today. There are some things they rarely discuss, and Dennis' mother is one of them.

Despite Dennis' lack of enthusiasm, John is happy to see his friend again. It has been several weeks since they've last spoken, even months since they've last seen each other, but that is nothing out of the ordinary. John has always said their friendship is somewhat like the water coming out of a kitchen faucet, sometimes on at full blast, other times just a slow drip. But the water is always there.

John remembers the first time he met Dennis. It was at the Martinsburg Mall, just days before the Moving Wall's arrival. The year was 1992. John was the new general manager at the mall and was hosting the replica memorial on the mall's front lawn. It was part of his marketing plan to generate interest and reach out to the heavily veteran laden community. John organized a town-hall style meeting, inviting local Vietnam veterans to be a part of the planning and logistics, and asked for a volunteer to chair the committee. No hands rose. Just as it looked like John would have no choice but to chair the meeting, a voice in the back of the room called out, "I'll do it."

John had looked up. The volunteer stood and walked to the front of the room; he had light brown hair, pale blue eyes, and a large barreled chest that one could only assume belonged to a bodybuilder. The man introduced himself. His name—Dennis Michaels.

John stood back and watched Dennis chair the rest of the meeting, coordinating the event's logistics with such ease that John was transfixed by his charisma and seemingly effortless ability to take charge. Within the hour Dennis had mapped out schedules, organized the ceremonies and presenters, determined who would help locate the names of the fallen on the wall, and scheduled veterans to volunteer for the nightly vigils. The veterans had already decided, once the flag was raised, the replica must never be left unattended.

In the days after the meeting, Dennis and John began to forge a friendship that continued even after the Moving Wall left Martinsburg. John joined Dennis, Jerry Brentham, and Sergeant Tom for lunches and long talks that soon turned into a weekly tradition, and for the first time in a long time, John felt like he belonged.

After he had come home from Grenada, people didn't exactly scoff, but they didn't take that military engagement very seriously either. It was like an old-time Banana War, a MOOTW—a military operation other than war—and the public didn't perceive it as being warlike as they did Vietnam. But John was a combatant in a war zone who lost his buddies and his own innocence as proof. He, too, suffered nightmares. He too thought of killing himself and ending it all. When he met Dennis, he found someone whom he could talk to, someone who could relate and understand. And because of that, Dennis became not only a friend and confident, but a symbolic godfather as well.

But it didn't take long for John to realize there was much more to Dennis than what appeared on the surface. His new friend epitomized the old saying "your greatest strength is also your greatest weakness." And Dennis' greatest asset and liability was his ability to "body bag" someone, to turn himself away from humanity, and shield himself from emotions. And John has the suspicious feeling that Dennis is doing that very thing right now, only this time John is the living corpse.

Mirror, Mirror

AN ELDERLY WAITRESS, wearing a drab gray wait uniform with beige stockings and hair pulled back in a tight bun, brings glasses filled with water to the table and takes their order.

Dennis orders first. "Meatloaf and baked potato." The usual.

"I'll have the same." They have long agreed; it's the best here.

"So . . ." John begins with trepidation. "You mentioned some sort of project? For the guys?"

Dennis waves it off, talking instead about the weather, the drive and work. The conversation is awkward and strained, uncomfortable even. John knows there is a problem lurking beneath the surface, but what? *Why isn't he talking to me? Is it something I did or said?* John can only wonder.

Dennis knows he is making his friend feel uneasy, which makes Dennis feel even worse. He feels guilt for having the capacity to treat those around him so badly, and he wears that guilt like an old, familiar coat. *What the hell is wrong with me?* Usually John is one of the only people in the world that he's able to really open up and talk to, but today, John is a blatant reminder of how badly Dennis treated his own mother. It's as though looking at John is like looking in the mirror. And Dennis doesn't like what he sees.

The truth is, Dennis never really hated his mother. The resentment he felt toward her was really the resentment he had for himself. He hurt her. Deeply. And it pained him to feel the flesh of that truth. He had lied to her.

He wasn't even supposed to be in Vietnam. In fact, the neck injury he sustained at Camp Pendleton all but guaranteed that he would not be sent into combat; it looked like his brother Dalton would go instead. But Dennis couldn't have anybody else fighting his war, so he ripped up his orders, told the authorities that he lost them, and requested that he be sent to "WestPac," the western Pacific theatre, home to the conflict raging in Vietnam. His request was granted.

He didn't tell his mother that he was in Vietnam until after she started sending letters to his battalion headquarters. When she found out the truth, she was devastated. Dennis tried to assuage her by writing to her as often as possible. The cut was deep, but she forgave him. Sweet Mrs. Michaels always forgave her son. No matter the slight, she always loved Dennis. But he couldn't handle that, because in his mind, he didn't deserve to be forgiven. He had lied to her. He went to war and became a killer. *Was she so blind to that fact?* But she loved him more. And he hated himself for not returning her love, for no longer being capable of it. So Dennis asked his "Brother John" to love her for him. He did.

After Dennis moved to northern Virginia, John began his daily routine of stopping over at Mrs. Michaels' house during his lunch break. He'd always bring her half of a sandwich, because that's all she would eat anyhow, and he'd pull up a chair at the kitchen table and listen to the old woman's stories. John fondly recalls Mrs. Michaels' sweet demeanor, and how her immaculately kept house and her front porch were always decorated for whatever holiday was in season. Every day until her death, John walked up the stairs of Mrs. Michaels' front porch. When it was blinking with bright Christmas lights, he changed a kitchen light; adorned with paper hearts for Valentine's Day, he shoveled her sidewalk and fixed a running toilet; when pastel Easter decorations garnished her lawn, she recounted her childhood memories, the first World War, and living through the depression. While he helped tack scarecrow decorations to the lamp post in October, she told John of her relief that her husband, Hunter, made it home from the "Big One," and how amazing it was to her that an American actually landed on the moon. She also showed John pictures of her children, Dalton, her oldest, and Dennis, her youngest, her baby.

During that time, John was aware of the anger Dennis harbored toward his mother; he knew Dennis had been upset with her and could understand why to some degree. But to him, she was just a lovable old lady. When she passed away, John helped Dennis make the arrangements, and together they buried her next to her husband in simple graves marked only by bronze plaques.

In that respect, many things that Dennis did in his life were textbook examples of what not to do. And John saw himself in Dennis. They were cut from the same cloth. Both grew up in military families that bred warriors dating back to WWI, and when the time came, both heeded the call to serve. And after their wars, they had built the same kind of barriers, experienced the same kind of loneliness, and dreaded the same fate. John identified with Dennis' constant need to overwork, his unbalanced romantic relationships doomed from the start, the psychological distance he kept from his family, no matter how close in proximity they were.

All of these things Dennis did to subconsciously protect himself were really a way to avoid intimacy. Yet the greatest paradox was that intimacy was the very thing Dennis wanted most. And he searched for it, yearned for it, coming so close he could feel a fleeting sense of true joy; but just as he reached out to grasp it, it would slip through his fingers like the grapes of Tantalus, and disappear before his very eyes. He was never able to achieve intimacy for the simple reason that he could not give it in return. And it was observing this irony in Dennis' life that inspired John to change the way he had been living, and more importantly, make amends with his own family.

John knows that it is sometimes easy to forget—rather, overlook—the fact that America has been, for much of its existence, a Spartan society, breeding generation after generation of warriors. For many American families, war has been and always will be a way of life. But the relationship with his family had suffered since he returned from Grenada. He was restless at home, aloof and perpetually agitated. His grandfather, a WWII veteran, was sympathetic, asking the rest of the family to show John patience, but after several years, even that wore thin. After one particular afternoon in which he spent his time moping around at a family function, his grandmother flatly told him, "Get over it." John stared at her in disbelief. "Get over it," she said again.

John had never felt more alone in his whole life, and he carried that acrid, empty feeling inside until the day he honored a promise to Dennis. It took the friendship of an old woman for John to realize that when his grandmother told him point blank to, "Get over it," it wasn't out of callousness or indifference, as John had at first perceived. No, there was more to it than that. It was a "get your *mind* over it."

So what he says next is out of love, not indifference: "The monkey's still on your back, huh?"

Still the Monkey

IT IS OFTEN SAID that people perpetually live in the moments in which they felt most fully alive. It is the mind's natural tendency to gravitate toward those moments and stay there, as if by the sheer proximity of thought, the moment will be recreated and can be re-lived. For Dennis, the early days he spent in Vietnam with Harry were the happiest of his life. It seems strange, because Vietnam is also where Harry died and his trauma lives. But the truth is, at one time he was happy being in Vietnam—happy that he was independent, happy that he had found a true friend, and happy that his life existed only in the here and now. Those early months defined the epic period of his life that radiated the true Dennis—his hopes, his dreams, his essence. Nothing in the past mattered; nothing in the future was guaranteed. The monkey was still.

And Dennis' mind has been stuck, paralyzed in the past, and in Vietnam, likely a consequence of the fact that he has never once been able to identify himself since. His mind has always been constantly barraged with questions such as: "Who am I? What am I doing? Why am I even here?" Astronauts who have ever left the Earth's atmosphere understand; those finite moments when they peered into infinite space are what they think about at night, what they think about when they daydream, what they think about when they identify themselves. So it is for warriors. Warriors think about their time in war. When it comes down to it, every veteran will forever "live" in the moments they were warriors, in moments where nothing else existed.

When Dennis first went to the VA in the early 70s, treatment was limited, and focused on trying to remove trauma from the mind. But what they found was that it—the reverberations of trauma—never really go away. Regressed and hidden maybe; dormant, but always there. Dennis knew he couldn't remove the trauma from his mind, so he looked into ways that he could remove his mind from the trauma.

Buddhists, masters of mind control, teach aspiring students the art of meditation by likening the human mind to a monkey, in that, left unchecked, it will swing back and forth from branch to branch like a wild monkey in the jungle. When a master tells his students to "still the monkey," it is a reminder to stay in the present moment, to still the mind, to keep the monkey from swinging too far to a branch of the past, or too far to a branch of the future.

Dennis had long ago learned to set limits for his mind—like a cage for the monkey—defining where it was allowed to go and where it wasn't. But after meeting Andy and going to that funeral, those limits have been blown wide open, and the monkey is now swinging back and forth to those forbidden branches with unrestricted access. Dennis' mind has officially gone there, and like the *Hotel California,* cannot get back. Not only is the monkey out of its cage, the monkey is on his back. And he is agitated because of it.

Ironically, when John said, "The monkey's still on your back, huh?" with the emphasis on the word "still." Dennis' mind immediately began to contort and twist those words around in his head. *Still dealing with Vietnam and PTSD after all these years. Still, the monkey is there no matter what the hell I do. Still the monkey.*

But he's never found a sufficient answer to what happens if, in the course of swinging back to a branch of the past, the monkey becomes so traumatized that it can no longer swing back. *Does it become the trauma itself?* For all he cares, that monkey can swing back and forth all it wants, it doesn't matter. It isn't ever going to go away.

Year of the Monkey

DRIVING HOME, Dennis mentally replays the question Andy had asked. "Why are you doing this?" He couldn't verbalize at the time, but the answer is, he's paying back his dues. He thinks about his life after Vietnam, the struggle, the guilt, and the things he's done that don't make sense. And he rationalizes that ninety percent of everything he has ever done is based on his belief that he must give back. Somewhere, someway, he's got to give back —he's got to pay the dues, even though sometimes he honestly doesn't know with what currency he supposed to pay. In some strange sense he feels like he *owns* his debt as much as *owes* it. It is his karma, his fate, his destiny, his purpose for being here and making it home alive. And he is just a pawn, a mouse, churning its little legs round and round the big wheel. Birth and death, death and rebirth, it's all the same. The question is when does the big ride stop?

One thing he knows for sure: living is a hard thing to make up for and pay back. He suspects that's why there were so many veterans who took their own lives in the years following the war. The true number of suicides committed is unknown, but some estimates are in the tens of thousands. It is the warrior's antilogy: dying is easy, living is the hard part. For several years, Dennis has recognized that his life and his bouts with PTSD have come in waves or cycles. And he has accepted the fact that he must live before death will come, before he can step off the karmic wheel. But lately he senses that, maybe, he is riding on the crest of his last wave, and he wonders if this is the reason for his current angst. *Is this how it feels before death? Is there an inner knowing? An internal clock that knows when your time is up?*

Dennis reflects on the major mile markers of his life, as Jerry calls them. The first was 1968, his first year home, and the realization that they were going to lose the war. Before 1968 there was no doubt in Dennis' mind that America would somehow, someway win this jungle war. But then Tet happened, and 1968 saw the beginning of Dennis' angry years. By 1980, he tried his hand at marriage and raising a family. But he was still angry for most of that decade, angry for being alive and at the way his life was coursing. His marriage deteriorated, and his anger continued to grow until 1992, when his heart nearly exploded. That was the year he met Jerry and began to understand PTSD. It was also the year he began reaching out to other veterans. His experience at the Moving Wall was a testament to that and in some strange way began the path that led him here today, to Andy. But instead of feeling evolved, Dennis feels like he's back at square one. Like the snake swallowing its own tail, his journey has formed a complete circle, with no beginning, middle, or end.

Dennis hears John's voice in his head, repeating over and over, "The monkey's still on your back, huh?" *That damn monkey.*

Dennis' mind flickers back to 1968, the Tet Offensive, and suddenly, he flashes back to a conversation he had with Harry. It was late fall of '66; they were still in Okinawa, waiting to go in-country. He and Harry were studying the Vietnamese culture at the base when they learned the significance of the Tet holiday. Marking the Vietnamese lunar New Year, it is considered the most important date on their calendar, and Harry was interested in the zodiacal animal symbols ascribed to each year. Dennis remembers Harry telling him that each animal symbol repeated itself every twelve years. Harry was born in the Year of the Pig, Dennis, in the Year of the Dog. 1967 was to be the Year of the Goat, and 1968, the Year of the Monkey.

Dennis tries to focus on the road in front of him, yet his mind is racing, careening toward a path that has no seeming destination. Twelve year cycles. Dennis again thinks back to the cyclical nature of his life post-Vietnam. Then it dawns on him. 1968, 1980, 1992 have all fallen under the Vietnamese astrological sign of the Monkey. *But what was it that Harry said? Something*

about those years ushering in periods of great change and powerful transformation?
And suddenly, it hits Dennis. 2004 is a Year of the Monkey.
   Is this my last transformation?

Divine Providence

SUDDENLY, A LOW-FLYING PLANE roars overhead. It flies over the car and into the distance over the hills directly in front of Dennis. In that instant the car, the driving no longer exists. Dennis is not here in the present moment. He is in Con Thien, and a phantom plane has just flown overhead to drop cluster bombs on the NVA. His first thought: *Where are the NVA?* And the following thought: *Napalm the hell out of 'em.*

But he quickly realizes the plane is not going to drop its payload, nor is it turning around to fly back to the base. He's not at Con Thien. He is in Pennsylvania, driving on the interstate. *We're not in Kansas anymore, Toto,* he chides himself, but inside, he knows his thought processes are not those of a normal person. He was re-wired in Vietnam, circuits were taken out, and there's no way to hardwire him back to normal.

He slips back into the monotony of driving, but with the specter of Con Thien in his head. His foremost memory of Con Thien is of a muddy firebase atop a dirt hill that takes up the space of approximately three football fields. It is late September, and the embattled Marines at Con Thien have been held under siege for several days. Inside the razor-edged concertina wire lining the base's perimeter sit fifty-five gallon drums of "fu-goo," a jelly-like mixture of diesel fuel and laundry detergent with a C4 explosive buried under it, planted there for insurance purposes. If the NVA succeeded in overrunning them, the barrel would be exploded and rain the goo on top of any

NVA unlucky enough to be entangled in the wire at that moment. If the Marines couldn't have Con Thien, no one could. Con Thien was to be held at all costs.

The base is populated with dirty and haggard looking Marines hunched over in ponchos as the torrential downpour relentlessly soaks them and everything around them. The artillery battery and the crew sit in flooded bunkers on the left side of the hill. The main entrance is a barbed wire gate. To the right of the gate sits the mortar crew—the 81s—located next to the dump and stacked high with ammo boxes. To the rear of the base, Marines lie belly-down in the thick mud looking down the barrel of their rifles.

Incoming rounds are pouring in all around the area. Smoke is rising up from the explosions. Shouts from the wounded fill the air. Dennis is atop the hill inside the observation post bunker. From his vantage point, he can see the NVA troops in formation. The first wave of attackers storms forward, sacrificing themselves as they fall down on the wires, enabling the second wave of attackers, carrying flame-throwers and RPG's, to press even further in their attempt to breach the wires and overrun the base. The NVA are trying to take the hill again.

Dennis radios to command post. "This is OP-1, do you read? NVA forces are advancing, I repeat, NVA forces are advancing."

A lieutenant rushes to OP-1 to see for himself the advancing attack. Incoming rounds are still thundering down all around them with deafening explosions. Flashes of light seem to be coming from every direction. The lieutenant looks down the hill through his binoculars. "How much ammo do we have left?"

"I don't know, sir. Motor pool hasn't been able to reach us since the flooding. We haven't been re-supplied in over a week," Dennis informs him.

"Get an ammo count."

Just as Dennis radios the battery, the Navy chaplain enters the bunker. "What's going on?" The chaplain asks, but he is cut short.

"Gunny, this is OP-1. What's the ammo count? How many rounds do we have left?"

"Seven rounds a man. 0-5s, no rounds left. Four deuces are out." There is a short pause before he adds sardonically, "We have a few frags left."

The lieutenant spits on the ground, worried. "Jesus. They're coming up over that friggin' hill, and we only have a couple of lousy friggin' grenades to toss over." He stops himself short, embarrassed about unleashing obscenities in front of the chaplain. "Sorry, father." He looks out at the flashes of light originating from North Vietnam. "How far away do you think those battery positions are?" He asks Dennis.

"I'd say about twenty–two or so miles, give or take a few. As of right now, we've got nothing that can reach em."

"That's what I thought."

Suddenly, a brilliant flash of light illuminates the sky.

Dennis and the others clearly see the explosion from OP-1. The NVA gun position in the north that was the main culprit for the barrage has just been hit, and is now a ball of fire that billows up into the clouds. The incoming ceases. Silence falls over Con Thien. The advancing enemy line quickly disenfranchises, and slips away into the darkness. Their cover has just been blown.

"What the hell was that?" Dennis asks. The same question can be heard echoing over Con Thien.

"I don't know, it must have been headquarters," the lieutenant surmises. He dials their frequency on the radio. "Be advised, thanks for the air strike."

The response quickly comes back. "There was no air strike. We can't get any planes up."

The lieutenant looks to Dennis, who is dialing the artillery frequency. "Be advised, thanks for the fire mission," Dennis radios.

"There was no fire mission. We didn't fire anything."

Dennis and the others are baffled by the response. "Well, if it wasn't an air or fire strike, what the hell was it?"

"I don't know what the hell just happened," the lieutenant shakes his head, "but whatever it was, it just saved all of our asses. If it hadn't hit that gun position, we'd all have been wiped out."

The chaplain looks up at the smoke-filled sky. "Divine Intervention," the chaplain says solemnly, bowing his head in reverence. "That's what it was. Never question Divine Intervention. It was God who saved us." *God?* Dennis wants to shout out. *We're out here blowing each other's heads off, and you think God is here?* But instead, he hears himself asking aloud, "What makes us so different from them, father? Why would God be on our side and not theirs?"

It is a rhetorical question. No one answers.

Dennis walks down to his bunker and plops down on his rain-soaked mattress. It doesn't matter that it's wet—nothing matters anymore. In his mind, he'll be gone soon enough. He looks up out of his bunker toward the heavens, and tells Harry, dejectedly, "I thought I'd see you tonight, buddy. I thought I was gonna join you."

How the hell did we make it? Questions fill his mind. *Where did that plane come from? Was it Divine Intervention? Like, Divine Providence?*

Dennis thinks back to a conversation he and Harry had when they were hunkered down in Quang Tri, at Camp Czzowitz, during the heavy rains last spring. They were bored out of their minds, as Vietnam had yet to become seriously dangerous. Harry picked up a dictionary, having already read everything else there was to read, and started memorizing words out of it. "I gotta prepare myself for college if I'm going with you next year," was Harry's excuse. He started at the back of dictionary, and leafed through some of the 'Z' and 'Y' and 'X' words and was now studying the 'V' section, silently memorizing the spelling and definition of different words.

Abruptly, Harry sat up in bed and announced the word "vine" as if it was a big deal.

Dennis was confused. "Vine? Yeah, so?" But Harry was excited. "Did you know that the word 'vine' means 'to travel?'"

"Huh, no kidding? No, I didn't know that."

"Di-vine," Harry pronounced slowly. Then, as if his brain were churning, picking up speed, climaxing toward a revelation, Harry looked at Dennis and whispers excitedly. "Don't you get it? Dio is Latin for God. Vine is to travel. Maybe 'divine' means to travel with God."

"Huh?" Dennis was confused. *Where is this coming from?* "Harry, what the hell are you talking about?"

But Harry paid him no heed, as he hurriedly flipped through the pages to the letter 'P' and looked up the word, "providence." A satisfied smile crossed his face as he read the definition.

"Harry?" Dennis looked at him sideways.

"Ah, nothing. I was just thinking about 'Ole Man Nelson. He was always talking about how Divine Providence led me to him. I always wondered what that meant. Now I know."

"Good night Harry."

Dennis had no idea that months later, he would replay that conversation over and over in his head that night at Con Thien. And he thinks about it again now, driving back to Virginia, on the eve of Veteran's Day.

Part X

Veterans Day
November 11, 2004

"We are not born all at once, but by bits. The body first, and the spirit later; and the birth and growth of the spirit, in those who are attentive to their own inner life, are slow and exceedingly painful. Our mothers are racked with the pains of our physical birth; we ourselves suffer the longer pains of our spiritual growth."

—Mary Antin

Scars, Walls, and Ghosts

DENNIS CAN SEE HIS BREATH crystallize in the cold morning air. Standing before his own reflection in the black granite columns, he quickly locates Harry's name etched in Trojan style letters. It is easy to find, especially since there are no crowds yet, which is the reason he came so early this morning. He wanted to visit the guys before all the tourists arrived for the Veteran's Day ceremonies. He doesn't care much for crowds. He never did.

It was crowded that day in 1982 when President Reagan unveiled the Vietnam Veterans Memorial and dedicated it as a gift to the country. Dennis attended the ceremony with a neighbor of his who was also a Vietnam veteran, a Marine from the Citadel, who had been shot several times. Dennis wanted to be there that day as a testament to the guys who couldn't. When he arrived, he could sense that nearly everyone there felt the same way.

The group of veterans led by Jan C. Scuggs, who had established the Vietnam Veterans Memorial Fund in 1979 to create a memorial honoring those who served and sacrificed, were there that day, as was the young woman who designed the memorial, Maya Lin. She was a twenty-one year-old senior from Yale whose design was unanimously chosen out of nearly fifteen hundred entries.

When Dennis was finally able to catch his first glimpse of the Wall, he was disappointed. *They're always trying to hide us,* was his first impression of the long black wall built into the ground itself. He didn't think it was visible enough, and felt it was just another effort to sweep Vietnam veterans under the rug. To him, it looked like a scar.

It was exactly what Lin had envisioned. She wanted the wall to appear as a "rift in the earth," with the black walls acting as a barrier that does not enclose, but rather exposes the names of the fallen, unifying them in their death. The names begin and end at the center; those that died at the beginning in 1959 touch the names of those last killed in 1975, bringing their war "full circle," as Lin described. Above all, she wanted the memorial to be a "park within a park for all to enjoy."

She had won based on the major criteria for design: that it be reflective and contemplative, that it harmonize with its surroundings, that it contain the names of all who died or remained missing, and that it make no political statement about the war. Maya Lin had achieved that and much more with her simple, evocative design.

Despite the emotions coursing through the vein of that afternoon, Dennis felt acutely detached, until a man on crutches tapped him on the shoulder. "You don't remember me. But I remember you. You put me on the chopper in Quang Tri."

Dennis looked at the man closely. He was wearing a dark overcoat and hat and had longish brown hair. He looked like a normal guy. Suddenly, Dennis recognized the man's eyes. He didn't know him then in Vietnam, but he remembers putting him on the chopper. This was the man with piercing blue eyes who was sitting in the LZ waiting for a chopper—hands shaking, smoking a cigarette, dazed and in shock, staring at anything and everything but the stump of his mutilated leg. Dennis looked down at the man's crutches. He was an amputee.

Standing in the middle of this park within a park, Dennis was hit full force with a revelation. *Walls are built usually to divide and create barriers—like Dye-Marker. But this memorial is a wall that unites and reunites.* In that moment, Dennis came to fully appreciate the Memorial. And every year since, Dennis has come to pay his respects and reunite with "the guys"—Harry, Dave, John—and even though her name is not etched on it, Lilly too.

Dawn has barely broken across the morning sky, but the gray clouds are starting to give way to the first rays of sunlight that glimmer off the western panels of the wall. It's going to be a nice, crisp fall day. Dennis pulls his coat tighter. He looks at his own reflection one last time. *Jesus, I look old.* But something else catches his eye. Shadows of early morning fog rising up from the earth now surround his reflection look like the smoke rising up from the red mud of Con Thien. For an instant it's as if he can see the ghosts of Vietnam in those shadows. It reminds him of Lee Teeter's famous artwork, "Vietnam Reflections," of the middle-aged business man who leans against the wall, pressing his hand against the hand of one of four fallen friends who are now ghosts within the wall. *That guy had it exactly right.*

Dennis focuses his attention now on the name etched into Panel 17. Harry. He kneels down, reaches out, and touches the etching of Harry's name. Then, he whispers something inaudible. Something only the ghosts can hear.

Witness

SUE TAYLOR IS IN the same position where Dennis found her yesterday morning, peacefully curled up in the corner chair, vigilantly watching over Andy's slumber. Sue looks up and mouths the words, "Hi. He's still sleeping," as she points toward Andy. Dennis walks over to the kitchenette table, and pulls out a chair—mindful not to rub it across the floor for fear of making noise—and sits down. Andy stirs.

Dennis is unsure if he should stay. He leans over and whispers to Sue. "Maybe I'll come back tomorrow and give you two a chance to spend more time together alone."

"Nonsense. Don't mind me. Besides, he's been looking forward to your visit today."

Dennis nods his head, "okay." He looks over at the cake and sees that a big, heaping piece has been cut out. He smiles.

"Hey," Andy's raspy voice calls out, rousing from sleep. "Thanks for the cake. It was damn good."

"Glad you enjoyed it."

A strange silence fills the room. Neither veteran is sure of what to say next. Andy breaks the silence. "Guess I should tell you 'Happy Veterans' Day.'"

Dennis groans a little. "Yeah, same to you."

Andy looks over to his mother. "It sounds weird doesn't it? Veteran? It's strange thinking of myself as a veteran. Veterans are supposed to be old guys—like Dennis."

Dennis smiles good-naturedly, "Don't worry; you're an old man, too. Just like me."

"How 'bout it," Andy says. His sentence tapers off, as if he is reflecting on something that is playing out in the theatre of his mind. Pensively, he stares off. Then, clearing his throat, he looks up at Dennis. Looking him directly in the eye he says solemnly, "I want to hear about Con Thien .... and about the birth."

Birth. It must have sounded strange to Sue, but she says nothing, instead continuing to rock gently back and forth in the chair, silently listening. She is a footnote now, a witness in the corner of the room now, as both men lock eyes.

"Alright," Dennis replies quietly. He sits back in his chair and looks up at the ceiling, asking his memory to recall a place in time that is so far removed, yet still so profoundly present. Dennis sucks in a deep breath and begins.

"There's not a place on earth that resembles what Con Thien was like in September '67. Nothing grew on it, nothing but dirt. The name Con Thien means 'The Hill of the Angels.' But for us, it was the most ungodly place on earth. Because being there was like being in a graveyard, only no one had told you that you were buried yet."

The Graveyard

DENNIS GRIMACES AS HE holds his head. *This friggin' headache.* He lights up a cigarette and takes a deep puff. Looking out over his sandbagged bunker, he can still see the ominous black smoke rising up from the direction of Dong Ha. They took a beating yesterday, as did Con Thien. For the past week, perpetual artillery and mortar attacks have pounded the Marine strong-point positions. Exhaling, he grimaces with pain; his headaches are getting worse, likely the result of consecutive concussions.

Yesterday, Dennis had awakened to the sound of incoming 82mm mortar rounds pummeling the base. All in all, nearly two hundred rounds of rockets and other assorted small caliber artillery and mortar rounds clobbered Con Thien. Rounds fell indiscriminately. That's the problem with constant shelling. There is no rhyme or reason to it, no tactic or logic that will ensure survival. It is random, ruthless, and unfair.

But Dong Ha was hit the hardest. The good news was that casualties were light. The bad news was that North Vietnamese Soviet 130mm field guns have wiped out the ammunition storage, bulk fuel farm, and damaged seventeen choppers, already in short supply.

Dennis throws down his cigarette and walks down to the eastern perimeter of the base where command officers are surveying the damage here at Con Thien. A bangalore torpedo has blown a gap in the wire on that side of the perimeter. The base is peppered with craters from bunker-busting

152mm artillery rounds. The range for bunker busters is only ten and a half miles, which means the enemy has set up shop right across the river and is lobbing artillery over like softballs.

One thing is for sure, Uncle Ho has definitely been stepping up his attacks. Dennis wonders if it had anything to do with yesterday's scheduled elections. South Vietnam had elected a new president, Nguyen Van Thieu, despite the widely circulated rumors that the electoral process would be dubious at best, and Thieu's government would in reality be a puppet government installed by the US. But on this morning, politics is the furthest thing from the Marines' minds, as most of them don't know, much less care, about the happenings in Saigon.

The only thing they care about is the fact that they are damn near out of food, supplies, and ammo—a precarious position, considering that much work still needs to be done to meet the November 1st deadline for Dye-Marker. Food rations are so low they are reduced to eating out of a number ten canister of cheese.

This is exactly what Dennis finds himself doing by mid-morning—slicing off hunks of cheese for breakfast. He's cranky, dirty, tired, and hungry. They all are; and mean for it. In fact, there's no better combination for making a mean Marine meaner than depriving him of food and sleep, Dennis surmises. For him, any beneficial effects of his "rest and recuperation" have long since passed. Thin, gaunt, and exhausted, he walks into the command post bunker to receive today's operation orders. He pulls out his maps to plot their upcoming patrol locations when he sees one of the corpsmen approaching the bunker. The sight encourages Dennis.

"Hey doc, got any aspirin on ya?"

The corpsman reaches into his jacket pocket. "Yeah, here you go." The corpsman flicks him a few pills of aspirin. Dennis pops them in his mouth and throws his head back, swallowing them instantly, anxious to feel relief.

"Thanks." Just as Dennis starts walking back to his bunker he hears a god-awful sound that stops him dead in his tracks: the portentous "*shooomb*" sound of a round being fired. He looks up and knows by the telltale smoke trails that six rockets are heading straight for Con Thien. Shouts ring out around the base.

"Incoming!"

Hell, this is going to be a bad one. Dennis sprints toward the closest bunker.

He has a surreal feeling that time is inexplicably bound by the distance he has to cover to reach that bunker just a few feet away; nothing else exists except running like hell, that bunker, and the whistling rounds descending upon Con Thien.

Dennis lands next to the ammo boxes, and slams his body up against the sandbags for support. He briefly takes stock of the bunker. He is surprised to see another Marine sleeping on a muddy cot, unaware of the incoming danger. Dennis yells over to him, but it is too late.

The next instant, a huge flash of light rips through the bunker. The explosion engulfs all extraneous sound in its deafening roar.

Dennis throws his arm across his eyes and tries to shield his face. The bunker collapses. The heat presses into him, searing his flesh, as the weight of heavy logs and sandbags crushes his legs. Then the world fades to nothingness.

In a world of pitch black, Dennis cannot see, cannot hear, and cannot move. But most alarming of all, he cannot breathe. He gasps for air, but his desperate attempts to inhale bring in mostly soot and debris. The burning bunker is getting hotter by the second.

The sick realization sweeps over him that he is buried alive. *This is how I'm going to die. I can't breathe.* His throat constricts with fear. He is suffocating. His body goes into panic mode, his heart races as he struggles to move his body from beneath the weight. But he can't move. Slowly, he feels his legs begin to succumb to numbness. Alarms start ringing in is head—a loud, throbbing ring that grows in his ears.

Lying there, pinned under the rubble of blackness, he thinks he can hear the faint warbling sound of voices. The voices sound like caricatures. "I'm in here!" he wants to shout out, but when he opens his mouth, nothing comes out. Instead, dirt and debris enter where nothing else can escape. *They can't hear me. They're never going to find me.*

He feels his ethereal body release itself from its physical cage, as if all it ever had to do was merely come unhinged from its fragile casing. *See . . . . This is how it works. Death is easy.*

Outside the burning bunker, Marines furiously dig through the wreckage. "He's alive; get him the hell out of there."

The Word

THE LIGHT AT FIRST appears in the distance, but as it reaches closer, it begins to emanate from all directions. In fact, he is the light too. Energy pulses through his entire being, pumping pure essence like a heart organ pumping blood through veins no longer bound by muscle, tissue, or skin. Free flowing and free moving, it beckons him closer. *Speak with me.* He follows. And then, in the chamber of light, he is touched.

A loud voice rises up and in one thunderous clap, it utters the Word.

Dennis is given the Word. That is all. That is everything.

The Word encompasses all meaning; it has no bounds. Nothing else is uttered, no instructions given; no orders are to be heeded. Yet somehow, Dennis instinctively knows he must never repeat this Word to anybody. This is his own Word, one given to him alone, bound to him for all eternity.

And a profound sense of peace sweeps over his being. The Word will carry him through. And it will carry him through life, just as it will carry him through death. All he ever needs to do is call upon this Word. And never, ever repeat it to another soul.

That point matters not to Dennis; besides, no one else would understand, even if he did say it aloud. The Word is found in no earthly dictionary.

Grand and Glory

"GET HIM OUT! Get him the hell out of there!"

Light streams in through the cracks of rubble now, as the Marines are able to pull Dennis from the smoking heap. Dazed and disoriented, he looks around. The entire base, masked in smoke and debris, is unrecognizable. *What the hell just happened?* The bunker he jumped in is gone, completely blown apart. Dennis looks down at his legs. He tries to move them. He groans in pain. One of them is broken, but he is thankful he still has them, despite the unimaginable pain. Dennis tries to talk. He coughs up blood and dirt. Finally, able to get the words out, he tells his rescuers. "There's another guy in there. What about the other guy?"

One of the Marines shakes his head. "He's gone."

Dennis looks over his shoulder. Behind him, thirty yards away, lies a broken and contorted body. The corpsman that gave Dennis aspirin is covering the body with a poncho.

The Marines carry Dennis to the landing zone to await a medivac. The corpsman rushes over to splint his leg. Incoming rounds are still shelling the base. Despite his broken leg and feeling dazed by the concussion of the blast, Dennis doesn't want to go.

The sound of a hovering chopper drowns out the timbre of the incoming barrage. The mechanical bird is flying so low it looks as if it's barely above the tree line. Cracking gunfire smacks the metal body, and Dennis wonders if they're even going to be able to land. It doesn't. Instead it hovers over the landing zone, parting the dirt below in a cyclone of dust. The corpsman and handful of Marines quickly hoist Dennis into the metal carriage. Dennis concentrates on the whirling vibration of the blades as he tries not to think about the pain emanating from his right knee.

The medivac transports him to a D-Med field hospital, a group of makeshift Quonset structures lining both sides of a dirt road. The location looks so foreign that Dennis has no idea where he is. The buildings have metal roofs and metal walls, and, inside, the bustling operating rooms and triages are filled with corpsmen and nurses, engrossed in their duty of tending to the wounded. Dennis is taken by stretcher into the triage area and laid down on what looks to be a sawhorse.

Dennis listens to the sound of choppers landing and taking off. He can tell by the number and frequency of landings that a lot of guys have been hit. He sits up a little higher on his triage table and positions his body so that he can peer out the crack of the metal door. Still woozy from the concussion, he is able to make out dead bodies being stacked up along the road. The bodies are stacked in a pile four feet high.

Fifty yards down the road, a corpsman is performing an amputation in the middle of the street on a guy who has just arrived on one of the medivacs. His hand was hanging on by a thread of skin. Dennis watches the corpsman sever it completely.

Disturbed, he cannot believe how fast this has gone wrong. This is so horribly wrong. It wasn't supposed to be this way. Just a few months ago, they were all healthy, strong nineteen- and twenty-year old kids. *Now, we're being mutilated and bleeding out all over some friggin' jungle street.* He feels like he's in a bad dream, a maniacal Alice in Wonderland kind of dream.

A corpsman walks over to Dennis and braces his knee, sufficiently taping it so as to immobilize the joint. "We need to operate on your knee. We'll keep you here until we can get you in for surgery later this afternoon."

Dennis punches the table with his fist. "What the hell good am I now?" he yells out, not caring who might hear him. An hour ago he was trapped under the weight of the rubble; in fact, he can still feel the tightness in his throat from his brush with death in the form of suffocation—and now? Now, he's trapped in a hospital with a bum knee, and then he'll be trapped back in the "rear with the gear," while the guys are still up on the hill taking a beating.

The thought sickens Dennis, and his new reality pushes his mind into over-drive. *I'm trapped. I let everybody down. The guys are still out there. I'm no good to anybody here.*

Suddenly he sits upright on the table. He leans over to massage his knee for a second, and then, as inconspicuously as possible, carefully places his good leg on the ground, then the other, grimacing in pain as he puts weight on his broken leg. He stands up, grabs his gear from under the table, and limps back out to the street. The triage is so busy that no one notices him slip through the door.

Outside, the trees and dust swirl mercilessly, as the circus of medivacs, corpsmen, and bloodied, mangled men perform out in the middle of an un-known dirt road. Dennis watches a chopper drop off more casualties. He hobbles over to the landing zone.

"Are you going to Con Thien?" Dennis asks the crew chief of the nearest chopper.

"Do you know what's going on over there right now?" the chief asks. Having watched Dennis limp over to the chopper, he is surprised by the re-quest.

"I don't give a damn. Are you going to Con Thien?"

"Yeah, hop in, we have to drop this guy off too," the chief says, pointing to a fresh-faced rookie huddled in the back. Dennis hops in, using his good leg to lift his weight.

The chopper rises up deftly above the circus, and flies over the tree line. Looking over the lush hills and valleys gracing the landscape of the Vietnam, it is hard to believe what lurks below. From several hundred feet away, Dennis can see Con Thien in the distance. It is still under heavy bombardment.

The flashes of light and the thunder of explosions can be seen and heard from inside the chopper.

Dennis looks down with a hardened gaze. He knows where he is going; he's been there before; he's descending back down into hell on earth. The rookie in the back of the chopper looks out toward the beleaguered base and whistles under his breath. "I hear Con Thien is taking over a hundred rounds of incoming a day. I bet when this thing is over, they'll be considered heroes just like the guys at Iwo Jima. They'll be Vietnam's 'Frozen Chosin.'"

Dennis is barely listening, but he bristles at the mention of the word "heroes." He has never thought of himself as one, nor does he think what he is doing right now is heroic—stupid maybe, but not heroic. He's not doing anything that any one of those guys down there wouldn't do.

The rookie carries on, not needing an audience. "But I guess if we're gonna find our grand and glory, Con Thien is the place to be."

Dennis breaks his gaze. He only knows only one thing for certain and he turns to directly face the rookie. "There is no grand or glory. There never was."

The rookie falls silent.

The McNamara Line

ANDY WATCHES DENNIS CLOSELY. Just moments ago, Dennis seemed lost in his thoughts, his voice seemed faint, almost distant, occupied in the encapsulated space and time that was September 1967, but now, his voice crescendos, and he leans forward in a state of near agitation.

"After the attacks on September 3rd and the logistical damage inflicted at Dong Ha, work on Dye-Maker was brought to a near standstill. Westmoreland was told that progress would continue to be impacted unless we received the materials and reinforcements promised earlier in the spring. But we never got them," Now, Dennis practically hisses through his teeth. "It bred suspicions that, maybe, there was never any intention to reinforce us in the first place."

Whoa. Andy is immediately taken back. *That's pretty heavy. Did they really feel abandoned out there, dangling like puppets on a string, a by-product of the rabbit in the grass perception?*

"McNamara revealed the Dye-Marker project to the public at a press conference on Sept. 7th. He old 'em that a 'plan was under way to build an electronic barrier south of the DMZ.' But by that time, the project was almost a year old and parts of it were damn near complete. The media had a field day with it. They christened it the 'McNamara Line.' Hell, even they knew the damn thing was futile. A waste of friggin' time, and an even bigger waste of men."

Dennis feels his throat constrict, sickened by memories that still taste like poison. It was difficult for him to come home and piece together what really happened, as his perspective of the war was entirely different from the media's portrayal, which seemed so utterly limited and inadequate. It was harder still to learn of the compromises that the Johnson administration made with the North Vietnamese. But the ultimate betrayal for Dennis was learning of Nixon's secret talks with the enemy, and the abandonment of the DMZ. Questions abounded for him and the many other veterans he talked to. *What the hell were we doing out there? What was the point?* Their hands were virtually tied behind their backs; they sat out on the DMZ like sitting ducks building the defense secretary's wall, and took enemy fire squarely on the chin. *For what?*

It took Dennis many years to distance himself from the anger he felt in those first years after the war. Controlling his anger was a hard lesson to learn. Even now, it is a subject that can provoke rage, and he mentally tells himself not to go there again. *Not today, not now.*

Everyday Heroes

"AMMO RUN!" For the men at Con Thien those words are like a lightning rod of hope, as the base is in dire need of food and supplies. But for the motor pool, running the gauntlet to Con Thien is dangerous and often fatal. Dennis hobbles as quickly as he can over to the perimeter to provide cover. The NVA surrounding Con Thien have already taken aim at the trucks driving up the road as fast as they can. Chances are that out of six trucks carrying out the mission, one or two will not make it.

The lead truck gets hit, and immediately explodes in a ball of fire. Dennis' heart sinks. A somber hush falls over the base as the Marines anxiously pray that the remaining five trucks can navigate around the burning heap without tripping a mine or otherwise meeting the same fate. Closer and closer the trucks race to the main gate. Louder and louder the Marines holler out, a mixture of encouragement, curses, and prayers. "C'mon, you sonuva-bitches . . . ! Drive!"

Luckily, the remaining trucks reach the base with no further casualties, speeding past the wire gates into the complex. Throngs of cheers surround the surviving Marines, as the men huddle around their motor pool comrades, slapping them on the back like returning heroes. Everyone knows the motor pool guys have one of the most thankless jobs in the Marine Corps, but today, they are heroes.

Dennis limps over to the huddle. "You just saved all of our lives," Dennis tells one of the drivers, giving him a hearty slap on the back.

"And you just saved ours," the driver responds, a proud smile spreads across his face. Today, they did something good.

At the time, no one could have foreseen that this would be the last supply mission any truck would make for several weeks. Soon, only choppers would be able to reach the Hill of Angels, and even they would have to bargain with the devil in order to do so.

Captain Brody

IN A TRENCH NEAR the rear of the base where the tanks are positioned, Dennis makes a fresh tin of morning coffee with the new rations along with Chet Lambert, who recently returned from Dong Ha. They enjoy the relative peace and quiet and catching up on stories as they watch a nearby tank unit work on their machinery. Tubes need cleaning, tracks need tightening, and considering the beatings the tanks have taken providing support to the grunts out in the fields and rice paddies around Con Thien, the units have a full morning's work ahead of them.

Captain Brody, a grunt captain, joins Dennis and Chet and the three men gulp down their bitter-tasting coffee as they watch a new officer work on one tank in particular. The track had been blown off the previous day, and the officer is clearly frustrated with the slow progress. After several minutes, he disgustedly throws down his tools and walks over to the trench.

"Hey," the lieutenant calls out to the trio sitting in the trench. "Do you guys have any C4s on you?"

"Affirmative," Captain Brody replies. He returns shortly with a five pound block of explosives.

"Thanks," the officer calls out over his shoulder as he walks back to his tank.

Just as the three Marines finish their coffee, they hear someone shouting from the direction of the tanks. Startled, they prepare to take cover, but realize no rounds have been fired. They watch as the tank officer, screaming loudly, sprints toward their trench, wildly flaying his arms. "Fire in the hole! Fire in the hole!" The officer shouts; his eyes filled with fear. He jumps into their trench and covers his head. Dennis, Chet, and Captain Brody look at the officer in bemusement. This is actual comedy for them, a rare thing indeed.

"What the hell did you put in that thing?" Chet asks the officer.

A loud explosion deafens the officers' response. All of the men hit the deck hard. When they peer above the trench, perfect "O's" form on their mouths as they stare at the entire underside of the tank. They stare in disbelief first at the tank that has just been blown up, then at the officer, and back to the tank, before they break into a fit of laughter.

"You stupid son of a bitch!" Chet hollers out, holding his stomach in stitches. "You just blew your own tank up!"

The officer is beside himself, holding his head in his hands, and moaning loudly. "Oh my god, how am I going to explain this?" He asks bewilderedly. He mysteriously looks to Chet for an answer. Chet just laughs even harder. He asks again, even more emphatically, "How am I going to explain this?' Then a look of horror sweeps over his face. "Oh shit, they're going to make me pay for it…" The officer stumbles out of the trench, wringing his hands now, and talking to himself.

"God, it feels good to laugh again," Chet says, wiping the tears of laughter from his eyes. He hasn't laughed that hard in ages.

"How about it," Captain Brody agrees.

Even Dennis is grateful for this little bit of comic relief; he knows it's probably the only thing keeping their sanity. It never fails to amaze him how they can experience absolute horror at times, and then, something like this happens, and it's downright comical how stupid they can be.

Without warning, rounds are fired in the distance. The three Marines' instantly recognize the sound. *The party's over. This one is heading their way.*

"Incoming!"

The Marines dive face-first into the trench and tightly cover their heads, praying this one will miss. A bunker ten yards away takes the direct hit, instantly going up in smoke and flames. Marines with bloodied faces and bodies crawl frantically on their hands and knees away from the engulfed site, while the Marines unlucky enough to actually be inside the bunker are now strewn all around, lying in various stages of shock.

Chet and Captain Brody scramble to their feet. Dennis is slower to stand, hampered by his broken leg, but suddenly, without any logical reason, he stops dead in his tracks.

No. Wait.

It is the voice again. The same voice he heard when he was buried alive in that bunker—the same voice that gave him the Word.

Dennis tries to shake it off, but he is overcome by a feeling of undeniable dread. Again, he hears, rather, he feels the voice. *Wait.*

Chet is just about to sprint over to the bunker when Dennis grabs him by his flak jacket and throws him back in the trench. "Wait. Don't go yet." Dennis reaches out for Captain Brody, but it is too late, he has already sprinted over to the bunker.

"*What!* What the hell are you talking about?" Chet screams. "We've got to get the hell over there and help them!"

"I said wait."

Captain Brody has just reached the burning bunker and is kneeling over the body of a wounded man. Three more Marines run over to assist and begin dragging the casualties out of harm's way.

BBBOOOOMMMM.

The very same bunker takes another direct hit.

Dennis and Chet hit the deck. Earth and debris fly up and rain over top of their heads. When they are able to look back up they see something that makes them want to vomit. Every single one of the Marines who were standing next to that bunker, including Captain Brody, is dead.

Oh my God, Dennis hobbles over to where Captain Brody had been standing just moments ago. The captain's head is missing. Dennis feels the urge to vomit, but something inside clicks, numbing his reaction. With his emotions mentally turned off, he walks over to where the decapitated head of Captain Brody has rolled, and nonchalantly picks it up off the ground. Chet and two other grunts pick up the truncated body and carry it to the medic parapet where they lay it across the sandbags to be tagged. Dennis places the head atop of the corpse, arranging it so that it looks like it still belongs on the man. It is the least he can do.

"You've got to be friggin' kidding me," the corpsman mutters under his breath.

But the joke has long been over.

The Hill of Angels

"ON THE SIXTEENTH OF September," Dennis continues, "the monsoons came, the heaviest monsoon rain in years. The rain was so heavy we slept in water, ate in water, and shit in water. The mud was so thick we could barely walk. Already swollen streams and rivers flooded, washing away some of the Dye-Marker bunkers and trenches, including the Cam Lo Bridge, severing Con Thien from the rest of I Corps. McNamara's Line and the DMZ became nothing but a quagmire."

Quagmire. Andy has an instant reaction to the word. He hates that word. If ever something epitomized a hot button for Andy, "quagmire" is it. And he is often annoyed by its use in conjunction with the war in Iraq. To him, saying that the war in Iraq is a quagmire is like saying their hard fought battles and spilt blood are nothing more than an impetus for political mudslinging. For Andy, it is a matter of dignity. But that's a place he's not willing to go today, not now. He looks at Dennis to continue.

"With the monsoons, came the NVA, and they laid siege to Con Thien, beginning the chapter of Con Thien that was just absolute hell. For ten days, the NVA fired more than five thousand rounds of mortars, arty, and rockets on us. By that point, it wasn't a matter of when or where you'd be hit. The question was: *How bad was it going to be?*"

Pandora's Box

NO PLACE IS SAFE at Con Thien. Rounds hit anywhere and everywhere. Nameless, faceless Marines walk by each other no longer acknowledging each other's existence. Choppers are no longer able to reach Con Thien safely. The entrenched Marines have no food, no supplies, and no reinforcements. The last container of wet cheese is nearly gone; rainwater is caught to drink. Ho Chi Minh is showing the teeth of his "Big Offensive," part of his plan to deliver a mortal blow by wiping out the American forces in the DMZ and taking over Con Thien.

The Marines look tired and ghost-like, dark circles are deeply etched under their eyes from lack of sleep. The unspoken thought on everyone's mind: "How much longer can we last like this?"

"Maybe tomorrow the choppers'll be able to make a run and drop off some food and some supplies, you think?" a young Marine asks optimistically. He is the one who flew into Con Thien on the chopper with Dennis, one of the last batches of rookies Da Nang has been able to station at Con Thien.

But they all know the deal—no choppers, no new reinforcements, no food. The veteran Marines have yet to answer the rookie, choosing to ignore him rather than dash his hopes. The young Marine tries to look into their faces, anxiously awaiting an answer.

Dennis is reminded of a saying that his father once told him: "Never take away a man's hope. Sometimes it's the only thing he has left." Hope. *Is it the consummate blessing, or the consummate curse?* Dennis wonders.

He doesn't know what is more miserable, the hunger, the rain, or the desperation.

Heavy Boots

THE FIRE DIRECTION CONTROL bunker is knee deep in water. Radio operators and plotters are standing in the red mud constantly shifting their weight so as not to sink down any further in the goop. Sores and lesions cover their feet. A plotter is trying to flip a large board to prevent it from getting too waterlogged. Radio operators hold their handsets high up in the air. Someone grabs a pan and begins filling it up with water.

Dennis is standing in front of half a dozen mounted radios. He is filling in as a radio operator now, a position he has held since returning to Con Thien, as his broken leg has rendered him useless out in the field. But his stint at artillery school prepped him enough to handle the radios in the FDC bunker and he deftly operates multiple radios. Receiving the incoming fire missions, he reads the fire mission aloud to the plotters on the board. The plotter assesses where the target is located, marks the map with pins and measuring with a slide ruler the distance of the target he calculates the elevation, powder charge, and deflection. Another radio operator is communicating with the battery to relay the coordinates and gun charges within seconds of the request.

Technically, Dennis isn't supposed to be up on the hill at all, and had escaped the attention of the corpsman until a week ago, when another radio operator at FDC required treatment for immersion foot. The corpsman didn't recognize Dennis at first; nor would he have, had he not looked down and saw Dennis' leg bandaged up in a green splint, "Stupid bastard," was all the corpsman said. With Con Thien under siege and no new reinforcements able to reach the base, no one, including the corpsman, is concerned with technicalities. Since September 18th, their war has been about two things, guns and mud—policies be damned.

For the gunners out in the open, conditions are the same. The battery parapet is completely filled with water. Even though their trenches are fortified with sandbags, the reality is they have no real protection. If they take even one direct hit, all the guns can be wiped out, and their ability to stave off an imminent ground attack will be reduced to zero. The NVA know this, and have been fishing for the bulls-eye, the battery, with frightening accuracy.

A Marine enters the FDC bunker with a status report. "Is the battery still able to fire?" An officer asks.

"Some of the hydraulics have been blown off the guns, but they're still firing."

One thing everyone knows for certain: Delta Battery will fire, no matter what. With the hydraulics burned out of the guns, there is no buffer to slow down the barrel from slamming back into the gun carriage with such a huge force, that the gun would literally jam and would need to be physically pushed back up into firing position. It is dangerous for the gunners themselves, as well as the guys out in the field, as the gun may no longer be accurate without the hydraulics. But the gunners are making do the best they can.

Several missions are coming in at once. "Bay Way Delta . . . Bay Way Delta." It is ordered chaos inside the FDC. Two more missions come in, including the adjustments, and soon, they are working on half a dozen simultaneous rounds.

The gunners out in the parapet fix the coordinates on their guns for the requested adjustments, "Right five, zero. Drop five, zero." And continue shooting out round after round.

After several hours of heavy bombardment, the incoming subsides. They have withstood yet another beating, but they know the NVA will come again, sooner rather than later. The enemy will not loosen its grip, nor will the Marines, until the back of Con Thien is broken.

With no further requests coming into FDC, Dennis throws down his handset on the table, and limps outside to survey the damage. So far, two Marines have been reported KIA. But the final casualty count has yet to be determined. Dennis notices a man lying against the medic parapet, obviously in shock.

The Marine calls out to Dennis. "Hey man? Can you help me?"

Dennis limps over to him. Standing before him, he sees that the Marine has lost his leg from the waist down and is bleeding profusely. Dennis balances on his good leg and kneels down. "Yeah, anything. What can I do for you?"

"Yeah man, my foot hurts. Will you fix my boot for me? I think it needs to be loosened up."

Dennis looks down. The man clearly does not have a leg. *Phantom pain.*

Dennis kneels over the Marines' missing limb, and pretends to loosen his boot as if it were really there. Dennis knows this man will likely die within the next hour, given how much blood he has already lost.

"Better?" Dennis asks.

The Marine looks up at Dennis with bloodshot eyes. "Yeah, thanks man, that's a lot better. Got a cig on ya?"

"Yeah, here," Dennis pulls out his pack, lights a cigarette, and places it in the Marines' mouth. The Marine slowly draws on it, with hands shaking, and eyes locked straight ahead. Moments later he is dead.

Phantom Pain

"I KNOW HOW that guy felt," Andy says gravely. "When I was hit, I could tell from everyone's voices that it was bad. I just didn't want to know how badly. I wasn't ready to admit that anything was wrong. At the hospital in Germany, I kept telling the doctors, 'Aw, nothing but a couple scrapes and bruises. Shrapnel cut me up, nothing to worry about.' But even before they told me I had lost my legs, I knew. Sure as hell, I knew."

Sue Taylor leans forward in her chair. Her only desire in the world right now is to get up and give her son a hug. Hold him close and tell him it's going to be all right. But she checks herself, deciding now is not the right time. *This is their time*, she tells herself. She is just their witness. A wave of gratitude washes over her, as she feels lucky to have this opportunity to see her son so candid. She relaxes back in her chair and quietly listens as Andy continues.

"I still get the sensation that my legs are still there—and I'll want to bend over and scratch my toes and massage my knee." Andy points down to those areas. "Every once in a while, in my dreams and such, I'll still feel—how do I explain this?" Andy searches for the right words. "I'll still feel the same. It's as if I exist the same way I used to, when I still had my legs and had everything and everyone about me. Then when I wake up, my mind snaps back to reality and I'll realize it's not really there. And it's never going to be there again."

Dennis nods his head and quietly confides, "Me too."

Third Heart

"THEY'RE COMING UP!" The first wave of NVA attacks the rear perimeter of the base. Marines run over to defend against the breach. They mow down the first line of advancing NVA soldiers. The second wave runs over the backs of their fallen comrades, undeterred by the barbed wire fortifying Con Thien. *This may be it. This may be the day everyone knew would come.* Within minutes, a Phantom plane flies overhead. It flies so low that the entire base practically shakes from its force, and the roar of the engine drowns out noise from the incoming fire. The Marines press their bellies to the ground and pray the pilot doesn't miss his target. Awed by the sight of the bomber, everyone watches as it flies over North Vietnam, turns back, and heads straight toward Con Thien. It drops its payload just seconds before reaching the base. The clusters hit the ground, and thousands of little grenade-size bombs detonate.

Dennis is operating the radios inside FDC when he feels the bunker shake from the Phantom's load. He braces himself for a moment and then continues yelling out coordinates for the fire missions. His leg is still bandaged up; he limps around the table gingerly, pinning positions in the map and performing other duties. He still can't run, and has frequently needed to tend to his leg to stave off infection from the wet conditions. But his broken leg is the furthest thing from his mind right now. All that matters is getting their missions out and the NVA off their backs.

Outside, a loud explosion rocks the FDC bunker. Moments later, a Marine runs inside with news the antenna is down.

"Damn it." An officer inside FDC spits on the ground. He is exasperated; the antenna for radio communication is vital. No antenna, no radio. "We need that back up ASAP."

Without hesitating, Dennis heads for the door. He hobbles as fast as he can toward the antenna tower. He passes the battery parapet along the way. He sees all of the gunners working hard.

Suddenly, for some inexplicable reason, he is overcome by the sense that time is warping, and his attention focuses on Gun Six loading in a round.

The barrel is slowly raised.

The sky is overcast and gray.

The gunner is moving his mouth. He has just shouted. "Shot Out!"

The round streaks through the gray sky like a small comet.

It is the last thing he will see.

A trio of heavy artillery rounds hit the base simultaneously. Dennis is bracketed by the rounds.

His body flies through the air on the impact, the concurrent blast hurling him against the sandbagged parapet of Gun Six. *You never hear the one that gets you.*

Dennis doesn't know what hit him. The only thing he knows is that he is sprawled against the battery parapet grabbing his leg with one hand and holding his head with the other. He struggles to recover his breath; the concussion of the blast has knocked the wind out of him. His vision is blurry, his ears ring, and his whole body hurts.

Incoming rounds continue to pound the base, but Dennis is no longer aware of the barrage. *That's it. That's your third. Tour is over.* He slumps forward, and loses consciousness.

The Birth

"WE'VE GOT THREE EMERGENCY medivacs and one ambulatory," Dennis hears as he begins to regain consciousness. The voice is unrecognizable to him; he doesn't know where he is, much less who is talking. He looks around. He is inside one of the steel-cased amphibious vehicles, an amtrac, one of the only vehicles on the base able to cross the muddy morass to the landing zone. The irony is not lost on him: an amtrac escorted him to the shores of Vietnam, and now an amtrac is showing him the door.

"Reappoint, put them out in the LZ and we'll get 'em," a chopper pilot radios.

Dennis reacts to those words as though he has just been sentenced to life in prison. His head feels like it's going to explode; between the verdict and the pressure building up inside his head from the internal swelling, he doesn't know which is worse.

I can't believe this is happening. Dennis can hear the chopper hover over the landing zone. Several Marines help him out of the amtrac and heave him into the chopper just as they start attracting fire. Rounds of sniper fire clip against the metal. The chopper lifts up and banks a sharp right. Careening over the tree line, it flies so low the blades almost touch the tops of the trees.

The corpsman on board attending to the wounded looks down at Dennis. "You're going home."

No! Dennis lunges forward to look down from the chopper at the hills and valleys below. For a brief flicker of a moment, he is taken by how beautiful and peaceful the surrounding country looks. Just then, a round hits Con Thien below. *Everything is an illusion.*

From his aerial view he sees a sight so grotesque to him that he literally feels his stomach retch—waves of NVA, several hundred strong running like ants up the muddy hill. His only desire is to fling his body out of that chopper and go back. But the corpsman places a steady hand on his shoulder, "It's okay, it's over now."

No it's not! Dennis wants to scream. *Never leave anyone behind!* He is overwhelmed by a gut-wrenching pain so intense that it does not even feel physical. It is a pain he has never before felt, nor is it one that he will ever feel again.

Dennis is born.

Survivor's Guilt

DENNIS STANDS UP ABRUPTLY. Andy and Sue watch silently as he walks over to the window as if in a trance. No one speaks. No on moves. Dennis stares out the glass pane at the neatly manicured lawn, but he is not looking out at the grounds of Walter Reed, rather, he is looking out over the hill of Con Thien. Several minutes of silence pass before Dennis finally turns toward them.

"The sickest, most painful feeling I've ever had in my life was looking down out of the chopper and seeing the guys still down there, still fighting. All I could think of was that no place was safe; everybody was going to die. And all I wanted to do was go back. As bad as it was, I didn't want to leave the guys behind."

Dennis takes a deep breath and sighs heavily, "There's no sicker feeling in the world, than knowing—the guys are still down there."

Part XI

Welcome Home

One Year Later
November 11, 2005

"If there must be trouble let it be in my day, that my child may have peace."

—Thomas Paine

The Hour Upon the Stage

ANDY WALKS SLOWLY DOWN Constitution Avenue, pulling his black fleece jacket closer to his body. The temperature is supposed to be in the fifties today, according to the weather report, but the north by northwest wind makes it feel cooler. Andy is meeting Dennis today to celebrate Veteran's Day. It is something they discussed a few times over the past year since Andy's discharge from Walter Reed, but they only solidified their plans three days ago.

Andy took a taxi the sixty-plus miles from Quantico, and actually stopped by Walter Reed earlier this morning. He had wanted to visit the team of doctors who performed his surgery and especially his physical and occupational therapists who had taught him how to function in everyday life, everything from the mundane going up and down stairs and getting into and out of the shower, to how to jog if he so desired. He didn't stay at the medical center very long; he knew they had busy schedules. Besides, he had spent enough time as a patient there already, nearly a year of his life. But he did have a chance to catch up with everyone, and of course, most of the talk was centered on the upcoming Base Realignment and Closure proposal, or BRAC, that Secretary Rumsfeld sponsored.

It is hard for Andy to believe that Walter Reed might not be here in the next five or six years, as its merger with Bethesda Naval Medical Center is scheduled to happen by 2011. This place is too real for him, too poignant, and Andy has followed the BRAC closings in the newspapers and television with bitter interest. It appears the decision to close the Walter Reed complex has been made final, having support from the Pentagon, Senate, and the White House; now the question in Washington is whether the campus will stay intact or be cut up in pieces and sold in chunks. Will it remain a hospital or be turned into a shopping mall?

Andy said his farewells at Walter Reed an hour ago and looks down at his watch. He is fifteen minutes early. He sits down on a bench in front of the National Science Building and happens to notice that the entranceway is decorated with a large bronze sculpture of Albert Einstein sitting in front of a zodiacal disk.

Andy finds it curious that the worlds' most preeminent thinker should sit in front of a zodiac. He ponders its possible significance, wondering if its hidden meaning is to illustrate that each person has his or her own cosmic time, their own predestined path in life that they must follow. If that's the case, it forces him to examine the belief that everything happens for a reason. *Was this supposed to happen to me? Was I supposed to lose my legs?* He is not ready for the answer, not now, and maybe not ever. The wound is too fresh, too deep, too much a part of his psyche to dissect and analyze at this point.

Andy looks up and sees a man walking toward him; he has the stature of a body builder with a thick neck, wide barreled chest, and big arms. It is Dennis. Andy stands up to greet him.

Dennis is taken aback at the sight of Andy standing on two legs. He never realized how tall Andy is, a little over six feet, or how handsome a young man he is dressed in everyday civilian clothes. Seeing Andy stand before him, Dennis feels a profound sense of pride. He also marvels at the idea that most bystanders seeing this young man would have no idea that he is standing on two titanium legs covered only by his blue jeans.

The two men embrace.

Then, together, they walk across the street to the western perimeter of the national mall. They walk past the Lincoln Memorial and the military memorabilia stand. The park is packed with veterans of all ages paying their respects on Veterans' Day and visiting tourists.

"Have you ever been here before?" Dennis asks.

"No. That's why I wanted to come here with you."

Dennis walks Andy over to the Wall. It is hard to see the full length of the long, black memorial with all the people impeding their view, but Andy can see, just by looking at the top of the panels, that though it carries the names of the dead, it pulsates with the life Dennis had described.

Dennis explains to Andy the inherent symbolism built into the Wall's design; the resemblance of a scar, the placement of the names, the beginning and the end of the war united at the memorial's core. "You guys will have your own memorial too, some day."

Andy nods. *Will we?* He doesn't know.

A group of teenagers walk by, chattering away on their cell phones and laughing loudly. Dennis and Andy exchange a quick glance. Dennis says quietly, "You see all of these people, and some of them, you have to wonder why it is they're really here."

"I think about that a lot," Andy says. "I always wonder if people really understand what Iraq and the war is all about. Do they really know what taking mortar fire, or getting hit with shrapnel, means? Or do they just see black words written on a white newspaper page, a blip on the radar, something they think about for a second or two, before they go on with their daily lives?"

"I wonder about that all the time. Truth is, I don't know."

"Dennis, why did you come to Walter Reed?" Andy asks. Andy said "Walter Reed," but what he meant was "Why me?"

"You don't know by now?"

"I think I do."

Dennis recites a Shakespeare verse, "Life's but a walking shadow; a poor player, that struts and frets his hour upon the stage, and then is heard no more: It is a tale told by an idiot, full of sound and fury, signifying nothing."

"Where have I heard that before?" Andy asks.

"Macbeth."

"What I told you about the day I left Vietnam, when I was in that chopper looking down . . . ," Dennis begins, as he looks into the waters of the reflection pool. "It took me a while to realize that I was born out of Vietnam's womb. Nothing could ever change what I had done, or what I had seen or been through. And I didn't know if anybody back home would ever understand that."

The Schoolyard

Early November, 1967

"THANK YOU FOR FLYING with Seaboard Airlines. Our destination is San Francisco, California," a friendly voice announces over the intercom in a polite southern drawl. "This is going to be a long flight—eighteen hours—so please sit back, relax, and enjoy our refreshments. We ask that you fasten your seat belts and remain seated for takeoff."

Dennis finds his seat and throws his bag in the cabin storage above his head. He sits down, uptight and rigid. It is still hard for him to believe he is going home. Mentally, he's not ready. He feels like a foreigner in his own skin, no longer able to trust himself, afraid of what he might do, of what he might say. A civilian passenger sits next to him and smiles. Dennis ignores the gesture, instead slightly turning his body so as to avoid future conversation. Staring out the window, he remains silent the entire flight over the vast Pacific Ocean.

By the time the red Golden Gate Bridge appears in the distance, Dennis legs are cramped and sore, his bum right knee throbs in pain. The stewardess announces over the intercom that the plane will soon pass over Alcatraz, the federal penitentiary famous for confining Al Capone. Dennis looks down over the rocky island that once was inhabited only by the pelicans. *Alcatraz.* It is ironic, he muses, that at this very moment, he can identify more with prisoners than he can the passengers sitting next to him. The prisoners are locked up, incarcerated, and so is he—in the jail of his own mind, of his own existence.

The aircraft touches down. Dennis grabs the olive green bag containing all of his worldly possessions and proceeds down the long corridor of San Francisco Airport to the Naval base station, where he is to receive his new orders. He keeps his eyes focused straight ahead, avoiding direct eye contact with anyone. His eyes dart around quickly, surveying his surroundings for any danger. The thousand-yard stare. He doesn't trust what he can't see. Things are different, signs, people. Dennis notices they have longer hair, different prints, and flared pants. *Welcome to the New World.*

The attendant at the naval station counter smiles as she hands him his orders. He does not return the smile. "Your flight to Newark boards in four hours. After your furlough you'll report to Quantico."

Dennis takes his orders and walks outside. He paces, unsure of what to do for the next four hours. *I'm not sitting in here, that's for damn sure.* He decides to go outside and walk around the airport, to get some fresh air. That is his plan; instead, moments after he hits the pavement, he hails a taxi.

"Where to?" The driver asks.

"Anywhere."

"Huh?"

"Just drive. I'll tell you when to stop."

"Whatever you say, boss."

The cabby drives Dennis around the various neighborhoods of San Francisco, pointing out various tourist attractions along the way. Dennis pays no heed. They drive for twenty minutes before Dennis ever speaks again.

"Stop here." He doesn't know where "here" is, but he wants to get out and stretch his legs. Dennis doesn't even look at the denomination of the bill he hands the driver.

"Are you sure?"

"Keep the change."

"Thanks! The taxi driver begins to drive away, then stops and sticks his head out the window. "Hey, uh, son . . . Thank you."

Dennis smarts, as if just stung by something unexpected.

He walks; not knowing where he is going, or why, he just walks. Up the hills and winding roads, he passes by the quaint brownstones and manicured lawns. He passes by single-family homes with bikes out on the front porch. Then Dennis passes by an elementary school. The American flag waves out front. He can hear children laughing and playing outside. *Laughter.* The sound of innocence. He is drawn to the sound like a magnet. It is recess. Dennis stops. He walks up to the fence, wraps his fingers around the chain links, and silently watches them play.

Immersed in their innocence, he loses track of time and pain as he watches them laugh and sing, run and skip. He can't stop the thought from creeping into his head. *I am never going to know this kind of innocence again.* And suddenly, Dennis' hands begin to shake. Deluged by a flood of emotions, his whole body quivers and his legs buckle, until finally he succumbs, deluged by a flood of emotions. His chest heaves with a great cry and he sobs uncontrollably.

Overwrought with guilt, he cries for the guys who didn't make it. He cries for their kids who, for all he knows, could be the very same kids he is watching play right now. He cries for the children in Vietnam who were killed, and for Lilly, the little girl with the red hat, who should be here playing with them. And he cries for himself, for how horribly, horribly, wrong it is that he should make it home instead of Harry and the others.

The bell rings. Recess is over. The children line up by the entrance and file back into the school. Silence fills the air, and Dennis is left with the echoes of children's laughter and the specter of Lilly.

Striations of Love and Hate

"THE BIGGEST PARADOX is that as I felt innocence leaving me, I began to crave those high levels of adrenaline, the fear, the excitement, living in the present moments of battle, unfiltered by anything else. And I could feel that as my innocence waned, my passion for that kind of existence grew. But we'll never know those levels again. And you'll miss it and spend the entire rest of your life searching for it. I think that's why they say, you begin to die the moment you are born," Dennis confides in Andy, as they walk around the park area.

Andy knows firsthand what Dennis is describing, as he has searched to find something that has a meaning or purpose, to replace the void of passion in his life since he returned from Iraq. In war, everyone has a job, a purpose; and on the battlefield, you are a warrior. *But what are you when you come home?* Andy does not yet know the answers, but he is thankful he has Dennis in his life to help him sort it out.

Dennis stops walking and looks directly at Andy. "That passion is love and hate. You can never love unless you've hated. And when the hate is gone, you're scared the love is gone, too." Dennis pauses and thinks about his next words carefully; it is something he has pondered for nearly forty years. "Some veterans," Dennis says slowly, "are always looking to hate. But, really, they're looking for the hate so they can find the love again."

KIA: Dye-Marker

DENNIS IS IN THE KITCHEN reading the morning newspaper. His mother is cooking a dead man's breakfast of steak and eggs. She is softly humming a cheery jingle to herself, oblivious of the rift in their relationship, or perhaps her song is a cover-u p, hiding a glaring hole, like spackling on a wall. She is lovingly adding salt and pepper to the eggs when Dennis jumps to his feet, slams his chair down and hollers, "Son of a bitch!"

Startled, she screams.

"Honey, what is it, what's wrong?" She asks, bewildered.

But Dennis has already stormed out of kitchen. She bends down and picks up the crumbled newspaper sprawled across the floor. She reads the headlines. President Johnson has announced the US has halted all bombing and incursions in the DMZ. Dye-Marker, the strongpoint obstacle barrier system that so many American men fought and died for, would soon be dead.

But the truth was Dye-Marker had been slowly dying ever since Tet, despite the significant progress made by the end of 1967. Highway 561 had been resurfaced and connected with Route 9 to Con Thien. Highway 566 ran parallel to the Trace and linked the strong-points. Over one hundred and fifty bunkers were completed, with an additional two hundred bunkers partially complete. Sixty-seven thousand meters of tactical wire were laid, and one hundred and twenty thousand meters of mine fields had been planted. Strongpoint A-1, controlled by the South Vietnamese' ARVN forces was finished, as was the combat operating base, C-2, south of Con Thien. The remaining positions of the system were eighty percent complete. All in all, the Marines spent 757,520 man days and 114,519 equipment-hours working on Dye-Marker. Yet Westmoreland still was not happy with it.

But it would be all for naught. The Tet Offensive happened in late January of '68. The NVA had invaded and sacked the ancient imperial port city of Hue, stunning the US and South Vietnamese forces. Despite warning signs that pointed to a full-scale invasion of South Vietnam, the Allies were caught off guard, misguided in their belief that Con Thien and Khe Sahn were the real targets. The NVA were repelled out of Hue after twenty- six days, while the fierce fighting at Khe Sahn lasted longer, but eventually, the Marines prevailed. The NVA and Viet Cong suffered massive casualties.

Yet even though they lost the tactical battle, critics overseas who came to view the American defense as soft, handed the NVA the victory in name; and it was the propaganda victory that proved to matter most in the court of public opinion.

McNamara had been ousted in February. The siege of Khe Sanh ended in April and Dye-Marker was officially put on hold shortly thereafter. Westmoreland was reassigned in June. And the South Vietnamese forces positioned to take over and man the strongpoint balked at the time of the transfer.

Later, General Tompkins would lament on the never-ending futility of the static fixed position barrier system. "The Third Division was responsible for Dye-marker, and if we were responsible for Dye-marker, then we had to have Carroll, we had to have Ca Lu, we had to have Con Thien, we had to have Khe Sanh. These are all part of this bloody thing . . . ."

But as Dennis learned on that early morning in November 1968, Dye-marker would bleed no more. *It was just a thing. Ain't nothing but a thing.*

Welcome Home

"THEY SAID THE DMZ could no longer be held. But we held it, God damn it." Dennis says through clenched teeth. "All those guys that fought up there, all those guys who died up there.... I can't tell you what it was like to hear that those positions no longer held a purpose. And it got me thinking. How many other 'Hills of Angels' were fought in Vietnam? Or was the entire war itself a 'Hill of Angels?'"

Andy has quietly listened up to this point, but something Dennis just said struck a nerve. Lately, he has increasingly found himself wondering about the fate of the War in Iraq, and how it will be written in the annals of history. And even though he believes in giving the Iraqis the opportunity to run their own country free of Saddam Hussein, he also recognizes the reality that Iraq is not a country that will be "held" for any length of time. Eventually, it will be turned back over to the Iraqis. *And then what?* Will it become a freely elected democracy, or will it slip into a three-way civil war between the Shiites, Sunnis, and Kurds?

Andy doesn't know what will happen, but he has been bracing himself for the distinct possibility that the strategic cities and outposts where they have spilt blood may not stand the test of time. And that many years from now, the casualties may seem mundane, their purpose gone; the old outposts just sandy "hills of angels" somewhere out in the desert. Andy is reminded of the Aristotelian philosophy that wars are waged for peace to prevail. It is, at least, what he dearly hopes is true, although he is beginning to realize just how precarious that notion may really be.

Dennis' last sentence still hangs in the air, resonating in Andy's mind: *Maybe the entire war itself was a 'Hill of Angels.'* Finally, Andy looks at Dennis and concludes, "Maybe all wars are."

"Maybe . . . ," Dennis quietly replies.

Then, Dennis and Andy walk over to a bench in front of the statue called the Three Servicemen, and sit down on the wrought iron seat. Dennis stares into the faces of the sculptures, frozen in that moment for all eternity, he sees their youth, but more so, he sees himself in their stony gaze. Still looking into their faces, Dennis says quietly, "I made it. Maybe so everything they went through over there wasn't a waste."

Andy turns to Dennis. "No, it wasn't a waste."

The two men ponder this in silence for a few moments before Andy is reminded of something that he has wanted to ask since the first day they met. "So what do you talk about? Those speeches of yours at the VA's?"

"Overcoming adversity."

Andy chuckles. "You're pretty good at it".

Dennis looks over at the wall. The crowd has thinned out. Dennis gets up and waits for Andy to follow, and leads him to a clearing just in front of Panel 17.

"There are over 58,000 names on this wall," Dennis begins. "You asked me why I am doing this. What is the purpose? Well, I'll tell you. It's for all the guys who came home—for all the guys who didn't—and for my son, so that one day he may understand." Dennis takes a deep breath. "The guys who were never really born are the guys on that wall. They never had a chance to be born."

Facing the black granite wall, they can see the reflection of themselves painted in shadows across the catacomb of names. Dennis steps forward and speaks directly to the wall. "Well guys, this is the one I was telling you about."

Andy stares into the granite at their reflection. He sees Harry's name etched into the wall. He stands back and watches Dennis lean over and touch Harry's name with his fingertips. Dennis closes his eyes, and whispers something inaudible. Then he straightens up and turns back toward Andy.

"What is it that you just whispered?" Andy asks.

"Welcome home." He pauses. "That's all we ever really wanted. Someone to welcome us home as the men we became, not as the boys we left. To welcome us home like they did our fathers. So now, every time I come here, I say it to them."

Andy likes that.

Dennis places his hand on Andy's shoulder. "Welcome home, son."

Epilogue: Trenton

DENNIS HESITATES. He's not sure which exit he should take. *Better double-check.* He fishes for the directions out of his jacket pocket, but a faded manila envelope containing a letter falls onto his lap instead. Dennis picks up the letter. It is hard for him to believe that it was written thirty-seven years ago, yet harder still to believe that he just read it for the first time last night. He knew it existed, knew who wrote it, but could never bring himself to read it. The envelope was post-marked from Trenton, NJ, and addressed to his mother. It reads:

May 13, 1967

Dear Mrs. Michaels:

I think I will never forget that wonderful letter you wrote to me just after Harry's sudden death while engaging the enemy in Vietnam. If I understand correctly, your Dennis is either through with or has completed his original tour of duty in Vietnam and also his stint for the U.S.M.C. or will have some time this month and will be back in civilian life once more, unless he, like Harry Williams, had his time extended for another six months or so. In Denny's case, being at the end of his enlistment, I don't suppose this could happen, unless he re-enlisted for another two or three years. So I am looking forward to a visit from him soon.

Among Harry's personal belongings returned from Vietnam was a Japanese

Yashica Lynx14 camera, which I suppose Dennis knows Harry had. I sent to New York for information about the camera and they sent a booklet. The price of it is less than $110.00. What they mean by such an expression, I don't know. I suppose either a few cents or not more than $4 or $5 dollars less is meant.

As I think I told you in my letter to you, Harry, or "Bunky" as our family called him, hardly ever told me anything concerning his life over there or his friends over there either. According to what he told others in the neighborhood, he thought I had enough troubles of my own without adding his on top of mine. But he didn't seem to distinguish very well between his troubles and his pleasures. There were several things he could have told me that would have been cheery news, one of which was that your Denny was his best pal in Vietnam, which to hear about from you and others, I had to wait until he was dead.

Since you have told me that Denny was Harry's best friend in Vietnam and Mrs. Pessolano—a sort of a third mother to Harry—received a snap of him and Dennis both smiling and looking at a piece of paper, a map, or something else. I've thought quite likely that Denny hasn't much that belonged to Harry and so would very much like to give him the Yashica camera with instruction book, if he would care to have it.

Along with the camera and other belongings were one roll of film of 20 exposures and 2 colored films of 36 exposures each. Another item among his belongings was a small leather pouch in which I placed the two color rolls—these were all unexposed and now I can't find the pouch or films. The black and white 20 exposure film is in the camera and a few snaps have been taken. The fellow who took them returned the camera to me to finish the film. He will then have it processed for me for nothing. So if Denny takes the rest and returns the roll to me I will give it to this friend to be processed and will return those to you, which he will have taken. The only thing I can think that could have happened to the pouch and 2 films is that somehow, unintentionally, they dropped into the carton of things I gave to The Salvation Army, as I've looked everywhere I thought they could be and in a lot of places I was quite sure they would not be but have not seen hide nor hair of them. It makes me feel terrible to know that the pouch and two quite costly 30 exposure color films are lost. I, many times, like to give things away, but detest losing anything. But that's what I get for becoming old and forgetful. So, as a brother-in-law has said, jokingly, many times, "Don't get old." Now he has Parkinson's Disease, poor fellow.

I may be wrong but somehow have the idea that Dennis didn't go along with Harry as a forward observer or scout. Harry changed in his ideas and actions to the very opposite of the way he thought and acted in the beginning of his boot training at Paris Island. He told me in a letter that he was going to volunteer for nothing. And in a letter to Mrs. Pessolano, he said, "If I had known what I'd have to go though in boot training, I never would have enlisted in the USMC."

Shortly after this, when he was asked to volunteer as a replacement in Vietnam, he, along with others—including your Dennis, I think—volunteered. Then I found out after his death that he had volunteered to serve another six months. And not as a member of his gun crew but as a scout, one of the most dangerous jobs he could ask for; and not only that, but he had promised Mrs. Pessalano not to go into the new assignment until after he had been home on furlough for the month of May and returned to Vietnam. But if my news is correct, Harry was on this new assignment 25 days before he was to come home, when he was shot April 5, 1967.

I've thought many times how strange that he should so completely change, until on the day in the store of the cleaning establishment around the corner a woman, a clerk told me that when they asked for volunteers for Vietnam-they practically brainwashed them into going to keep from feeling like heels. So, if this was what happened in the USA why not in Vietnam, when they badly needed volunteers again. A major in Trenton tells me that he doesn't think Harry was urged but that he freely volunteered. I hope it's the truth, but doubt it. It gives me no pleasure at all to know that Harry died for his country and is now considered to be a hero. If he had stayed with his gun crew, quite likely he would still be among the living.

I'm glad that when quite young I accepted God's great and wonderful plan for our Salvation through Jesus Christ who died that we might begin to live here and then live with Him forever. He also rose again and ascended into heaven to make our resurrection possible and our place with Him assured, as soon as we repent of our sins and turn our lives all over to him for him to direct and keep. I've never been much of a man, in the eyes of the world, and if it were not for God's love and compassion would not stand a ghost of a chance of ever seeing my loved one and especially of seeing and dwelling with Him eternally. Thank God, that even though I was so unworthy of any love and blessing from Him, I am His (blacked out word) because I have repented and after turning everything of self and possession, talents, if I have any, and life over to His care and keeping He accepted me as His Son.

Don't forget to let me know if Dennis is not getting out this month and that I am looking forward with pleasure to your son's visiting with me soon.

I am sincerely your Friend in Christ,
C. S. Nelson, Sr.

P.S. Maybe I should more fully explain that war these days of fast transportation and advanced technology are idiotic. If what we have been told is the truth, about our containing communism and keeping them from entirely overrunning and staying all of the East, then I believe our boys must stay until the job is done. As to our boys giving their lives for our country and the rest of the free world, not one of them went over there with the intention of giving their lives, but of helping to do a rotten job and getting it over with. They don't give their lives. Their lives are taken from them, and they have taken many also of the enemy. I suppose to save the free world is noble, but I am not patriotic enough to rejoice that Harry is now a hero.

P.S. I just discovered today that the purple heart must have been sent to Harry's father instead of to me. Another not unexpected disappointment. Because the flag that draped the casket was given to Harry's father, who jumped in and took charge of his funeral after ignoring him as much as possible all during his short life. The MC gave me another one, but the Gov't must have sent the Purple Heart directly to his father. If it had come to Trenton it would have been given to me.

Dennis tucks the letter back in his jacket pocket, and pats it twice for posterity. He exits off the New Jersey Turnpike, and drives north on Route 29 along the Delaware River's eastern bank toward Trenton, a blue-collar manufacturing town that also happens to be the state capital. Dennis smiles. Only five more miles.

A bridge appears in the distance, connecting New Jersey and Pennsylvania. In large white block letters that contrast against the green bridge, the city's motto reads like a billboard: *Trenton Makes, The World Takes.*

"Hang on, Harry. I'm on my way, buddy. I'm finally on my way."

Author's Note

MY PASSION FOR WRITING this story began in the summer of 2003 when I spent time at Walter Reed Medical Center managing video crews hired by the USO-Metro and their media partner to document various celebrities visiting the young, wounded veterans being treated at the facility. Before that experience, I had never seen the reality or consequences of shrapnel and IED wounds. Reading reports in newspapers—black words on a white page—could not compare with what I saw at the hospital. I had been ignorant of what war looked like up-close and personal and I will never forget the far-off look on the faces of the amputees who sat out on the hospital porch in wheelchairs.

Shortly thereafter, I met a former combat Marine named Dennis Butts at a business luncheon. Still haunted by the images of the young veterans sitting on the porch, it struck a nerve when Dennis revealed he had spent nine months in Vietnam. "War is war. It doesn't matter where it's fought or even when. It's all the same," he said, referring to Vietnam, Iraq and Afghanistan, and also of the wars waged in veterans' minds.

Over the next several months I interviewed Dennis to better understand the psyche of warriors and the life-long implications of living with PTSD. I am forever grateful to him for his willingness to share his stories of fighting for country and friends, as well as the forty-year battle he waged against an invisible enemy, PTSD. While a number of the experiences Dennis shared are recounted, and the chronology of events in Vietnam as presented in this book is historically accurate, many scenes and characters are fictional, as is the character of Andrew Taylor.

The story setting of two warriors meeting at Walter Reed over a ten-day period in November, 2004 I felt was fitting as that month had been the costliest of Operation Iraqi Freedom in terms of deaths and casualties at that time. I did not interview any of the Iraq veterans I had met at Walter Reed, or any of the veterans Dennis had briefly mentored. I felt it would be too exploitative. Instead, I read every blog site I could find on the Internet, from servicemen still in the combat zone to those of amputees blogging about their rehabilitation experience at Walter Reed.

Aspiring to keep the theme and purpose for writing the book intact as I wove together the various stories, histories, and news snippets, I found myself referring often to a conversation I had with Dennis the first time we discussed Vietnam. "Nine months," I had said, "that's the same amount of time it takes a woman to give birth to a child." Dennis looked into my face, our eyes deadlocked, and I continued, "I bet that's what it must have felt like—going into a war as a nineteen year old, and coming out a completely different person—almost like you were born again."

"Exactly," Dennis had whispered, "except this time, I wasn't born with my innocence . . . . I was born without it."

The first edition of this novel, entitled *Still the Monkey, What happens to Warriors after War*, was completed in March of 2006 and published in March, 2007. Since Dennis was unable to read the book himself, I read it to him aloud. He especially liked the ending. Dennis has yet to visit his friend Harry's grave in Trenton.

Author's Resources

THE FOLLOWING is a list of materials read and referenced to ensure historical accuracy:

Operation Buffalo: The USMC Fight for the DMZ, by Keith W, Nolan (Dell, 1992); *The March Up: Taking Baghdad with the United States Marines*, by Bing West and Major General Ray L. Smith, USMC, Ret., (Bantam Books, 2004); *On Killing, The Psychological Cost of Learning to Kill in War and Society*, by Lt. Col. Dave Grossman, (Little, Brown and Company, 1995); *Fighting Elite, US Marines in Vietnam 1965-73*, by Charles D. Melson and Romiro Bujeiro (Osprey Publishing, 1998); *Not Going Home Alone: A Marine's Story*, by James Kirschke (Ballantine Books, 2001); *13 Cent Killers: The 5th Marine Snipers in Vietnam*, by John Culbertson, (Presidio Press, 2003); *Con Thien, The Hill of Angels*, by James P. Coan (University of Alabama Press, 2004); *Bloods: An Oral History of the Vietnam War by Black Veterans*, by Wallace Terry (Ballantine Books, 1985): *Bernard Fall, Memories of a Soldier-Scholar*, by Dorothy Fall (Potomac Books, Inc., 2006).

Online book sources also provided historical information, such as, *The US Army in Vietnam*, by Vincent H. Demma, (American Military History, Center of Military History, United States Army, Washington DC, 1989, Chapter 28, www.ibiblio.org; *The Defining Years*, "History of Dye-Marker Construction & III Marines '67-68, eHistory at the Ohio State University, (http://ehistory.osu.edu/vietnam/books/); *The Marine War: III MAF in Vietnam, 1965-1971*, Jack Shulimson, U.S. Marine Corps Historical Center, (www.vietnam.ttu.edu/vietnamcenter/events/1996_Symposium/96papers/m arwar.htm)

In addition, the following essays, websites, and archives provided background information: "The Walking Dead" (www.thewalkingdead.org). "Attack on Con Thien" (1stbn4thMarines.com/delta-company/conthein). "Battle for Baghdad Begins" Defense Tech (www.defensetech.org). For military jargon and Marine Corps terms, United States Marine Corp (www.usmc.mil) and USPharmD (http://uspharmd.com/usmc). For official statistics and archived material: United States Department of Veterans Affairs. (www.va.gov), United States Department of Defense (www.defenselink.mil), United States Department of State (www.state.gov), and United States Central Command (USCENTCOM) (www.centcom/mil).

Reference material was also obtained from the following websites: Amputee Coalition Organization (www.amputee-coalition.org). National Center for PTSD (www.ncptsd.va.gov/). The Moving Wall www.the movingwall.org, and www.virtualwall.org. Vietnam Veterans Memorial Fund (www.vvmf.org) and (www.teachvietnam.org). National Park Services (www.nps.gov). Global Security Organization (www.globalsecurity.org). The Fourth Rail; History, Politics, and the War on Terror (www.militarywebcom. org). Voices in the Wilderness (www.vitw.org). Global Policy Forum, UN Security Council (www.globalpolicy.org). Iraq Coalition Casualties (www.icasualties.org). Disabled American Veterans (DAV) www. dav.org. Stars and Stripes (www.estripes.com). Wounded Warriors Organization (www.woundedwarriors.org).

Information and references from news outlets include: Newsweek, MSNBC, Fox News, NY Times, Washington Times, Washington Post, ABC, CBS, CNN, BBC, Associated Press, and Reuters.

And lastly, the following blogs provided a wealth of insight and information, and enabled me to immerse myself in the daily lives of combatants at war and at home. "The Memory Hole" (thememoryhole.org); "Milblogging. com: The World's Largest Index of Military Blogs" (www.milblogging. com); "One Veteran's Voice: A Group Blog by Veterans of Iraq and Afghanistan" (www.oneveteransvoice); "IAVA Blog: Iraq and Afghanistan Veterans of America" (www.optruth.org).

About the Author

ALIVIA TAGLIAFERRI is an author, publisher, producer and documentary filmmaker. Her first documentary *Beyond the Wall: Homeless Zone* (DVD; 30 minutes) was produced by Ironcutter Media, a company she founded to create media that matters, and establish a platform for other artists to share important works with social value. A native of Williamsport, Pennsylvania, she received a Bachelor of Arts degree in History from Pennsylvania State University in 1999. She currently resides in Washington, D.C.

Visit her site at www.aliviatagliaferri.com.

Other Titles and Works by Ironcutter Media, LLC

UPROOTED: Searching for Serenity, A Poetry Collection
by Michelle McCloskey-Alicea
ISBN: 0-9788417-1-9

This stirring four-part collection of poems recounts the long and arduous path of survival Michelle McCloskey-Alicea and her family journeyed after the War on Terror hit close to home. Speechless, poetry became her voice. Coursing the experiences of her family feeling emotionally uprooted by the tragedy of war to their survival, revelation and search for serenity, this beautifully evocative collection is capped by Michelle's tribute to her brother and our country's servicemembers and families. (www.uprootedpoetry.com)

Beyond the Wall: Homeless Zone (a social documentary), produced and directed by Alivia Tagliaferri.

Nearly one in four of our nation's homeless is a veteran. Relevant, real and raw, this social documentary explores the contributing factors that lead to or increase the risk of veteran homelessness by meeting two Iraq War warriors who lived on the streets of Washington, D.C. and learning from the Vietnam veterans who support them. (www.beyondthewallhomelesszone.com)

The Mrs. Pea Children's Book Series by Kat Parrish.

Giving children a voice while promoting literacy and life lessons, The Mrs. Pea Children's Book Series embeds social lessons and topics often hard for children to understand or parents to discuss, bringing to light important issues that engage the whole family. (www.mrspea.com)

Speck's Amazing Adventure
ISBN: 0-9788417-4-3
Speck, a simple piece of sand, wants to be important. But how does one piece of sand find worth when it is one of literally trillions? No matter how small and insignificant we may sometimes feel in such a large world, Speck proves even the smallest piece of sand can make a world of difference!

Blake the Brontosaurus and Timmy the Boy
ISBN: 0-9788417-5-1
Blake the Brontosaurus is taller than any of his play friends. Sometimes being so tall makes Blake feel out of place. Until the day his friend Timmy makes a wonderful observation. Blake is so tall that he is able to pop his head through the clouds and see heaven! Sad endings turn into new beginnings with the proper perspectives and the support of true friends.

The Ant Who Defeats His Bully
ISBN: 0-9788417-6-X
Abe the Ant is being bullied at school by Butch the Anteater. Silenced by fear and nightmares, Abe's ordeal soon spirals out of control. But with a little courage and a lot of love and support from his parents and trusted adults, Abe learns how to break the cycle of abuse and defeat his bully.

Ironcutter Media, LLC is an independent publishing, media and event production company based in the Washington, D.C area. Visit www.ironcutter media.com to learn more about these authors and upcoming titles.

Beyond the Wall: The Journey Home
(Formerly titled 'Still the Monkey, What Happens to Warriors after War')

Reviews

"DESPITE VOLUMES WRITTEN about war and its effects throughout the ages, it is difficult to convey the experience to those of us who have not experienced combat. Through the story of Dennis, a Vietnam Veteran, this compelling novel engages the reader from the first page and allows us into the world of honor, courage, loyalty, and commitment, as well as the brutality of war, and the pain of its consequences.

"It is at its best in conveying what we clinicians refer to as 'survival guilt,' a short cut term that can barely begin to describe the aftermath of the combination of intense and almost sacred bonds formed during combat with the brutal loss of those so uniquely loved. Although as civilians we will never fully understand what it is like to live through and beyond combat, this important book will help us to appreciate the living consequences of those who have."

Dr. M. Tracie Shea | Professor, Psychiatry & Human Behavior, Brown University

"ONE OF THE YEAR'S BEST" (2007)
The National Alliance on Mental Illness (NAMI)

"A POIGNANT AND POWERFUL NOVEL..."
Midwest Book Review, April 2007 Fiction Shelf

"A MOVING NOVEL"

VVA Magazine April 2008 Issue (Vietnam Veterans of America)

"AS A THERAPIST who treats veterans with post traumatic stress disorder, I found this book powerfully wields a new pathway for teaching others about combat trauma...it is cathartic and poetic all at once."

Jerome Beightol | PTSD Therapist and Veteran

"TAGLIAFERRI WAS A HISTORY MAJOR in college. Today she's an author and entrepreneur... (her) book tells the story of a Vietnam Vet and how he came to know a young Veteran of our current conflicts who had lost both legs in Iraq. The issue of PTSD (The Monkey) and the impact on their lives is front and center and makes for a good read, even if often shockingly brutal and true to life.

I was curious how she (Tagliaferri) had learned so much about us and even more to the point, I was fascinated with the degree of historical accuracy she provides. I'm not known to be particularly shy so I contacted her and we talked. We talked longer and in more depth than I could have imagined. She's a civilian with scant connection to anything military but it was quickly apparent that she gets it."

Jim Strickland | VA Watchdog, 5/2/07, EVERYTHING YOU EVER WANTED TO KNOW ABOUT FILING A CLAIM FOR PTSD — Advice from Veterans' Advocate Jim Strickland

"I AM AMAZED at the depth of understanding and obvious compassion of your character(s). I am also extremely impressed that you could present this material without it devolving into a crass political statement, a failure too often experienced by writers whose work—unlike yours—I found immature and of little value. I cannot explain to you the emotions I felt reading parts of the book, and how I feel about you for having written it the way you did. The words that come to mind would sound trite or inappropriate. You have done a great service to many veterans."

– Dr. David Rathgeber, Retired USMC

"A REALISTIC, INFORMATIVE and mind-rattling account of war (Vietnam and Iraq)—and the human costs. Tagliaferri hits the nail dead center."

– Walter T. Steinbacher, A.Co. 1st Bn. 26th Marine, Vietnam, '66-67